# My Kind of Scoundrel

## Rogues of Fortune's Den
Book 4

### ADELE CLEE

***My Kind of Scoundrel***
Copyright © 2024 Adele Clee
All rights reserved.
ISBN-13: 978-1-915354-37-2

Cover by Dar Albert at Wicked Smart Designs

He's more myself than I am.
Whatever our souls are made of,
his and mine are the same.

—Emily Bronte

# Chapter One

*The Olympic Theatre*
*Wych Street, Drury Lane*

Theodore Chance dropped into the red velvet chair in a private box at the Olympic Theatre. Madame Vestris, the principal actress and manager, had addressed the audience, and her company of actors had finished singing the verse and chorus of "God save the King!"

Theo had not come to watch Madame Vestris don breeches and make a parody of a classical play, or to laugh until his sides hurt. He had come to prove a point to his estranged uncle, the Earl of Berridge. Despite being shot in his shoulder by a thug mere weeks ago, Theo was still a man to fear.

As the gaslights dimmed and the burgundy curtains parted for the first act, his sister-in-law Naomi tapped his shoulder. "Most men are here to watch the famed Miss Baker perform, though I hear she only has eyes for you."

Theo shot his brother a questioning glare. Aramis had

been gossiping to his wife again. He was obsessed with the woman, forever whispering in her ear, always touching her hand. If a hard-hearted rogue like Aramis could be tamed, all bachelors were doomed.

"As I'm sure Aramis told you, I have taken a vow of chastity." If Theo avoided romantic entanglements, he could not fall into a matchmaker's trap. "While Miss Baker invited me to dine with her tonight, I came only to humiliate our uncle and spend time with beloved family."

Aramis snorted. "How long do you mean to keep up this charade?"

"Charade?" Theo clutched his chest as if mortally wounded.

"The pretence that you've abandoned your roguish ways. Your moniker is the King of Hearts, not Virtuous Victor. Avoiding women won't prevent destiny from knocking on your door."

"Destiny deems I shall die a bachelor."

A shiver chased down Theo's spine. Over the course of a few short months, three of his siblings had married. He was next in line. Doubtless fate lurked in the shadows, gripping a noose, ready to string him up by the *proverbials*.

"Look what happened to us. We didn't expect to fall in love." Naomi stared at Aramis as if he were a god amongst men. A curious combination of lust and longing encompassed them like a halo of gold. "We never believed we could be so happy. When you meet the right person, Theo, you will know true love, too."

Theo turned his attention to the stage and feigned interest.

He would rather rot in hell than trust a woman.

Bitter thoughts of Lucille Bowman clawed their way out of the dirt and into his heart. Painful memories were never truly buried. They lay like the undead in the darkness, waiting to grab a man by the ankle and drag him to his doom.

Being his usual intuitive self, Aramis was quick to grasp the problem. "Lucille Bowman was not the right woman for you. She toyed with your affections to frighten her father. She kept you dangling like a puppet. You were never good enough. You're not heir to a title."

The words hit hard—no man wished to think himself inadequate—though Theo kept his arrogant mask in place. "Don't spare my feelings. You may as well twist the blade and sever an artery."

"I'm your brother. I'll not serve the truth like a sweet treat on a lace doily. You were never in love with her. The sooner you realise that the better your life will be."

The urge to curse the woman stung like acid on his tongue. Deceit was a sin he could not tolerate. But he was the King of Hearts. Should he not be a man of great empathy? Should he not have an emotional intelligence above that of other mortals?

Perhaps he needed a different moniker.

Engaging with one's heart made a man weak.

He should be the King of Loathing. The King of Tragedies.

"What about Miss Darrow?" Naomi said above the crowd's sudden shriek of laughter when a donkey in a periwig appeared on stage. "Aramis said she came to Fortune's Den looking for you last night, though she wouldn't say why. Only a woman driven by an obsession would risk visiting a gaming hell after dark."

Mention of the modiste had Theo grumbling under his breath.

Miss Darrow was obsessed, but not with him.

"Perhaps she came to offer an apology. She lied to me. She made me coffee and flirted outrageously, all in the name of deception."

It was partly Miss Darrow's fault he got shot outside her shop. He had gone to the dressmaker's to chaperone his sister, Delphine. Unbeknownst to him, she wasn't there for a gown fitting. It was a ruse arranged by Miss Darrow so Delphine could meet a man in the yard.

Miss Darrow had used him and treated him like a fool. She was no different to Lady Lucille. They were both conniving cats.

"Miss Darrow merely came to her client's aid," Naomi said, showing her unwavering support for womanhood. "Surely the days spent nursing you are reparation enough. Besides, everything worked out perfectly in the end. Were it not for Miss Darrow's intervention, Delphine would never have met her husband."

Seeing Delphine happy and in love was indeed a blessing.

"Nothing pleases me more than knowing Delphine is content." Theo rubbed his wounded shoulder and winced. Perhaps he should be grateful he'd gained a scar. It did add a certain ruggedness to his physique. "But being shot makes me look weak. Every coxcomb drunk on arak will think he has the strength to pummel me now."

Aramis found the notion amusing. "You could do with honing your pugilistic skills. Admit nothing brings you greater pleasure than thrashing a few arrogant lords. We

4

could put you in the fighting pit and take bets on the outcome."

It was no laughing matter. Another attack was imminent. He could feel it in his blood. This time, he would be prepared.

"I shall consider fighting in the pit once I've won our current wager." Theo met his brother's gaze, and they both grinned.

Their latest bet involved Miss Darrow.

Miss Darrow had helped nurse him back to health as part of her penance. She'd closed her shop and spent hours at his bedside while he recuperated at Mile End—now his sister's marital home. Yet he'd often wondered if the modiste had another reason for wanting to leave town. Throughout her vigil, she was never without her mysterious wooden box.

*You hug that sewing box like it's a beloved pet.*

*These threads are expensive.*

*Who in their right mind would steal haberdashery?*

*You'd be surprised.*

One might ask why a simple sewing box came with a small gold key. Or why the modiste wore it on a red ribbon fastened around her neck. When feigning sleep, he was certain Miss Darrow had retrieved something from her bodice and buried it beneath the threads.

It was a puzzle he longed to unravel.

So, in an act of retribution, he stole the box and hid it in his bedchamber at Fortune's Den. The longer he kept it, the closer he came to winning the wager.

Not that he cared about the prize. Toying with Miss Darrow was part of his recuperation. A means to heal his wounded pride. Indeed, he would make sure the modiste never lied to him again.

"What made you think your uncle would attend the theatre tonight?" Naomi glanced into the auditorium. The crowd's laughter proved contagious, and she chuckled, too. "Would he not have arrived in time for the performance?"

"The aristocracy likes to make a statement," Aramis said, settling his wife's gloved hand on his thigh. "They come to be seen, not to watch Madame Vestris and her amusing burlesques."

Excitement coursed through Theo's veins. He lived to wipe the smile off Berridge's face. "And when he finds us in his private box, this horde will watch the pompous Earl of Berridge reduced to a laughingstock."

Berridge had been goading the men at White's to make bets as to which one of Theo's brothers would die first. It didn't matter that Theo had been hit with the lead ball. The fact a fool had found the courage to fire weakened his family's defences.

They did not have to wait long for the battle to begin.

Yet it was not the pathetic Earl of Berridge who barged into the theatre box, eager to cause a scene. It was the devious Miss Darrow.

"Good evening, Mr Chance." Swathed in a pink satin cloak, the lady projected an air of confidence while pinning Theo to his seat with her intense green gaze. "You're a hard man to find."

*Damnation!*

How the devil had she known he was at the theatre?

"Missing me already, Miss Darrow?" He cursed inwardly, vexed by the prospect of being publicly berated by a shrew. "I should think you've seen enough of me to last a lifetime."

As part of her nursing duties, she had changed his

6

bandages and mopped his brow. He'd drawn the line at a bed bath. He'd not give the woman the satisfaction of knowing her touch roused a cockstand.

The lady whipped back her hood, revealing waves of lustrous red hair—the mark of a vixen. "I prefer your temper to your teasing, sir. You know why I'm here. After all I have done for you, I demand you stop treating me like a fool."

Miss Darrow had the devil's cheek. She had kept him talking in the shop, offering her little witticisms while Delphine conducted an illicit encounter in the yard. Doubtless she giggled at his naivety every time she escaped to the fitting room.

Arching a brow, he attempted to look bewildered. "Forgive me if I have given you the wrong impression." He turned to Aramis, keen to make this woman pay for every wicked lie she'd told. "Nurses often become infatuated with their patients. It's a common malady. As you can see, poor Miss Darrow is desperate for my attention."

Mischief—the harmful kind—swirled in Miss Darrow's stormy green eyes. "Only a woman lacking in self-respect would seek the company of a libertine."

Theo clasped his injured shoulder. The damn thing still pained him. "You wound me, madam. Though it would seem we have some things in common. Arranging secret meetings and lying to hide your deception are the traits of a scoundrel."

A sly smile touched her lips, lips he'd admired before discovering they belonged to a devil. "You make an excellent point, sir." She slipped the gold button on her cloak, drew the garment from around her shoulders and draped it over the empty seat beside him. "Perhaps keeping you company is the best way to achieve my goal."

Aramis and Naomi grinned. Apparently, they found the situation more entertaining than the farce on stage.

"I don't recall inviting you to sit," Theo said when the lady gathered her skirts and settled into the plush velvet chair.

Miss Darrow leaned closer, filling his nostrils with the sweet scent of jasmine. "As you said, I am suffering from a dreadful malady. An obsession with my patient. An addiction I cannot control." Her voice dropped to a dangerous whisper. "I mean to hound you night and day until you give me what I want."

Oh, he would give her what she wanted, and he wasn't referring to the silly sewing box. Despite trying to avoid staring at her soft breasts, pressed enticingly against the fashionable pink gown, his traitorous gaze dipped.

*Merciful Lord!*

This woman would make a monk question his vows.

Thankfully, her perfidious character lessened her appeal.

"I know what you want," he uttered, draping a languid arm over the rail of her chair. "But I have taken a vow of celibacy and have no plans to make love to any woman, least of all you."

Her eyes blazed. "No. The only thing you make love to is your own reflection. I suspect there's an enormous mirror at the foot of your bed, littered with smudge marks where you've practised kissing."

A chuckle burst from Aramis' lips, though he quickly averted his gaze to the stage when Naomi nudged him.

"You'll never know, Miss Darrow." Theo's blood simmered with the need to prove a point. "Be assured, I'm no amateur when it comes to kissing." He could have the lady panting in seconds.

The flash of curiosity in her eyes accompanied her satisfied grin. "The truth is, Mr Chance, I know exactly what you keep in your bedchamber at Fortune's Den."

It was a lie. Women weren't permitted inside the gaming hell, let alone given leave to search their private rooms. "Feel free to enlighten me." This was another attempt at manipulation, a common stratagem of the fairer sex.

"There's a large gilt mirror propped against the wall," she remarked casually, diverting her attention from him to the unfolding farce on stage.

"Most people keep such an object in their chamber."

"The entire room is painted midnight blue. I suspect your carved ebony bed came from France. The opulent rug is Persian."

*What the devil!*

His pulse rose a notch.

The minx excelled at this game.

"No doubt Delphine has been exercising her tongue again." What had his sister said about him? Perhaps she had spoken of his selfless deeds, the kind gestures that made a man look feeble. "They say a woman shares her deepest secrets with her modiste."

The lady looked at him, the shadow of an unknown burden dulling her eyes. "Yes, you'd be surprised what information people entrust to a stranger. I admit, Delphine told me your room was blue when we spoke about the colour of her favourite gown."

While Miss Darrow's confession brought a triumphant smile to his lips, a subtle undercurrent of disappointment left him perplexed.

Was it wrong to wish she had been a more formidable

ADELE CLEE

adversary? Why did he enjoy these verbal tussles? What was it he liked about this cat-and-mouse game?

"And I'm quite certain I mentioned my bed during my convalescence," he said. Having been force-fed opium by the doctor, he'd been drowsy at the time and could have told her anything. "That's how you know it's ebony."

"Perhaps." There was a playful glint in her eyes as she proceeded to taunt him with facts. "You might wonder how I know you sleep with your right leg out of the bedsheets or that the third board from the door creaks."

His heart leapt a little.

But he firmed his jaw and studied her intently.

"The cufflink box on your chest of drawers is made of leather and brass," she continued, almost gloating. "You possess every cologne one might purchase from Floris, though you favour sandalwood and clove. You keep an empty bottle on the bottom shelf of your armoire." A sensual sigh breezed from her lips. "Everything smells of you."

Theo straightened. The lady had his undivided attention, but the constant howling from the audience made it hard to think. "What else do you know about me?" He prayed Miss Darrow had mystical abilities because the alternative meant she had been in his room.

Impossible.

"You keep a tincture of opium on your nightstand, though your desire to prove you're as strong as your brothers prevents you from taking the tiniest drop. Even when your shoulder pains you, which it does most nights."

Devil take it. He must have spouted nonsense in his sleep. No wonder she'd barely left his bedside. She'd been rubbing her hands in glee while he mumbled like a drunken fool at the fair.

10

"You feel safe in the dark," she added.

The comment had him jumping out of his seat.

He had not uttered those words to a living soul.

"Excuse us for a moment." He didn't look at Aramis as his fingers encircled Miss Darrow's upper arm. The softness of her skin sent an unexpected surge of awareness coursing through him. Damn the woman. Something about her stirred a complex mix of emotions. Evidently, the line between desire and disdain was perilously thin. "This conversation demands discretion."

He guided Miss Darrow into the candlelit hall and yanked the curtains closed. Never had he felt so exposed.

"How did you arrive at that conclusion?" He drove her back against the wall and braced his hands above her head. She was at *his* mercy now. "It's certainly not something I would say."

Perhaps she was a mystic who could see into a man's soul.

Maybe she had read the leaves in his teacup.

She blinked rapidly. "It was merely an observation. I dress people for a living. There's a vast difference between the person they present to the world and the one they keep hidden."

"You dress women, Miss Darrow. Men are a species unto their own." Yet he wondered what the complex knot in his cravat and his penchant for new coats said about him.

"That's not true." She swallowed hard. Clearly, his proximity unnerved her. "An alluring gown might be a lady's weapon of choice. Men choose arrogance. Both serve the same purpose."

"Is that why you've come armed to the teeth tonight?" Lured by the rapid rise and fall of her breasts, his errant gaze skimmed the neckline of her gown. "Did you hope your pretty countenance would leave me defenceless? That you would force me to surrender and admit I have your beloved box?"

"Do you have it?" Her sudden alertness came as no surprise, though the flicker of hope in her eyes tugged at his conscience. "Tell me, Mr Chance. I have been mindless with worry."

"Over spools of expensive threads?" It made no sense. She was hiding something, though he'd be damned if he knew what. After picking the lock on the box, he'd found nothing valuable.

"It's a family heirloom."

Theo knew enough about antiquities to know that was another lie. He'd get the truth from this woman if it killed him.

"Then one wonders why you were careless enough to lose it."

"I didn't lose the box." A fire ignited in her eyes, and accusations flew like hot sparks from her tongue. "You stole it from under my nose. You crept into my room while I slept. It was on my nightstand when I went to bed and was gone the next morning."

Guilt weighed heavily in his chest.

Yes, he wanted to keep the box and win his wager with Aramis. He wanted to punish Miss Darrow for making him coffee and smiling at him over the top of his newspaper. Both were devious tactics she'd used to cover her tracks.

"Have you searched the rooms at Mile End? Have you questioned the staff? One of them may have moved it."

"With your sister's permission, I scoured every room."

Keen to drag a confession from her lips, he said, "If it

makes you feel better, I shall buy you a new box. Pick whatever threads you need and send the bill to Fortune's Den. Choose something expensive. It's the least I can do."

She shook her head and seized his gold waistcoat in her fist, gasping like a drowning sailor struggling against the tide. "You have my box. I know you do. You'll give it to me tonight, or I shall sneak into your room at Fortune's Den and shoot your good shoulder."

While he should demand to know how she planned to enter the club without a key, the threat of violence intrigued him.

"So the vixen breaks cover and bares her teeth."

"Had you been civil, we might have joked about this over a bottle of claret and a game of piquet. As it is, you force me down a road I had hoped to avoid. I mean to reclaim my box, Mr Chance, by wicked means if necessary."

He wasn't the least bit fazed. "Challenge accepted. You sound like my kind of scoundrel, Miss Darrow, and I am more than willing to play your game."

Indeed, he could not recall when he'd last felt the potent thrum of excitement coursing through his veins. Any hopes of outwitting her evaporated when he noticed three people appear at the end of the long corridor.

The popinjay leading two ladies towards them was not the Earl of Berridge but his only son and heir, Viscount Wrotham—Theo's inept cousin. The beauty gripping his arm was none other than Lady Lucille Bowman. The deceitful wretch who'd refused Theo's suit so she might marry the heir to an earldom.

Panic ensued.

He could handle Wrotham, but the sight of the woman

who had tricked him brought bile to his throat. His arrogance, once a sturdy coat of armour, had taken too many hits to be effective.

"Are you well, Mr Chance?" Miss Darrow's worried tone jolted Theo back to the present. "You look like you've seen a ghost."

She was still gripping his waistcoat in her dainty hand, still standing so close they looked like lovers. That's when he realised there was a way to bolster his defences. A way to slake his curiosity, too.

"Shall we make a trade, Miss Darrow?"

"A trade?"

"I shall tell you where you can find your box." Resisting the urge to glance over his shoulder, he held Miss Darrow's gaze. Her eyes had a tranquil allure, like a verdant meadow beneath the moon's soft glow. "In exchange, I have a demand of my own."

Miss Darrow was near breathless when she said, "What could you possibly want from a lowly modiste, Mr Chance?"

He smiled to himself.

"A kiss, Miss Darrow. That's what I want from you."

# Chapter Two

"A kiss?" Eleanor was convinced she had misheard. A minute ago, they had been waging war. Now, the man who haunted her dreams stared into her eyes and offered the one thing she craved. "Have you lost your wits?"

Perhaps he *had* taken a dose of laudanum tonight.

Maybe he'd downed a bottle of claret before the performance.

"There's no time to explain." Theodore Chance bent his head until his mouth was mere inches from hers. "Kiss me now, Miss Darrow. The more authentic the caress, the more information you'll earn."

Authentic? She had never kissed a man in her life.

But as she locked eyes with him, she found herself lost in the beauty of his cerulean gaze. A lady could dive into the fathomless depths and never resurface. One might be hypnotised into forgetting danger lurked below.

"Miss Darrow?" he pressed, his warm breath breezing over her lips.

Three figures emerged from the left, catching her eye. In

a world where social connections were currency, it paid to know every fashionable lady in town. Thus, she knew the golden-haired beauty on Viscount Wrotham's arm was a woman Mr Chance admired.

"You plan to use me to annoy Lady Lucille Bowman?"

She would tell him to go to the devil if she wasn't desperate to reclaim her sewing box. Without it, she might not survive the night.

"Does it matter? We've contemplated kissing each other before."

"Have we? Perhaps you've mistaken me for someone else."

A sly smile played on his lips. "Your feminine qualities have not gone unnoticed. I've seen the way you look at me, Miss Darrow. I'm experienced enough to know you've thought about more than kissing."

The conceited devil.

As her life depended upon bringing a swift end to this game, the time for honesty was nigh. "You have many fine qualities, Mr Chance." Her heart had melted upon hearing the loving things he had said to his sister, Delphine. He would die to protect his family. Both were attractive attributes. "I may have admired your countenance, but that was before you stole my box. You're like a fine wine that proves disappointing on the palate."

"If you want it back, you'll kiss me. I believe you'll have a different opinion when you do."

Eleanor stared at the face that made women swoon. Could she trust Mr Chance to keep his word? Did she want to kiss her tormentor? In all fairness, he was unaware of the dangers she faced. He didn't know the heavy price she must pay for being part of his foolish game.

"And you will keep your word?" she said.

"I will tell you exactly where you can find the box. It is up to you to retrieve it." Aware the viscount was fast approaching, he added, "It's now or never, Miss Darrow."

Her heart skittered. Lady Lucille was a prestigious client. One she would likely lose after this debacle, but living to see another day was more important than filling the coffers. The ladies of the *ton* were fickle. One exquisite design would have them swarming to the shop like bees to blossom.

"Very well. One kiss. That is all."

Mr Chance grinned like his horse had won the Derby. He moistened his lips. "Close your eyes, Miss Darrow. Remember, I shall be in your debt if you make it look authentic."

There was no time to reconsider.

Theodore Chance captured her chin and slanted his lips over hers in a kiss that proved quite shocking. It wasn't a rough, carnal mating of mouths. It wasn't a prelude to something salacious. It was soft and slow and tender. A heart-stopping kiss that sang to a lady's soul, not her senses. A thief's caress.

He robbed the air from her lungs. He pilfered her hopes and dreams and replaced them with ones in his own image. He stole every wicked misconception she had ever had about him.

Then he pulled away, taking a tiny part of her with him.

Their eyes met.

"You seem surprised, Miss Darrow." His gaze lingered on her lips as if he yearned to reclaim them. "What were you expecting?"

She had expected to be mauled by a selfish scoundrel.

She had expected a libertine's lewd advances.

She had hoped to feel disgusted, not moved and utterly intrigued.

"Now I know why you bear the King of Hearts moniker," she said. Beneath his formidable exterior lay a beautiful fusion of gentleness and strength. "Once a lady has kissed you, no other suitor would suffice."

Before he could reply, Viscount Wrotham interrupted their intimate interlude. "Why in blazes are you lingering outside my box, Chance?" Despite his attempt at annoyance, a note of unease tinged the viscount's tone.

Mr Chance ignored him and continued gazing at Eleanor's lips. "You're not without skill yourself, Miss Darrow. Despite your obvious inexperience, a fiery passion simmers within."

Lord Wrotham cleared his throat. "I say, this isn't a bordello. Take your fornicating to the alleys of Covent Garden."

"I'm glad you approve, sir." Eleanor leaned into Mr Chance's hard chest and whispered, "Once we're rid of our audience, you will keep your word and give me back my sewing box."

"I confess, I find your presence here quite disturbing, Miss Darrow," Lady Lucille stated, her cheeks flushed with a fiery rage reminiscent of the rubies dangling from her earlobes. "Tell me, how does a woman of your occupation find time for frivolity?"

"A woman can always find time for love, my lady."

The comment earned Eleanor a wink from Theodore Chance.

"Some ladies prefer the chill of jewels around their necks to the fervent caress of a passionate man's lips," Theo said.

The viscount nudged his maternal aunt, Mrs Dunwoody,

a matron of some import. "We know what sort of woman prefers the latter."

Mr Chance turned so quickly the weasel-faced lord stumbled back. "Insult my betrothed again, Wrotham, and you'll face me at dawn."

Eleanor fought to stifle a gasp.

His betrothed?

What was the man thinking?

"Your betrothed?" Mrs Dunwoody fluttered her fan as if warding off a dreadful stench. "I suppose a modiste is a step up from those who sleep in the gutter. Your poor grandfather must be turning in his grave."

"One can live in hope," Mr Chance countered. "I pray he's fodder for the worms. A man who disowns his kin deserves to rot in hell."

"Your father was the devil incarnate," the snooty woman snapped. "He deserved to lose everything. There is always one scoundrel in a litter. You've proven you're no different."

Unable to hold her tongue, Eleanor said, "The Lord holds everyone to account, Mrs Dunwoody. When the day of reckoning comes, the Earl of Berridge will need to atone for leaving his young nephews on the street."

How could anyone sit idly while four boys were thrown out of their dead father's house and left to fend for themselves in the rookeries?

Mr Chance snorted. "I could not have worded it better myself, Miss Darrow."

He did not question how she knew his family history. A modiste was party to all manner of gossip. She knew many of the *ton*'s secrets. Why else would she be in this terrible predicament?

Mr Chance offered Eleanor his arm. "Now, if you will

19

excuse us, we must return to our box." Before the lord could protest, Mr Chance parted the curtains and gestured for her to sit in the plush velvet chair.

Being a coward of the highest order, the viscount dithered while Mrs Dunwoody stormed into the box. Her beady gaze fell on Aramis Chance and she faltered. "This is a p-private box belonging to the Earl of Berridge. You will vacate it immediately."

Aramis Chance ignored the woman.

Theodore Chance remained standing. "Berridge is our uncle. We are permitted to occupy the family box."

Mrs Dunwoody pressed her case. "What poppycock. Your father relinquished the right to call himself family thirty years ago when he stole the silver and shot a man in Hyde Park."

"Two men in Hyde Park," Theodore corrected. "Though I believe it was self-defence."

"I shall fetch the manager and have you forcibly removed."

"Before you do, I suggest you read the contract. As a blood relative, I have a right to sit in this box."

Viscount Wrotham found the courage to take up the reins. "King George himself decreed your father should be disowned. You're no longer family. You've no claim here."

Members of the audience shifted their attention to the box. Midway through her soliloquy, an actress glanced their way, too.

Theodore Chance grinned. "George is no longer king. One could argue he was not of sound mind sixteen years ago. For reasons I cannot discuss, our family has King William's favour. Let us take the matter up with him. I believe he will agree there was a conspiracy to oust us. By rights, my eldest brother is in line to inherit an earldom when your father meets his maker."

Mrs Dunwoody blanched.

Viscount Wrotham struggled to muster a reply.

"You're playing into our hands, Wrotham. Aramis will call your father out for slandering our name and inciting men to murder us. I shall call you out for insulting my betrothed. While you're rotting in a shallow grave, our brother Aaron will be the next Earl of Berridge."

A tense silence ensued.

"Is this how you mean to seek vengeance?" Lady Lucille said, jumping to the same conclusion most conceited women would. "If you're doing this to hurt me, it won't change anything between us."

Mr Chance chuckled as if the notion were ridiculous. "The fact you think this is about you tells me everything I need to know. Go home, my lady, and take your weak-chinned affianced with you." His expression darkened. "Go now, else there'll be hell to pay."

The craven trio backed out of the box.

Mrs Dunwoody uttered something derogatory as a final farewell, but a scream of laughter from the audience drowned out the cutting remark.

Eleanor breathed a sigh of relief. She was one step closer to reclaiming her sewing box. Yes, Lady Lucille would prob-ably warn her friends to find a new modiste, but Eleanor would not die tonight.

"Well, thank you for an entertaining evening, Mr Chance, but I have business elsewhere." Having wasted enough time, she bid his family farewell and gathered her cloak. "May I have a private word outside?"

The amusement in his eyes confirmed he was unaware of the secrets hidden inside the box. "Of course."

He drew back one curtain but blocked the exit so she was forced to squeeze past him. This time, it wasn't the divine smell of his cologne that made her heart flutter but the man's sheer size.

Theodore Chance might be the youngest of four brothers, but he was no less intimidating. He stood tall and robust, a perfect monument to maleness. His powerful presence would make any woman feel safe. What a shame he was her enemy and not her ally.

The devil grinned as he joined her in the corridor. "I suppose this is where you demand I keep my end of the bargain."

"You made such a fuss about being deceived. I'm confident you're a man of your word." She straightened. Something about his manner made her wary. Perhaps he liked this game and had no desire to see it reach a swift conclusion. "I did everything you asked. It is imperative that you return my box to me tonight."

He drew his thumb across his bottom lip as he studied her. "You did more than I asked, Miss Darrow. I asked for a kiss, but you gave me a glimpse of something more intriguing."

Heavens above!

This man would test a nun's patience.

"Do not mistake me for those simpering misses who hang on your every word." She tried to dismiss thoughts of their kiss, but the touch of his lips had left an indelible imprint in her memory. "I am immune to your flirtations and flattery."

"I beg to differ." He raised his chin, his eyes shining in

silent challenge. "You may lie to yourself, Miss Darrow, but you cannot lie to me. Had I deepened the kiss, you would have welcomed me into your mouth."

The mental image of him pressing her against the wall and ravishing her senseless was entirely unhelpful. Fortunately, the fear of being slain in her bed snapped her back to reality.

"I thought you had taken a vow of celibacy."

"I'm willing to bend the rules for you, madam. You're not inclined to marry, and perhaps you'll find an illicit liaison more satisfying than sorting the spools in your sewing box."

If she had nothing better to do than tidy the threads, she might agree. His comment meant he didn't know the box had a hidden compartment. Her survival depended upon the secret notes reaching their recipients.

"The only satisfaction I seek is having my box returned to me."

"Yet your eyes tell a different story."

As if in agreement, the theatre erupted in a symphony of applause. As the audience prepared to flood the halls, eager to stretch their legs and find refreshment, she spoke with an air of finality. "No more games, sir."

Mr Chance inclined his head in acquiescence. "Your box is wedged between the mattress and headboard in my bedchamber at Fortune's Den."

The weight of her burden lifted from her shoulders. "Bring it to my shop in New Bridge Street tonight and we can put this sorry business behind us." If she did not deliver the blackguard's note by six o'clock tomorrow, she would have to leave London.

Mr Chance chose to be pedantic. "I agreed to tell you

where to find the box. If you wish to reclaim it, you must do that yourself."

With her relief short-lived, she firmed her jaw but felt like throttling him with his starched cravat. "You will be the ruin of me, sir, and not for any romantic reasons I may have once envisioned."

He narrowed his gaze. "Ruined over a few threads? Is there something you're not telling me, madam?"

*Confess,* the logical voice in her head cried.

She was out of her depth, drowning in a quagmire of deception, sinking in a swamp of secrets. Telling the truth meant admitting she was involved in immoral schemes and wicked charades. He would think less of her than he did already.

"I'm tired, Mr Chance." She had barely slept since realising her precious notes were missing. "What do you want me to say? That I shouldn't have helped Delphine? That I shouldn't have lied to you?"

"You let me think you enjoyed my company." As he spoke, she caught a fleeting glimpse of sadness behind his stoic facade. "You let me believe our conversations were the highlight of your day."

"I am truly sorry." To say anything else meant admitting she held him in high regard—well, she had before he began his quest for vengeance. "Delphine is my client and my friend. How could I refuse her request?"

He remained silent, though the hum of conversation echoing from the auditorium built to a crescendo. People poured out of the private boxes. Many stared in their direction.

Her blackmailer might be amongst them—a devious dog

in a docile pack. She had no clue whether the villain was a man or a woman.

"Come with me, Miss Darrow." Mr Chance parted the curtains to the earl's box, spoke to his brother and left abruptly. "If I didn't know any better, I'd think Aramis was glued to his wife's lips."

With a firm grip on Eleanor's elbow, he led her to the foyer, pushing past those loitering on the grand staircase. All eyes were upon them as he opened the wooden doors and led her outside into the cool summer night's air.

He inhaled deeply. "I would rather watch libertines lose at the card table than endure the nonsense on stage."

His remark was a cue to ask an important question.

"Is the club closed tonight?" she said, gauging how and when she might force the lock on the front door. "I'm surprised your eldest brother could spare you."

Aaron Chance was a hard taskmaster. Fooling him to gain entrance to Fortune's Den would be no mean feat.

Being astute, he gave a playful wink. "I suppose you're considering how you might force your way inside. This would be much simpler if you were honest and told me what's so special about the box."

Unwilling to take the blame for him being attacked a second time, she politely told him to mind his own business. "My troubles are my own. Might you summon a hackney? There is somewhere else I desperately need to be."

Mr Chance obliged by whistling to the jarvey parked farther along the narrow street. He retrieved an ornate iron key from his coat pocket, captured her gloved hand and placed it in her palm.

"Don't lose heart." His teasing grin made her wonder if the move was a strategic part of his game. "I agreed to oblige you if you made the kiss look authentic. This is your reward, Miss Darrow." He curled her fingers over the key but did not release her hand.

Something passed between them.

Something other than frustration and annoyance.

Something that made her heart race wildly.

"I presume it's the key to your club, sir, though I don't see why you cannot bring the box to my modiste shop."

He leaned closer, filling her head with his intoxicating scent. "Giving you the box means I lose the wager. If I keep it in my possession until midnight tomorrow, my brother must pay me a hundred pounds."

"A hundred pounds?" She almost choked on the words. Theodore Chance had caused her untold misery because of a stupid bet?

The hackney cab drew up beside them. Mr Chance opened the door and offered his hand. "Come to Fortune's Den after midnight tomorrow, and you may reclaim your prized possession."

Tomorrow was a day too late.

She needed the secret notes tonight.

Keen to leave and put her plan in motion, Eleanor ignored his proffered hand and climbed into the vehicle. "New Bridge Street," she said to the jarvey before facing Theodore Chance. "Thank you for the key. It makes entry into London's most dangerous gaming hell a little less impossible."

He glanced at her lips and smiled. "Approach from the east. Have the hackney park on the corner of Houndsditch. Aaron will be in his study until the lights at The Burnished Jade have dimmed."

Suspicion flared.

Why had he decided to be helpful?

"I must be better at kissing than I thought," she said, praying he did not return home until the early hours. Encountering Theodore Chance in his bedchamber would be any woman's fantasy, but she could not afford any mishaps tonight. "Had I known that was the price for your benevolence, I would have tried harder."

He laughed, giving her a glimpse of the exuberant man she used to admire. "You could not have done more to please me," he said.

Annoyed that his praise should cause a soft fluttering in her chest, she huffed. "Good night, sir. I shall try not to wake you when I come for my box."

"Have no fear. How could I sleep with the prospect of you sneaking into my bedchamber?" He moved to close the hackney cab door. "Until tomorrow, Miss Darrow. I shall await your arrival with bated breath."

# Chapter Three

Theo left the Olympic Theatre twenty minutes after Miss Darrow and returned to Fortune's Den. The club was still open. Gas lamps cast a warm glow over the mahogany card tables, where fifteen elegant men sat engrossed in games of chance. Cigar smoke hung spectre-like in the air, obscuring the men's vision and blinding them to the risks.

Their avarice knew no bounds. The thrill of outwitting one's rival proved more intoxicating than the pursuit of wealth. Losers left with mounting debts and no semblance of pride. Winners paid homage to the green baize until their luck ran out. Some players wore masks of concentration, while others had the same conflicting look Theo had seen in Miss Darrow's magnificent eyes—a curious blend of determination and fear.

What was the lady's secret?

He knew one thing with absolute certainty. Miss Darrow would not wait until tomorrow to enter Fortune's Den. The flash of fire in her eyes said she wanted her sewing box tonight. All he had to do was warn Aaron, dim the lights, climb into bed and await her arrival.

He saw Aaron speaking to the glum Lord Deacon. The peer stood on shaky legs and almost swooned when Aaron gestured to the study across the hall—a formidable place where men signed away their souls to settle their debts.

Aaron caught Theo's gaze and gave a nod of recognition. He warned Lord Deacon not to move a muscle before crossing the room. "Back so soon? I trust the evening went as planned."

"Wrotham arrived with Mrs Dunwoody. Wiping the smug grin off his face brought immense satisfaction." Not wishing to dredge up the ghosts of the past, Theo made no mention of Lucille Bowman. "I assume Deacon's debts are mounting and you're about to give him an ultimatum."

Aaron glanced at the lord and muttered a curse. "Until Deacon's affairs are in order, he's barred from the club. Had I not intervened tonight, the fool would have staked his Mayfair abode on one game of whist."

A sudden cheer at the Hazard table stole their attention. The Marquess of Rothley—a devilish gentleman in his own right—wrapped his arms around the mountain of coins and vowels on the table and gathered it to his chest like a beloved child.

Aaron called a footman to fetch a bottle of their best Burgundy and deliver it to the marquess' table, then faced Theo. "Watch the croupiers while I have a private word with Deacon. I'll not have these devils accuse us of cheating."

"Is Christian not here?"

Their brother lived with his wife in Ludgate Hill and usually remained at the club until the last patron staggered over the threshold.

"He left half an hour ago. I can manage these profligates on my own. Most deserted the tables when Rothley announced he would empty everyone's purse."

"No doubt the marquess needs the funds. They say he keeps a harem at the aptly named Studland Park." If anyone needed advice on how to embrace bachelorhood, they should ask the Marquess of Rothley. "Perhaps that's how he gained the fresh scratch on his cheek."

Suspicion lurked in Aaron's dark eyes. "Rothley is hiding something at Studland Park, but I doubt it's a harem."

Theo pulled his watch from his fob pocket and checked the time. By his estimation, he had an hour at most until his nemesis arrived. "Do you have any objection if I close the club? I'll persuade the players they have a better chance of recouping their losses if they return tomorrow."

Aaron narrowed his gaze. "As few men will sit down with Rothley tonight, your suggestion has merit, though the shifty look in your eyes says you have an ulterior motive."

He gave Aaron a brief account of the night's events, omitting the part where he had traded information for a lingering kiss and lied about being betrothed to Miss Darrow.

"I expect Miss Darrow will come tonight," he said, dismissing the pang of excitement as simple anticipation. "Like Rothley, the lady has something to hide. I'm determined to discover what."

"Why do you care?" came Aaron's direct reply.

The question stumped Theo.

The wager had nothing to do with the contents of the box.

Besides, how interesting could the modiste's secret be?

"Delphine credits Miss Darrow with helping her find

happiness," he said, struggling to think of another answer. "Though I have a personal gripe with the woman"—which had vanished into the ether when they'd kissed—"I respect their friendship. I would hate to think Miss Darrow is in trouble." Particularly since he had been treating their verbal spars like a game.

Aaron did not dismiss the notion as folly. "Although Miss Darrow expressed regret over the shooting outside her shop, I found it odd she abandoned her work to nurse you. When she comes for the box, I suggest you ask her directly."

He had every intention of doing just that. "I've given Miss Darrow a key. She should arrive within the hour. All I ask is that you remain in the study and allow her to reach my chamber unchallenged."

Witnessing Lord Deacon edging covertly towards the door, Aaron said, "I need to deal with that reprobate. I'll ensure Sigmund knows not to wrestle Miss Darrow to the ground. Come to my study once she's left. I expect a full explanation."

Theo nodded, though he doubted Miss Darrow would tell him her darkest secret. They had forged their bond in the fires of distrust. Every wary glance and guarded word was a testament to their fragile relationship.

Besides, there was nothing sinister in the box. Perhaps the threads concealed small gems, the simple cotton wrapped around her life's savings. Perhaps she was toying with him, keen to rouse his concern and teach him a lesson.

After ushering the last gambler out of the club and securing the door, Theo could not shake the suspicion that he was a mere pawn in her intricate game.

Should that be the case, his next move would be seduction.

At the very least, he would claim another kiss tonight.

That thought kept him warm as he stripped off his clothes, washed and climbed into bed. He looked inside the box and studied the wooden appliqués on the sides and lid but found nothing of interest.

Then he waited in the gloom.

Miss Darrow was right.

When a boy was forced to sleep on the streets, he used the shadows to hide from predators. At night, it was easier to evade detection. In the darkness, he was the same as everyone else, not the weakest of the pack.

He must have told her that while mumbling in his sleep. Lord knows what he'd said while dosed with opium. Miss Darrow undoubtedly had more weapons in her arsenal. It was just a matter of time before she used them.

Theo cupped his hands behind his head and relaxed against the mound of pillows. Midnight came and went. Every creak and groan drew his attention to the bedchamber door. The anticipation roused a host of erotic thoughts.

Miss Darrow had a body made for sin.

She had luscious lips and bountiful breasts.

All made sweeter by the fact she had no need to marry.

Those thoughts occupied him for a few minutes. He made no excuse for the subject of his fantasies. Tonight's game with Miss Darrow had sparked a fire in his blood.

Long minutes passed.

He climbed out of bed, strode to the window and peered through a gap in the curtains. Across the road, candlelight shone in an upper window of The Burnished Jade. Perhaps that was the reason for Miss Darrow's hesitance. Was she waiting for the lights to dim, knowing that's when Aaron would drag himself from the study and fall into bed?

More time ticked by as Theo studied the deserted street.

Miss Darrow wasn't coming. Having honed his instincts over the years, he felt it with absolute certainty. It made no sense. The desperation in her eyes and voice was undeniable.

*My troubles are my own.*

An icy chill shivered down his spine.

Had those troubles caught up with her tonight?

He would not rest until he knew.

Dressing quickly, he snatched the box off the bed and descended the stairs to the study. He found Aaron lounging in his throne-like chair in the dark, cradling a large glass of brandy, watching Miss Lovelace's club.

Theo didn't dare question his eldest brother's actions. Aaron's preoccupation with the beautiful owner of The Burnished Jade was his own business. Only a man with a death wish would demand to know why.

"I have a strange suspicion Miss Darrow isn't coming," Theo said. His breathlessness came as no surprise. His heart raced, the sound beating in his ears like a drumroll. A sudden sense of foreboding gripped him, refusing to let go. "I've decided to return the box to her tonight. I'll not bother rousing Godby." He could not wait for their coachman to ready the carriage. "It's a thirty-minute walk to Miss Darrow's shop, and I could do with the air."

If he quickened his pace, he could cover the distance in fifteen minutes. Yet a persistent voice in his head told him to run.

Aaron stood and returned his glass to the drinks tray. "To win the wager, you must keep the box until midnight tomorrow. That's what you told Miss Darrow. Perhaps you were mistaken and housebreaking isn't on her agenda tonight."

"Then why come to the theatre?" No, she was desperate

to see her treasured item returned. Why else would she kiss a man she despised? And in a public corridor, to boot?

Aaron perched on his desk, where he had a clear view of The Burnished Jade. "Why spend days at your bedside mopping your brow? She is using the box as an excuse to see you. The woman turns doe-eyed whenever you enter the room."

Yet nagging doubts took root in his mind. Miss Darrow had melted into the kiss, though it said more about his skill and her intentions than any genuine desire.

"Since I took her box, she cannot abide me."

"Can you blame her?"

Guilt stabbed at Theo's conscience. The knock to his pride had left him eager to prove a point, though it was time to do the gentlemanly thing and make amends.

"When Aramis suggested the wager, I was in a dark place," he confessed. The camaraderie had helped him forget how perilously close he had come to dying. He would be cold in the grave had the thug aimed an inch lower.

Aaron stood and gripped Theo's shoulder. "There's a reason I gave you the King of Hearts moniker. When someone hurts you, you feel it deeper than most. Remember, Miss Darrow isn't blameless. But you're right. You need to return her box tonight."

A pang of remorse twisted in his gut.

Oddly, it had nothing to do with losing the wager.

He would miss playing this game with Miss Darrow.

Aaron heaved a long sigh when Miss Lovelace extinguished the light in the upper window of The Burnished Jade. "I shall accompany you to Holborn. Since there are bets at White's on which one of us will die first, we must expect an attack from at least one debt-ridden wastrel."

"I can defend myself." He'd been shot because he was in the wrong place at the wrong time. The blackguard had caught him by surprise. It wouldn't happen again.

"You fight like a warrior, but a boy brought down Goliath. A woman defeated Samson." Aaron's gaze shifted to the window as if Delilah lived across the street. "Besides, the night air will do me good, too. For once, I might fall asleep before the cock's crow."

They left Fortune's Den, blades tucked into sheaths strapped to their shins, the box hidden in a leather satchel draped across Theo's chest, and traversed the gloomy streets to Holborn.

A drunken fool called to them from a shop doorway, begging for a spare shilling. Aaron flicked him a sovereign. A constable disappeared into a grim alley, preferring an illicit encounter to patrolling the pavements. Not that it mattered. Theo would rather police this problem himself.

Anger ignited beneath his calm facade as he strode along New Bridge Street. He had not visited Miss Darrow's shop since the day of the shooting. Every approaching step brought an influx of memories; Miss Darrow's lies, the thug's vicious threat, a whiff of sulphur tainting the air, the pain searing through his shoulder seconds before he hit the ground.

"It seems Miss Darrow had no intention of committing burglary tonight," Aaron said, stopping outside the prestigious dressmaker's shop and studying the facade.

"It's not burglary if she has a key and owns the object." Theo glanced above the swinging sign sporting an image of a gold needle and thread—a symbol of Miss Darrow's artistry. Darkness shrouded the upper windows of the four-storey townhouse.

A sinking feeling settled in Theo's gut.

Something was wrong.

Aaron tried the front door and found it locked. He knocked three times. No one answered. "Perhaps she has a lover, and they met after she left the theatre."

Theo kicked the thought from his mind. "She told the jarvey to take her to New Bridge Street."

"People often change their minds en route." Aaron glanced over his shoulder at the row of shops across the street. "She may have struck up a convenient friendship with the silversmith or cobbler. A woman living on her own must crave company. Miss Darrow works long hours. Like every woman, she has needs."

Theo's fingers tightened into fists. Was Aaron trying to provoke him? Though why Miss Darrow's private affairs bothered him remained a mystery.

"I wonder if Miss Lovelace does a similar thing when The Burnished Jade is closed on Sundays." Theo noted the instant flicker of annoyance in his brother's eyes. "Such an intriguing woman cannot be short of offers. The Marquess of Rothley asked about her tonight. Perhaps he wants to invite her to join his harem."

Theo thought he felt the ground rumble beneath his feet.

Aaron firmed his jaw and growled, "Rothley can go to the devil."

"Rothley could coax the birds from the trees while you have the charm of a wilted bouquet." Theo would have laughed were it not for the gnawing unease in his chest. "If you want her, you'd better do more than gawp at her through the study window."

"Mention her again and your tongue will be food for the

dogs. I suggest you focus on finding Miss Darrow. It's your fault she's missing."

The comment proved sobering. "You're right. We should check the rear entrance. We can access the yard via Water Lane. I'll not return to Fortune's Den until I'm certain all is well."

Maybe Miss Darrow would call tomorrow as planned.

The thought offered a sliver of hope until he strode into the dingy yard and found the back door to the premises wide open. The splintered wooden frame indicated that someone had kicked it with brute force, shattering the glass pane and scattering shards across the flagstones.

Coldness swept through him, the icy tendrils coiling around his heart. "We should enter the building," he whispered, praying Miss Darrow *was* at the cobbler's shop taking supper and the fellow was old enough to be her grandfather.

Aaron drew his blade from its sheath and insisted on leading the way. As the eldest, he lived to protect his siblings, and Theo knew not to argue.

They passed through the dark corridor to the fitting rooms and saw nothing untoward. The elegant gowns displayed in the shop window remained untouched, but someone had ripped every pair of gloves from the drawers in the glass counter. The doors to the walnut cabinet were open, the ornate combs thrown to the floor.

"We should fetch a constable." Aaron glanced at the ceiling, the deathly silence making him frown. "Miss Darrow employs three seamstresses. Do you know if any live on the premises?"

"Delphine said they only stay when work demands it." Theo learnt that much while considering who might have shot him in the street. "Though Miss Darrow has barely opened the shop since her return from Mile End."

"During your convalescence, did she mention being afraid?"

"No, though tonight she said she would reclaim the box by wicked means if necessary." He thought she'd meant seductive means and was merely teasing him. "Had she told me she was in trouble, I would have come to her aid."

"We must check the upstairs rooms." Shadows of unease passed over Aaron's rugged features. "Prepare yourself. There's every chance she's here."

A bleak image burst into his mind.

Less than two hours ago, they had shared a memorable kiss. Now, Miss Darrow might be lying sprawled on the landing in a pool of blood, her eyes gazing at heaven, not him.

Nausea roiled in his stomach as he followed Aaron into the gloomy hallway. They crept upstairs to the first floor, their footsteps as silent as whispers in the night.

Every room had been ransacked. Bolts of silk ripped from their cotton covers, exposing them to dust and damp. Every chest prised open, an assortment of material spilling over the floor like it had been spewed from the belly of a beast.

"Perhaps they were looking for her box," Theo said, his heart heavy with regret. "It's fair to say Miss Darrow is hiding something more precious than threads."

"Then why the devil didn't she say so?"

"Because she believes the people who did this are capable of murder." It explained why she closed the shop and stayed at Mile End to nurse him. "She feared the villains who shot me had come to abduct her, not Delphine." And every day he'd kept the box, she must have been out of her mind with worry. "This is my fault. If only I'd not been so bloody angry."

Aaron raised a silencing hand. "We're all to blame. Aramis and Daventry encouraged you. None of us could have known what was inside the box."

"There's nothing inside but spools of thread. I've searched through them ten times or more." He removed his hat and dragged his hand through his hair. The most important thing was finding Miss Darrow. Then they could worry about what she kept in the damnable box. "We should check the upper floors."

Aaron nodded and led the way.

With each step, Theo dreaded what the blackness might reveal.

There were three bedchambers on the second floor, all conveying scenes of utter disarray. It was like a storm had swept through the house, scattering personal objects over the floor, upending furniture and untucking the bed linen.

"This is Miss Darrow's room." Theo recognised the enticing scent of her perfume. "I pray she didn't come home to this." He wasn't sure anything could be salvaged. "I pray she was somehow delayed."

"With the absence of a body, we should be grateful for small mercies," Aaron said in his usual blunt manner. "Though she may have been abducted. Does she have any friends that you know of? Might someone offer her sanctuary?"

They were typical questions an enquiry agent would ask but Theo was clueless. "She never mentioned friends or family."

Miss Darrow had spent days at his bedside, talking about

history, food and books while he slipped in and out of a drug-induced slumber. He knew she disliked macaroons and preferred the poems of Keats to Coleridge, yet he knew nothing of her personal life other than she designed dresses for a living.

While Aaron left to summon a constable, Theo roused the cobbler across the street, who confirmed he had seen nothing untoward. He woke the cabinet maker, who agreed to secure the premises by boarding the back door.

It was almost three in the morning when they returned to Fortune's Den. A constable had taken their statements and scoured the premises looking for clues. With no sign of Miss Darrow's body, the peeler refused to rouse the magistrate from his bed, at least not until noon.

Aaron gave Theo a reassuring pat on the back as they lingered at the bottom of the stairs. "We'll visit Mile End tomorrow and make sure she's not hiding there while Delphine is visiting her grandfather in Chichester."

The theory she could be at Mile End brought mild relief. Had Miss Darrow arrived home to find looters in the house? Had she fled for her life and hailed another hackney to take her across the Thames to Walworth?

"Get some rest," Aaron added. "Miss Darrow is a resourceful woman. Instinct tells me she's alive. It's fortunate you still have her box. Had the blackguards found the valuable item, she may have paid the ultimate price."

Aaron's confidence was reassuring.

"I know you're right, though I doubt I'll sleep tonight." He should return to the Olympic and question the jarvey. Perhaps he had delivered her to a different destination.

"We'll find her. If need be, we'll hire Daventry's enquiry agents."

Theo forced a smile and bid Aaron good night. As he trudged upstairs to his chamber, his conscience urged him to load a pistol, return to Miss Darrow's shop, and begin the search again, though he could not risk taking the sewing box. Indeed, he removed it from the leather satchel, held the dratted thing in his hands and cursed his stupidity.

That's when he heard a gasp from a dark corner of the room.

He swung around and peered into the blackness, his imagination running riot. Had the villain come for him, too? "Who's there?"

A flash of pink silk drew him to the washstand, where he saw a woman huddled in the corner, hugging her knees to her chest.

"Forgive me. I had nowhere else to go." A sob caught in Miss Darrow's throat. "I've lost everything, Mr Chance, my dreams and aspirations crushed like ants beneath a blackguard's feet."

Despite the thread of fear in her voice, a sense of calm washed over him. She was alive. Nothing else mattered.

"You speak of the damage at your shop? I have just returned from New Bridge Street. I assume you know someone broke into your premises."

"Why else would I be here?" The hint of contempt in her tone said she had not come to listen to his flirtatious banter or endure another breathtaking kiss.

"Take my hand." Tucking the wooden box under his arm, he reached for her. "Let me help you."

"No one can help me now," she uttered, slipping her ice-cold hand into his and letting him haul her to her feet.

With a sigh of regret, Theo offered her the box. "You should have told me what this meant to you. I would have respected your need for privacy. By nature, I'm distrusting, though that is no excuse." A boy left to survive in the rookeries became suspicious of people's motives.

She stared at the box, though she did not snatch it from his grasp or sag in relief. "I need you to do something for me, Mr Chance."

"Anything," he said, a vision of her ransacked home bursting into his mind. "The game went too far, and for that, I am truly sorry. I'll do whatever it takes to put this right."

She met his gaze in the gloom, her tear-filled eyes shimmering like stars in the night sky. She seemed so distant now. Any connection they'd shared had evaporated into the ether.

"Will you see me safely to Dover? I believe you owe me that." Tears traced a silent path down her cheeks, and he fought the urge to dash them away and insist on a different course. "I need money. You may raid my shop and sell anything of value. An established modiste will purchase the lace and gold brocade."

The knot in his chest tightened. "Where will you go?"

She seemed a shadow of her former self as she hung her head. "Wherever the first ship out of port will take me. Anywhere far, far from the home I love."

# Chapter Four

Mr Chance stood clutching the box he had stolen two weeks ago and stared into her eyes. He was no longer grinning like the sinful scoundrel who had kissed her at the theatre. He offered no teasing retorts or wicked suggestions. From his strained expression, he knew nothing he could say would make this right.

"The destination is unimportant," she lied, her throat tightening at the thought of abandoning everything she had worked so hard to achieve. How many ladies of six and twenty had the skills to dress London's elite? "I don't care where I go as long as it's far from England's shores."

"May I ask why?"

"You may not." It was too late to care now. He sealed her fate when he stole her box. "The secret might cost me my life. I'll not place you in danger. Not when I bear some responsibility for you being shot outside my shop." Having seen her beloved home ravaged by blackguards, surely he knew to heed her advice. "See me to Dover—or Portsmouth if you prefer—then put this dreaded business behind you. Forget you ever met me."

"It's not that simple." He opened the box and peered inside as if it were something of the devil's own design. "I cannot forget the part I played. My thoughtless actions are the cause of your ruin. I will—"

"Greed was my downfall, Mr Chance. Greed, and an elevated notion of being the most famed modiste of the decade. The fight for financial security can cloud a lady's judgement."

Guilt plagued her, too. The crippling guilt that came with knowing she had stolen someone else's life. Every breath she took was not her own but made in her beloved mother's memory.

"It's not a sin to want a stable future," he said, unaware of the real issue. "To excel, one must take risks. I assume that's how you're in this predicament. Do you owe a debt you cannot pay?"

A fear of failure was the root of her problem.

The risk of bankruptcy was great indeed.

Thieves stole silk from shipments. Bolts arrived ruined. The middle-aged clerk at the shipping office tried to bribe her with reduced costs on imports if she dined with him each Friday.

One sly remark at a ball was enough to relegate her design to the compost heap. Gowns would need unpicking and altered. Eleanor would spend endless hours trying to save the expensive material. All while her father's dying demand was like the prod of a pistol in her back.

*Your mother dreamed of having her own shop. You'll do it for her. Don't let me down, girl. You owe her your life. It's the least you can do.*

Though her father had died five years ago, his veiled contempt was still a crushing weight on her shoulders. His gentle jibes still hurt more than the stab of a blade.

"While your actions have made it impossible for me to remain in town, Mr Chance, I got myself into this regrettable mess." Much like his silly wager, what began as an innocent game had cost her everything. "There remains but one way to evade my tormentor."

"You're fooling yourself if you think you can escape your problems." He retreated to the dim depths of his chamber. Perhaps he thought she needed space to think. Perhaps he hoped to entice her to confess every wicked secret. "Is that how you want to spend your life, always looking over your shoulder? Forever living in fear?"

"If I live to see tomorrow, it will be a blessing."

He fell silent as he sat on the edge of the carved ebony bed. Bracing his arms on his muscular thighs, he turned the box over in his hands and examined the carved appliqués.

"In my defence, there is nothing here to warrant concern," he said, looking a little baffled. "How could I have known what this meant to you?"

"You couldn't. As a modiste, I'm an expert illusionist."

She dared to move from the safety of the shadowy corner, where she had sat crying for an hour because the box was not wedged between the mattress and headboard as he'd claimed.

"What you do with pearls and lace is short of a miracle."

She couldn't help but smile at the inflated compliment. "A skilled seamstress can find work almost anywhere. Though if I'm to have any future, I must leave town tonight."

He said nothing for a moment, and left her tuning into

was an understatement. "I doubt there's a person alive who considers you weak."

"I think I am weak, and that's one person too many."

The day of the shooting flashed into her mind. Mr Chance had refused to hand his sister over to the armed thug. He acted as a human shield and risked his life to save Delphine. It was the action of a courageous man, not a coward.

"I am yet to see any evidence to support your claim, sir."

"Do you know what my father did to Aaron?"

"Yes, he made him fight in the pits and used the purse to pay his gambling debts." Delphine had confessed while being fitted for a new gown, though the memory had left tears streaming down the lady's face, wetting the silk.

"Aaron was twelve and fought men three times his age and size," Mr Chance said, contempt for his sire deepening his voice. "My father would wake us upon their return. Force us to light the lamps and gaze upon our brother's bruises. He aimed to make Aaron fight harder so we wouldn't have to witness his pain."

Eleanor put her hand to her mouth in disgust.

Compared to his father, hers was a saint. Yet she knew how it felt to stare into the eyes of a man who professed to love you, only to discover it was a lie.

"I would close my eyes, screw them so tightly my head hurt," he added, repeating the action as if he were back in that room. "I would count the seconds until I could extinguish the lamps and banish the sight of my brother's suffering." A mocking snort escaped him. "I ask you, Miss Darrow, is that not the sign of a weakling?"

It was the sign of a child with a pure heart.

An innocent soul being corrupted.

"You were a boy forced to face an ugly truth."

She'd recently had a similar awakening. There was nothing romantic about delivering secret letters. Love affairs were like a poison, infecting those involved and ravaging relationships. She had been no one's saviour but an instrument of destruction and despair.

"I suppose you're wondering why I am telling you this." He placed the offending object in her lap. "How does it relate to me stealing your precious sewing box?"

What made a man reveal something so personal?

To gain her trust?

To explain his lack of empathy?

To mend a broken bond?

"I have no notion, Mr Chance, but I'm sure you're keen to tell me."

Again, he gazed at the rug, which in itself was a blessing. His magnetic blue eyes had the power to bend people to his will. She remained steadfast in her decision to leave town.

"Had I shown my father that I was unaffected by his game, that I could cope with whatever villainy came my way, I would not spend my days living with regret."

Still a little confused, she said, "If you're asking me to stay and face my problems, know that is not an option." Her blackmailer had lost patience. Why else would he ransack her home?

Mr Chance cast her a sidelong glance, the look in his eyes conveying the confidence of someone used to dealing with scoundrels. "I am asking you to light the lamps and open your eyes, Miss Darrow."

She gave a mirthless chuckle. "I assure you, my eyes are wide open to the dangers. Had I used the front entrance and not seen the broken door and shards of glass in the yard, I might be dead."

Yet she had crept into the shop, desperate to assess the damage. The sight had torn her heart in two. Expensive gloves tossed over the floor like rubbish. Drawers upended. Tortoiseshell combs snapped. A mirror smashed. The banging above stairs made her take to her heels and run.

"Your eyes may be open, madam, yet you see nothing but failure. Allow me to help you. Believe you can overcome your difficulties."

Silent seconds passed as she stared at him.

She couldn't ask him to risk his life without offering a reward.

While she envisioned every tragic scenario—her possessions lost when her enemy razed her house to the ground, her being kidnapped and tossed into the Thames—his optimism was like the glimmer of a dawn horizon, the warm rays chasing her doubts away.

"And how can you help me when I am clueless myself?" That was the nature of secrets. She had no idea what was written inside the notes. "I don't know who raided my home, nor do I have the faintest idea why they targeted me."

He frowned as he stood and faced her. "You speak in riddles, Miss Darrow. How can you be insensible to the problem? Surely it has something to do with your sewing box."

*Tell him!*

For heaven's sake, she should tell someone.

If she died, the culprit would go unpunished.

"Why should I trust you?" she said with a weary sigh.

"Because I already know half the story," he was quick to reply. "Because I have people at my disposal capable of solving the crime. Because I mean to make amends for any torment you have suffered on my behalf, even if I die doing so."

His impassioned entreaty left her speechless.

What lady wouldn't want such a commanding figure fighting her corner? Perhaps he meant to atone for closing his eyes to his brother's torment. Perhaps he had another motive for coming to her aid. If he did, he had no intention of confessing.

"If I tell you," she began, the four simple words sending her pulse soaring, "you must respect my wishes. The problem is mine. If you mean to help me, you will not treat me like a hapless female incapable of mopping up her own mess."

A smile touched his lips and he nodded. "And you will accept that my experience with crooks and villains gives me an insight you do not possess."

Not wanting to wrangle over who was wisest, she focused on the one thing lacking in this alliance. "We need to learn to trust each other. I suspect honest communication is the key."

Mischief shone in his eyes. "How honest would you like me to be?"

"As honest as you have been tonight."

He put his hand over his heart. "I can do that."

She dared to let hope blossom in her chest. Upon hearing her story, he may reconsider his position. Even the best enquiry agent would struggle with the lack of clues. Yet instinct said Mr Chance had the brains and brawn needed to help her with this problem.

"I'm not entirely sure where to begin." Her fingers shook as she ran them over the lid of her sewing box. How strange that one tiny piece of paper could destroy a person's life? "Perhaps this is the best place to start."

He observed her closely as she gripped the sides of the box in her hands. She rested the soft pads of her thumbs on the two fleur-de-lis decorations. If one pushed them simultaneously towards the centre, and with the exact same pressure, the hidden drawer clicked open.

Mr Chance inhaled sharply at the sight of the velvet-lined compartment. "You're right, Miss Darrow. You're a master of illusion. I suspected a hidden cavity but never found one."

"I bought it from a man at the Bartholomew Fair. He said it was a lovers' box, somewhere a lady might hide secret letters." She removed the three folded notes—all a mere one-inch square and sealed with a different wax or stamp—and placed them on the coverlet. "If only he'd said it was a sewing box, then it would not have sparked the idea that became the cause of all my woes."

"We need light." Mr Chance took a friction match to the oil lamp on his chest of drawers and the candles on his nightstand. He returned to the bed, retrieved one note and held it between his long fingers as if it were as innocuous as a sweet biscuit. "Am I to understand you didn't write these letters?"

"I am paid to be a messenger, sir."

"Paid? By whom?"

"My clients. It began with Lady Summers complaining about her nosy maid. I offered to deliver a note for her and accept a reply."

If only it had stopped with one simple transaction. But Lady Summers was a veritable gossip and responsible for an influx of new clients visiting the shop. None cared about the design of their new gowns, only that Eleanor act as a courier for their sordid missives.

"As there are three notes, I assume they're not all from Lady Summers." A frown marred Mr Chance's brow as he examined the tiny paper folds. "Whoever wrote them has very little to say."

"They had no choice in the matter. If I am to hide a note in the pocket or hem of a garment, it must be small."

"And the shades of wax and different stamps?"

"Are a means of identifying the sender."

Mr Chance gave an appreciative hum. "It's a rather ingenious way of making money, Miss Darrow."

"Not so ingenious. It has become a troublesome venture made worse by public demand. Many of my clients are harridans posing as respectable ladies. A woman harbouring a secret can be merciless."

"I cannot disagree," he said, the words as bitter as bile.

"One client threatened to ruin me when I failed to deliver a note on time. She insisted on telling those who would listen that my designs are outdated." More than that, she had complained the material was of inferior quality.

"That's the gamble one takes in the game of deception. I trust you have a valid reason for playing with schemers."

She explained the rising cost of silk, ruined shipments and the constant pressure to please the rich. "It was my father's dying wish that I should succeed in this business." It was a demand, not a wish. "It's why I accepted a job from an anonymous source."

The stranger had twisted her arm quite literally.

The fiend—dressed in black and wearing a hooded cloak—had appeared from a darkened corner of the yard. He had grabbed her from behind, plastered his gloved hand to her mouth, a metallic smell overpowering the earthy whiff of leather, and given her an ultimatum.

*You'll deliver my notes where and when I tell you.*

*If they fail to arrive, you'll die.*

*If they arrive open, you'll die.*

*If you tell anyone, you'll die.*

"Ah, now we're getting to the crux of the problem, Miss Darrow." Mr Chance captured her chin and insisted she look upon his handsome visage. "Your trembling lips tell me all I need to know."

"And what is that?"

"You're afraid of this person. You presume they're responsible for the damage at the shop. Is that why you need the box? Is that why you came to play nursemaid during my recuperation?"

She doubted he'd appreciate the truth, but he needed to hear it.

"If we're to learn to trust each other," she began, "I must confess that I fled the shop fearing I was the intended target."

The crack of pistol fire had preceded his sister's scream. Remorse had flooded her chest like a relentless tide, yet her first thought was for her own survival.

He released her chin as if he'd scorched his fingers on a brazier. "I knew you'd not nursed me out of loyalty or guilt."

"I sat at your bedside, made you a healing broth and cleaned your wound because I was genuinely sorry for what happened. Once I learned why you were shot, I knew it was safe for me to return home. Had you not stolen the box, I would have had time to deliver the notes, and we would not be standing here now."

He had the decency to look ashamed. "I suppose that makes us even in this game of subterfuge."

"Yes, if you help me as you agreed."

He glanced at the pathetic pieces of paper, the contents as lethal as a blade. "Put the notes away and leave the box on my nightstand. We will visit Lucius Daventry and explain everything to him." He arched a knowing brow. "Including the details you have failed to mention. You're tired. I'll not press you for an explanation now."

What could Mr Daventry do?

How did one find a nameless blackguard?

"But it's almost dawn. Do you not require sleep?"

One look at his black carved bed and the pulse in her throat thumped harder. While she had caught more than a glimpse of his chiselled chest, any woman would give their right arm to see Theodore Chance sprawled naked between the sheets.

"I plan to sleep until ten, Miss Darrow, but we must tend to a personal matter first."

A personal matter?

Did he mean to offer another trade?

Another kiss in exchange for his assistance?

Heat crept up her neck to warm her cheeks. "In an attempt to strengthen our fragile bond, I must be honest. Nothing you could offer would persuade me to kiss you again."

His gaze fell to the opening of her cloak, a smile forming on his villainous lips. "Having kissed you once, I know that's a lie. Rest assured, I have no plans to share my bed with anyone, least of all a woman who cannot abide me."

Should she admit that kissing him had been nothing short of extraordinary? Should she confess her disdain for him did not rage as fiercely as it ought? If she meant to be true to her word, the answer was yes. But he straightened his coat and took a fortifying breath as if preparing to leave.

"If you plan to sleep until ten, why do you look like a man on a mission? Where is it you need to be, Mr Chance?"

"We have one rather large obstacle to climb if we're to get any rest tonight. You cannot return to your shop. As Delphine no longer resides here, her room would be perfect for you."

Live at Fortune's Den? She supposed there was nothing to fear. Her reputation was already in tatters, and he spoke as if she were a visiting aunt, not a woman he was desperate to bed.

"You're suggesting we live under the same roof again?" Eleanor managed to sound jovial despite the flare of heat in her belly.

"If I'm to help you, I need to keep you close." His tone lacked the warmth she felt coursing through her blood. "I assume you have nowhere else to go, no relatives to speak of."

"No. I have no friends or family in town." She had no one out of town either. Was that why the blackmailer targeted her?

Mr Chance clapped his hands and rubbed them vigorously. "Let us head to my brother's study. You'll need to sway him to your cause." His gaze dipped to the opening of her cloak. "Your feminine charms will give you no advantage. Aaron has eyes for only one woman, but he will listen to reason."

Aaron Chance was sitting in the dark when they entered his study. His gaze moved over her with cool indifference.

"I'm glad to see you're still breathing, Miss Darrow. Sigmund informed me you had entered the premises."

Sigmund was their man-of-all-work, a beast of a fellow who dealt with drunken lords and daring intruders.

"They say Sigmund has the nose of a bloodhound. Truth be told, I was expecting to encounter him before I reached the stairs, sir."

"Theo asked that I grant you a pass."

Eleanor cast Theodore Chance a sidelong glance. He had been expecting her tonight. Evidently, he wanted to make amends.

"I need to prey on your kindness and beg one more courtesy," she said, knowing few people would dare to ask Aaron Chance for a favour. "As you know, I cannot go home."

"I'm sure Theo has told you to use Delphine's room, and now you seek my permission." Aaron snatched the crystal glass off the desk and downed what looked like brandy. "I want a detailed account of your problem, Miss Darrow. I'll not risk my business by harbouring a criminal."

"You can trust my brother," Theodore said.

Knowing she had little choice in the matter, Eleanor explained what she kept in the box. The Chance family rallied together when presented with unknown dangers. Aaron Chance's support was vital if they hoped to find the blackguard who'd broken into her shop.

"We will seek Mr Daventry's advice and proceed from there," she said.

Aaron gave a humourless chuckle. "Daventry will guide you, I'm sure. He has a knack for fixing things that are broken."

"Then you agree Miss Darrow can stay?"

Aaron shrugged. "Who am I to argue with fate?"

# Chapter Five

*Hart Street, Covent Garden*
*Office of the Order*

As the master of a group of skilled enquiry agents, Lucius Daventry had witnessed many astonishing sights, yet he seemed most intrigued by Miss Darrow's unusual box.

"Can you describe the man who sold it to you?" Daventry said from behind his imposing desk. His dark eyes narrowed as he closed the secret drawer and placed his thumbs on the wooden appliqués.

"I'm afraid he was quite nondescript, sir."

Miss Darrow rose from the chair and showed Daventry how to open the drawer. The old blue pelisse she had found in Delphine's armoire hung loosely from her narrow waist, and she had spent thirty minutes this morning adjusting the hem and sewing a makeshift belt. The teal boots were too big, and she had stuffed the toes with old stockings. Still, she could wear a grain sack and still look exquisite.

"Think, Miss Darrow," Daventry said in his usual blunt

way. "It may be a crucial piece of evidence. The villain who ransacked your shop may have deliberately targeted you."

"Targeted me?" The lady frowned. "I don't see how. It was my idea to deliver Lady Summers' notes. Had she held her tongue, I would not be in this predicament."

"Lady Summers knows how to use her title to her advantage. The subtle art of persuasion is her forte. And let's be frank, you have not been entirely honest, madam."

Theo suspected the same but had decided against forcing a confession. While he had persuaded Miss Darrow to face her fears, he knew she would rather leave London than tackle the culprit.

Theo leant across the arm of his chair and touched Miss Darrow lightly on the forearm. "We're here to help you, but you must tell us everything you know. Hearing half-truths will hinder our progress."

"Half-truths lead to flawed reasoning," Daventry added, though grinned when he heard a click and saw the velvet-lined compartment pop open. "I'll not risk an agent's life. And I'm sure Mr Chance wishes to avoid taking another shot to the shoulder."

A sad sigh escaped her. She stared at Theo, not Daventry, an almost apologetic look in her mesmerising eyes. "A man attacked me in the yard. It was dark. I did not see his face, but he grabbed me from behind and said if I did not deliver his letters, I would die."

A knot tightened in Theo's gut. There was nothing more despicable than a man who used his physical strength to suppress a woman.

His mind drifted to the night his mother died. Did she trip over her nightgown and tumble down the stairs? Had his father pushed her during another heated argument? Was it a coincidence that the devil's first wife had suffered the same fate? He would never know.

Daventry placed the box on the desk and gave Miss Darrow his full attention. "You said you purchased the box at the fair. I assume that was last summer."

"Yes, sir. In August."

"And when did you offer to act as Lady Summers' messenger?"

Miss Darrow tapped her finger to her lips as she considered her answer. Feminine vulnerability lay beneath her indomitable spirit. The contradiction proved more fascinating than seeing the hidden drawer in her sewing box.

"I cannot recall when exactly, but she instructed me to place the note in a bible and leave it on a certain pew in St Audley's Church. It must have been February during Candlemas. People were taking candles to church to be blessed."

"And you don't know what was written inside the note?" Theo said. Being suspicious by nature, he would have waited to glimpse the recipient. "You weren't curious enough to linger in church?"

"No. I assured Lady Summers I would deliver the note and leave. Besides, the less I know of her business, the better. A working woman cannot afford to anger her client."

It had been that way when Aaron first opened a gaming hell, but he soon realised the lords of the *ton* liked the exclusivity of a members' club. The night he refused Lord Bretton entrance was the most intelligent decision Aaron had ever made.

Once Theo had helped solve Miss Darrow's problems, he would give her some sensible business advice.

"Hence you agreed to deliver notes for a host of other society ladies." Daventry glanced at the three tiny missives visible in the secret compartment. "Have you ever opened a note?"

A blush touched her cheeks. "No, but the barrow boy has."

"The barrow boy?" Theo inhaled sharply. Everyone knew a child could not keep a secret. "Someone else knows about your lucrative exploits? Why did you not say so before? I presume it's the same barrow boy you were waiting for the day I was shot."

She nodded but was quick to defend her position. "I needed help. Jules is twelve and provides for his ailing mother and younger sibling. Curiosity got the better of him. I don't know why. He cannot read. Then he dropped it in a puddle. I had to forge Mrs Brampton's handwriting and begin again. Thankfully, she was none the wiser."

"What did the note say?" Theo was more than a little intrigued.

"Royal Oak. Seven. Wednesday." Miss Darrow waved her hand impatiently. "Or something to that effect."

Doubtless the message referred to an illicit liaison. If Miss Darrow wasn't careful, she might be called as a witness to adultery. No lady in London would dare purchase her gowns then. The only person crossing her threshold would be the bailiff.

Daventry drew a piece of paper from the desk drawer and took up his ink pen. "We will need a list of those who paid for your services."

Miss Darrow's head jerked up. "Why? They paid in good faith. I will be ruined if word gets out. Surely the focus of our investigation should be the devil who threatened me in the yard."

"In my experience, the obvious suspect is rarely the

guilty party." Daventry dipped the nib into the ink pot. "Their names, Miss Darrow. Whatever you reveal shall not be spoken beyond these walls."

After mumbled complaints and an obvious wrestle with her conscience, she pulled back her shoulders. "Miss Fresson —though she has delicate sensibilities and won't take kindly to being questioned."

"I'm sure you will know what to say to her."

"Lady Chapman. Mrs Langdon." Miss Darrow mentioned three other names before pausing to catch her breath, but the list went on. "Lady Clementina Morley—"

"Daughter of the Duke of Farnborough?" Theo almost fell off his chair. Did the lady not know she was dicing with danger? Farnborough would slay an entire village to protect his daughter's reputation.

Daventry's expression turned grave. "Then we will add the duke's name to the list of suspects. I shall need time to decide how best to proceed. The matter requires tact and diplomacy."

Theo's pulse rose a notch and he gestured to Daventry's list. "This is more complex than I imagined. If any of these women discover we know about their notes, Miss Darrow will be driven out of town."

Worse still, someone may seek to silence her for good.

One kind gesture had opened Pandora's Box. According to myth, the only thing left inside was hope. It would take a miracle for Miss Darrow to survive this mess unscathed.

"Let us focus on the blackguard who attacked you in the yard," Theo said. They would begin by questioning the barrow boy. A child desperate to feed his family could be easily bribed.

"There is another lady's name to add to the list." She met

Theo's gaze, her verdant green eyes losing their sparkle. Then she bowed her head and revealed the name that made his blood boil. "I—I delivered notes for Lady Lucille Bowman."

Anger burned in Theo's veins. Why was he surprised? Lady Lucille was a devious devil who valued a prestigious title more than her fickle heart. What grated most was he'd made a damn fool of himself.

"You should have told me," he snapped.

"When? We've barely had time to breathe since I stole into your bedchamber last night."

"You could have mentioned it on the carriage ride to Covent Garden." Theo felt the weight of Daventry's inquisitive gaze but continued, regardless. "How are we supposed to work together if you insist on keeping secrets? Where is the trust?"

"It's not a secret. But I know how fond you are of her. You're all she spoke about during her last fitting. I was simply trying to find the best time to tell you."

"The only thing I feel for Lucille Bowman is disdain."

"Are you quite certain? Your actions at the Olympic last night suggest otherwise. You wanted to make her jealous. Was that not the reason for our intimate trade?"

Their kiss may have started as a means to bolster his defences, but the touch of Miss Darrow's lips made him forget anyone else existed. Time had stood still. Nothing else had mattered. Hell, he'd not stopped thinking about her since they'd parted.

He would kiss her now should the chance arise.

During their ride across town, his mind ran amok as he imagined dragging her onto his lap and settling her restless spirit.

"Do you know who Lady Lucille was writing to?" Daventry said, adding to Theo's discomfort. "Ladies of the *ton* like to gossip."

Miss Darrow released a sweet hum as she pondered the question. "No, though I got the impression she was annoyed with someone."

"Doubtless the lady is keeping another gentleman dangling by a string," Theo said but was quick to change the subject. "Perhaps you should explain the barrow boy's role in this debacle."

Daventry agreed. "We need to understand how your operation works. I assume you keep a record of every transaction."

"Yes, in a diary at home, though it may have been stolen."

Was the villain looking for the book or the box? Had a seamstress stumbled upon the information and used it to line her coin purse?

"We'll return to the shop when we leave here." He would not hide behind Aaron like a lily-livered fop. If men wished to attack him, they could try their luck. "We'll search for your diary, and you can pack a valise. I know you're eager to collect clean clothes."

Miss Darrow nibbled her lip. "Just the two of us?"

"Just the two of us." The lady had courage abound. Did she not say she wished to mop up her own mess? Was she not a woman of action? "I can give you a pocket pistol. Sadly, I don't have an iron skillet to hand. I'm told it was your weapon of choice when I was shot outside your shop."

Her eyes brightened. "I grabbed the first thing I could find. When used with force, a skillet is lethal. Though I confess, I cannot fire a pistol with any accuracy."

Theo smiled. "All you need do is point it and cock the hammer."

"We must visit Jules," she said as if she'd only just realised the boy might be in danger. "I've not seen him for a few days. What if the villain discovered where he lives?"

Daventry pushed a piece of paper across the desk and offered her a pencil. "Note down the boy's direction. I'll have an agent visit him now and move his family to a safe location."

Giving a relieved sigh, she did as instructed. "Jules delivers the notes to a place of the client's choosing. He collects them from the same place. Sometimes, I'm required to hide them in a seam or tucked inside a hat or glove and deliver the garment to an address. The process is different for every client."

"What about the fiend who attacked you?"

The lady shivered as if the beast had trampled over her grave. "He leaves them in the yard, slipped inside a leather-bound book which he hides in the coal shed. I have delivered three in total, though there is never a reply."

Theo pointed to the three tiny letters on the box's velvet tray. "One of these must be from the man in question. You seem so certain he was responsible for the damage to your shop."

With shaky fingers, she pointed to the note sealed with black wax, a colour typically used for mourning. "That is the note I was supposed to deliver two weeks ago. But you stole the box, Mr Chance. I had no way of informing my client. He was waiting for me the night I returned from Delphine's wedding."

While a gnawing sense of remorse filled Theo's chest, Daventry said, "Did he hurt you?"

Miss Darrow winced. "A little."

Theo shot out of the chair. "You should have told me." He ripped off his hat and thrust his hand through his hair. "I would have returned the box and helped you defeat this devil."

She looked up at him with a sad expression, her eyes glistening like dew on a meadow. "I'm used to fending for myself. It's hard to know who to trust." Her gaze fell to her lap, a silent testament to the trials she must have endured.

Though the situation was not as harrowing as seeing Aaron hurt as a child, it pained Theo to know Miss Darrow had suffered while he'd been sleeping peacefully in his bed.

"I promised to deliver the note this evening." She looked at the mantel clock and seemed relieved it was only midday. "He insisted I bring it personally and said there must be no more mistakes. I'm to place it inside the book he left in the shed and deliver it to the travelling library at six o'clock."

"The travelling library?" Daventry narrowed his gaze. "You speak of Mr Pickering's elegant wagon? Only the wealthy can afford to pay for his services."

"Pickering used to call at Fortune's Den before my brother Christian moved to Ludgate Hill." Theo returned to his seat. From his recollection, Pickering would move mountains to please his prestigious customers. "The fellow sourced rare books on Ancient Egypt. It saved Christian endless hours of research."

"Do you always deliver the villain's notes to Pickering?" Daventry said.

Miss Darrow nodded. "I hide them beneath a paper bookplate I glue to the inside cover."

Theo found that odd. "Why does the villain not hide it

66

there himself? Then you would have no need to handle the note."

"Because he has been known to change his mind." She paled and clutched her hand to her chest. "I woke to find he had been in my bedchamber. He left instructions to say I must deliver a different note. So I can only imagine he does not wish to deface the book."

"The devil broke into your house?" Theo could barely sit still. When he caught the miscreant, he would wring his damn neck. "When?"

"A month before you were shot outside my shop."

He could understand why Miss Darrow thought the armed thugs had come to kidnap her and not Delphine. The lady was up to her neck in the mire. Now it was up to him to ensure she didn't sink.

"You have an obvious problem," he said, though it was one of many. "I see no sign of the book. How are you supposed to deliver the note at six this evening?"

"I pray it is still at the shop."

Daventry stood abruptly and snatched the paper with the barrow boy's direction. "I'll catch D'Angelo before he leaves and have him visit the boy. While I'm gone, decide if you wish to open the letters or use them as bait."

Daventry departed.

Barely a second passed before a subtle intimacy enveloped them, one born from their shared goal. This unspoken connection prompted Theo to reach out, his hand finding hers, offering a reassuring squeeze that spoke of their newfound bond.

"We will fix this, and you will dress the ladies of the *ton* again. I give you my word." He looked at the box and the three letters resting on the burgundy velvet. "Who do the other notes belong to? You must tell me the truth. You mustn't be afraid to confess your darkest secrets."

Miss Darrow glanced at their joined hands. He expected her to tug hers free, but she did not. "It must be comforting to be part of a large family. There's always someone there to ensure you remain on the right path. Someone to tell you your decisions are foolhardy."

Yes, his brothers did not mince words.

"Is there anyone I might contact on your behalf?" Was there someone in the world who cared about her? A parent or sibling? "A person you trust enough to help you with this matter?"

Her gaze rose to meet his. Though she smiled, he knew the look of loneliness in a woman's eyes. "There is no one, Mr Chance. My parents are dead." There was a tinge of guilt in her tone, as if she had been the one to slay them. "It's just me, battling the world alone."

"No. We are battling this fiend together."

She swallowed deeply and pursed her lips like she might cry. "Which goes to prove one cannot foretell the future. I'll never forget how you looked at me all those weeks ago when you stormed into the yard. I pray I never disappoint anyone like that again."

*I can tolerate many things, Miss Darrow, but never deceit.*

*I'll not trust another word from your lips.*

The crux of his anger had stemmed from his fears for Delphine.

"You proved yourself my match when you barged into the theatre box, threatening to use wicked means to over-throw me." And she had. One kiss had left him craving another. He would wring every last whimper from her lips if she'd let him. "I think that makes us even."

"I always hoped we might be friends before tragedy struck as it did. You were amusing company."

"I'm still amusing company. I see no reason why we cannot be friends now." Hell, he had told her the one thing he'd never revealed to another living soul. "I heard you used to find me charming."

She laughed. "Who told you that?"

"Delphine."

"Your sister exaggerates. Although the way you came to her rescue was rather gallant."

"Does that mean you'll consider kissing me again?" He couldn't help but tease her, though the answer mattered more than it should.

"Why would I? You have nothing with which to barter."

"Trust me. I shall find something."

"That sounds like the beginnings of a game, Mr Chance."

"Perhaps it is, Miss Darrow." While her rosebud pout held him captive, her gaze traced the breadth of his chest. "A game of seduction. Let us see who submits first."

A spark of intrigue flashed in her eyes. It was the happiest he had seen her in weeks. "Very well. But there is only one rule."

"Which is?" Why did he find a simple challenge so arousing? They had troubles abound but this proved the perfect distraction.

"Honesty. Lies result in a forfeit."

Theo couldn't help but grin. "Agreed. I've said it before, but you're my kind of scoundrel, Miss Darrow."

"Let's pray you're as magnanimous when you lose."

He couldn't lose. There was pleasure to be had in playing the game. "When do we begin?"

She shrugged. "There's no time like the present."

"Very well." He released her hand and captured her chin, stroking her soft skin gently with his thumb. "It's good to see you smile again."

Suspicion flashed in her eyes as she attempted to determine if he spoke the truth. "Why?"

"The world seems brighter when you do."

"I might doubt your word and force you to cluck like a chicken."

"But you won't because you know I speak in earnest."

Daventry returned, though he lingered outside the door, giving Theo the split second needed to release Miss Darrow.

"D'Angelo is leaving now. I'll inform you of the situation once he has visited the barrow boy." Daventry pointed to the notes in the secret drawer. "Well, are you opening them or using them as bait?"

"Miss Darrow must decide what's best."

"Agreed." Daventry picked up the note sealed with green wax. "I'm confident when I say a gentleman's wife or daughter sent this. Green wax is reserved for the clergy and members of government."

Miss Darrow cast Theo a nervous glance.

That's when he knew the sender's identity.

"Lady Lucille wanted the note taken to an address in Finch Lane, Cornhill," she said. "I was supposed to deliver it weeks ago. When she came to the shop last Friday, I lied and said I had delivered it myself."

Theo didn't grit his teeth or silently curse the deceptive Lucille Bowman. It amused him to know she manipulated

Wrotham like a virtuoso did a tuned fiddle. "If you agree, Miss Darrow, we may as well open the note."

Daventry handed it to her.

Without hesitation, she broke the seal. A frown marred her brow as she squinted to read the small writing. "*Hyde Park. Noon Wednesday. At the Achilles statue.*"

Theo recalled the times the lady had sent him secret letters. They had met on the Row early one morning, met one afternoon at the British Museum to observe the exhibition of Tantric objects. He would not hear from her for weeks, and then another letter would arrive.

Aramis was right in his observations.

Theo was more in love with the idea of besting the aristocracy than with the lady herself. He was more annoyed at being treated as an inferior than of losing something precious.

"It's as I suspected." Theo couldn't keep the bitterness from his voice. "Lady Lucille has another fool dangling like a marionette."

"It would appear so," Daventry said.

Miss Darrow retrieved the letter sealed with red wax. "The image of the laurel means this belongs to Mrs Langdon." She opened it carefully. "*Same place Wednesday evening.* That's all it says."

Most people used Miss Darrow's service to conduct illicit liaisons. If they wanted a note back, they merely had to ask. The theory meant there was but one line of enquiry to pursue—finding the villain who attacked her in the yard, made threats and turned her shop upside down.

"We will focus on Pickering," he said, resisting the urge to break the black seal and read the scoundrel's missive. "As all the notes are passed through him, we will persuade him to give us a name."

Daventry's gaze flicked between them. "Have a care. Something tells me there's wickedness afoot, and I'm not talking about the immoral exploits of the *ton*."

"What is there to fear?" Theo would keep Miss Darrow in his sights until they had the devil in custody and she could return to her shop.

"You'd do well to remember one important fact." Daventry's tone carried the weight of his warning. "Only the dead keep secrets."

# Chapter Six

With the rear entrance of Eleanor's shop boarded to prevent intruders, they had no choice but to park the carriage outside the premises on New Bridge Street.

She shuffled to the edge of the seat, impatient to alight. Debtors' prison awaited her. Salvaging the silk and Chantilly lace might raise enough funds to keep her from the Marshalsea.

"What's the hurry?" Mr Chance opened the door and was first to the pavement. He extended his hand. "Allow me to assist you."

The man was a monument to contradiction. Despite being a dangerous rogue who co-owned a gaming hell, he possessed a gentleman's breeding. Goodness lay beneath his sinful facade. It was an attractive combination.

"Time is of the essence. There's not a second to lose." She poked her head out of the carriage and glanced left and right. The villain could be lurking in the vicinity, waiting to pounce.

Was that why she shivered?

Was she scenting danger?

"It's four hours until your appointment with Pickering and his mobile library." Mr Chance's warm fingers grasped hers, his gaze falling to her ankles as he helped her descend. "We've plenty of time to attend to matters here."

"We should avoid drawing undue attention." The hairs on her nape prickled. Someone had their beady eyes fixed on them. Living with a distrustful father taught one to have a second sight.

"You fear the villain might be stalking the premises?"

"Yes, if he is keen to retrieve his note."

"But you're to deliver the note today. The damage caused to your property was to ensure you kept the appointment." His gaze moved to the loose curl escaping her simple chignon. "I'm only grateful he took his temper out on the cabinets and not you, Miss Darrow."

Although Mr Chance had seen her without a bonnet before, she felt a little naked beneath the weight of his stare.

"Doubtless he meant to frighten me." The villain wasn't her only problem. "The local shopkeepers will demand to know what happened last night. Gossip spreads like wildfire. Mudlarks who scour the Puddle Dock raided the cobbler's yard last month. They will suspect the same happened here."

Indeed, as she retrieved the door key from her pelisse pocket, the silversmith hurried across the street, calling her name.

"Miss Darrow. Thank heavens you're well." Mr Franklin —a man of thirty with wavy brown hair and a countenance that left her clients drooling—had thrown his coat on in a hurry, for the collar was askew. "I saw two constables searching your premises early this morning and haven't slept a wink."

Since the shocking theft at the cobblers, Mr Franklin kept his nose pressed to the window most days, searching for the elusive culprit.

"They suspect a vagrant entered my shop, hunting for food." She hated lying but could not confess to being attacked in her yard and hounded by a devious devil. Wielding spades and batons, the shopkeepers would charge down to the Puddle Dock, determined to make someone pay for the crime. "Based on the damage caused, the vagabond must have been ravenous."

She introduced Mr Chance and the air turned frosty.

The men scrutinised each other with obvious suspicion.

"You're the gentleman who was shot by that thug last month," Mr Franklin said, eyeing her companion. "Being so close to the Thames, we get all sorts of riffraff wandering up from the barges and merchant ships."

Mr Chance hardened his stare. "I was shot while protecting my sister. Indeed, I'm duty-bound to ensure Miss Darrow receives no further trouble." He drew his calling card from his pocket and thrust it into Mr Franklin's calloused hand. "Miss Darrow will reside with a friend until her affairs are in order. Should you notice anything untoward, do your civic duty and report it to me."

Mr Franklin arched a brow as he read the elegant script. "You're a gambling man," he stated with a touch of disdain.

"I run a gaming club. Only a fool stakes his future on the dice."

Mr Franklin clearly feared for Eleanor's safety. He leaned forward, his brows furrowed in quiet concern. "If you'd like to remain in Holborn, we have a spare room. Anna would be glad of your company. You've been of great help to my sister. Her needlework is much improved."

Eleanor smiled. "That is most kind, sir. Miss Franklin is an excellent student, but I hope to return home in a day or two. I have merely come to assess the damage."

Mr Franklin looked a tad disappointed. "Well, the invitation stands if you change your mind."

"I doubt she will," Mr Chance said bluntly.

A tense silence ensued before the silversmith mentioned the vagrant. "I suppose the rascal ruined your silk. I saw Emily moving the bolts this morning. Well, I say this morning, but it was just before dawn. The poor girl was up with the larks."

While Eleanor reeled from the surprising news, Mr Chance said, "Emily?"

"A seamstress I employ when work demands it." She kept a calm tone though many questions danced in her mind. Emily had no reason to visit the shop, and certainly not at the crack of dawn. "Emily mentioned borrowing her father's cart, hence the early hour."

That was another lie.

But how else was she to gain information?

"Yes, she came with an older man I didn't recognise."

"I'm visiting Emily this evening to take an inventory of the stock she saved. I'm sure she will be relieved to learn business will resume soon." She thanked Mr Franklin and bid him good day.

Mr Chance waited until the fellow crossed the road before offering his expert opinion on the minds of men. "Franklin wants you."

She wasn't being vain when she said, "I know."

"I expect many women think he's handsome."

"I expect they do." Her fingers shook as she unlocked the

door. A fear of what she might find was the cause, though Mr Chance presumed otherwise.

"Does Franklin always make you nervous?"

She might have fed him a tale as part of their game but could not risk paying a forfeit. "He doesn't make me nervous. You're the only man who raises my pulse."

"I am?"

"Don't sound so pleased. Most of the time I'm angry."

The overhead bell tinkled as Eleanor entered the shop. The once welcoming melody had a sad ring to it now. Her gaze fell to the mess on the floor, her property scattered like the remnants of a shipwreck washed ashore. She doubted anything was salvageable.

"It grieves me to admit it, but I have made a dreadful mess of everything." Tears welled. Misfortune had plagued her since birth. This shop was her mother's dream, her father's legacy. Disappointed, her parents must be turning in their graves. "I have felt powerless many times. None more so than now."

The stab of failure cut deep.

The gentle touch of Mr Chance's hand on her back preceded his thoughtful comment. "Things aren't as bad as they seem. I could have the place straightened in no time."

To prove the point, he retrieved two pairs of gloves, dusted them off and placed them neatly on the glass counter.

The man's charm was impossible to ignore. Confidence oozed from every pore. Eleanor stole a glance at his muscular thighs as he crouched to complete the task. While the sight roused heat in her belly, the kind gesture made her heart race like a runaway carriage.

She bent down to help him.

Their fingers brushed as they reached for the same glove.

"You don't need an excuse to touch me," he said, a teasing twinkle in his eyes. "You don't even need to ask."

Like a moth to a flame, his allure was irresistible. "After our interlude at the theatre, why would I want to touch you again? You satisfied my curiosity."

His smile turned sinful. "Did I? I don't see how. The things a man can do with his hands are limitless."

It took mental strength not to conjure an erotic image.

"Mr Franklin said a similar thing only last week." The lie left her lips before she could reclaim it.

Being as sharp as a tack, he grinned. "You owe me a forfeit, Miss Darrow." He looked at her lips, and she felt sure he would demand another kiss. "I believe I shall claim it now."

"What do you want me to do, Mr Chance? Cluck like a chicken?" She wasn't ready to kiss him again. Not when he weakened her defences.

"Where's the pleasure in that?"

She swallowed hard. "What would give you pleasure?"

"Education is everything, is it not?" Still crouched, he flexed his fingers. "The touch of a man's hand was the catalyst that brought down Troy."

She suspected the feel of his hand would be her ruin, too.

"Let me begin with something simple to prove my point," he said softly. "Let it be an exercise in the power of anticipation."

He waited for her permission to begin.

"I'll not stop until you demand it," he warned her before caressing her cheek in slow, mesmerising circles.

The heat of his skin warmed her face and soothed her restless spirit. She closed her eyes briefly, finding solace in his touch. Tenderness was a potent drug for a lonely heart. Everything about this man was addictive.

"Relax," came his whispered command.

Her shoulders sagged as if willed by the gods.

"I've never seen lips so plump," he said, an undeniable hunger in his gaze as he traced the shape with his thumb. He worked closer to the seam, seeking entrance. "I'll never forget how soft they were. You'd drunk wine before coming to the theatre. That, or you always taste like dark berries."

"You'll never know."

His languid smile stole her breath. "There's always a way to achieve one's goal," he said, penetrating the seam where her mouth was moist. He wet his thumb before taking it in his own mouth and sucking hard. "Hmm. I feel a thorough inspection is needed. But not today."

Her heart pounded now.

Perhaps he saw the rapid beat of her pulse in her throat. Perhaps he knew the muscles in her abdomen were tight. That heat pooled between her thighs.

Exploring further, he drew featherlight fingers down over her lips and chin, down the column of her throat.

The hairs on her nape prickled. Tingles ran down her spine. She thought of halting his in-depth study, but the thrill of anticipation left her eager to know what he planned to do next.

He paused, his fingers lingering at the base of her throat, his brow rising in silent challenge.

"Is something wrong, Mr Chance?"

"Not at all."

"Does that conclude the end of the lesson?"

"Not quite. Shall I continue?"

The answer should have been no, but she nodded.

Those dangerous digits moved again, trailing slowly southward, leaving a scorching path in their wake. His wicked blue eyes remained fixed on her, waiting for her to say stop.

He paused again when he reached her left breast.

She arched a brow, daring him to continue.

The pads of his fingers grazed her nipple.

She inhaled sharply. Not because she felt his touch through the layers of material or because lust had her in its powerful grip. The fire in his eyes stole her breath. The slight tremble of his fingers said these feelings were not one-sided. This wasn't part of the game.

"I think that concludes the lesson for today, Mr Chance."

A sensual hum escaped him. "Thank the Lord. You're killing me, Miss Darrow."

Eleanor smiled to herself as she gathered more gloves off the floor and rose to her feet. "I concede. A man might work miracles with his hands if his partner is willing."

"A fact we may explore if you lie to me again, madam."

"I won't make the same mistake, sir," she said, placing the gloves on the counter. They couldn't be sold as new, but that was the least of her concerns.

"Mistakes are regrettable." He rose and adjusted his trousers. "Nothing that happened between us a moment ago could be deemed so."

Being careful not to lie, she said, "No, you did a superb job of proving your point. There's a reason they call you the King of Hearts. I'm told you collect hearts and break them. I mean to guard mine with my life."

"You, of all people, should know not to listen to idle gossip. Particularly when it comes from the mouth of Lady Lucille Bowman." He did not give her an opportunity to refute the claim. "Where did you leave the book the villain placed in the coal shed?"

"Under the boards in my bedchamber." Glad of a distraction, she dusted off her hands and beckoned him to follow her upstairs. She realised the room might be in a dreadful state, too. "Did you happen in there last night?"

A muscle in his jaw twitched. "Yes."

His tense shoulders told her all she needed to know.

"Prepare yourself," he said, mounting the stairs beside her. "The room is a shambles. The intruder left no stone unturned in his search for your box."

Part of her wished she had inspected the upper floors last night. Then she would know the face of her tormentor— assuming she had lived to tell the tale.

A whimper escaped her when she peered inside the store-room and saw the empty shelves. The small tapestry boxes had been tossed aside. Gold and pearl buttons littered the boards like pretty shells on a beach. She stood rigid, gripping the doorframe before her knees buckled and she collapsed in a heap.

"I'm ruined." The words were a whisper, but they hit her like a punch to the gut. "I pray Emily took the silk for safe-keeping. I have no hope of raising the funds to replace what's lost."

Mr Chance stood behind her, his warm hand settling on her shoulder. Like a sturdy shelter in a storm, his presence brought a sense of calm.

"Write a list of what's missing and I shall have it replaced." His thumb moved in soothing circles on her nape. "You have troubles enough without worrying about bankruptcy."

"I cannot take your money."

"You can and you will. I'm to blame for this debacle."

"You're to blame for taking my sewing box. You're not to blame for this. I agreed to play the messenger. My father always said I lacked my mother's common sense."

"I imagine he would eat his words if he knew you dressed the most prestigious ladies in London."

"He would find fault. Nothing was ever good enough. I could never reach the mark." There was always room for improvement. The beef was never tender. The chunks of apples in the pie were too big. She read too slowly. Ate too quickly. Walked with a sloppy gait.

"Criticism is rooted in insecurity. Perhaps your father blamed you for his own failings. Noting your flaws boosted his own sense of worth."

Eleanor faced him, confusion and wonder fighting for supremacy. She had been conditioned to believe the problem lay with her.

"You surprise me, Mr Chance. I never expected you to be so—"

"Sensible?"

"Wise."

"We all play roles, Miss Darrow. How does the youngest of four fearsome men find his own identity?" He answered before she could. "He becomes what his brothers are not. Playful. The jester. The King of Fools. An amusing distraction amid life's troubles."

"You do yourself a disservice."

"I do?"

"You're a better man than you claim."

Love for his sister had shone from him like a brilliant beacon. His kindness towards Delphine knew no bounds. He was fiercely loyal. Strong. Dangerous. Unafraid to fight for what he believed.

"You have seen the best and the worst of me, Miss Darrow. You're one of the few people who knows me as I really am."

While she still felt the imprint of his teasing fingers, his remark fostered a deeper intimacy. Warmth gathered in her chest, not her loins.

"In a world where most people wear masks, know you can always be yourself with me, Mr Chance."

His slow smile said he had mischief on his mind. "I'm glad you said that. Veracity is something to be admired. Might you permit a scoundrel to show his gratitude?"

The sudden pounding in her throat made her swallow. "I spoke the truth. There is no need for me to pay a forfeit."

"This has nothing to do with our game," he said, wetting his lips. "I cannot concentrate on any task until I've paid homage to the only woman who understands me. Consider it my way of saying thank you."

"You're referring to a kiss, I trust?"

"I wouldn't presume to ask for anything more."

"Very well." Suppressing a grin, she offered him her cheek. "You may kiss me, Mr Chance. After which, you will pay a forfeit."

"For what?"

"You don't want to kiss me out of gratitude. You've had the same sinful look in your eyes since you touched me downstairs."

He laughed and slapped his hand to his heart. "I confess, you have the measure of me, madam, though you're wrong. I've had the same sinful thoughts since our interlude at the theatre."

That kiss had stayed with her, too.

She had been out of her depth, floundering in a wild sea of emotions. During those amorous seconds, the weight of her burden had lifted. The touch of Mr Chance's lips had made her feel like someone worth loving.

She would do well to remember it was all an illusion.

A strategic move in his game.

Eleanor pointed to her cheek. "Well? Will you kiss me? We have work to do and cannot dally all day."

A shiver raced down her spine when his fingers brushed her waist. His mouth was hot on her skin, the pressure light. He didn't kiss her once but worked his way across her cheek, each featherlike touch lingering a little longer.

Her eyes fluttered closed when he reached the corner of her mouth. It was a mistake. She should have prised them open because Theodore Chance was an overload on a lady's senses.

The sound and feel of his breath stirred the hairs on her nape. The sweet, aromatic scent of sandalwood flooded her nostrils. He was everywhere, his masculine aura teasing every nerve in her body to life.

Seeking more, she turned her head a fraction.

Then their mouths met—a sudden desperation igniting.

Eleanor had felt many emotions in her life: shame, guilt, a profound inadequacy. She had never felt a rush of passion so strong it almost knocked her off her feet.

The kiss they'd shared at the Olympic had been slow and tender.

This … this was raw. Unbridled.

This was lust, a greedy battle to feed the hunger.

Heaven help her. She couldn't resist him.

She gripped his coat lapels as he pushed her back against

the wall. They kissed in an open-mouthed frenzy. Heat pooled low and heavy. The pulsing between her thighs was like the incessant beat of a drum.

*Sweet mercy!*

This was madness.

"Mother of all saints! Tell me to stop," he panted but claimed her mouth again with a need that defied logic.

A sweet moan rumbled in her throat.

He cupped her nape and deepened the kiss.

There was something savage, something reckless about the way he drank from her. Like she was the only woman who could slake his thirst. Every kiss was a desperate attempt to ease an ache, to sate a longing that knew no bounds.

The thought proved sobering.

Keen to guard her heart, she dragged her mouth from his, gasping to catch her breath.

Mr Chance looked at her, his gaze smouldering, his lips moist. "I suppose now I must pay a forfeit," he said huskily.

"Don't look so pleased. I might ask you to wrestle a wild dog." In truth, she had no idea how to make this game enjoyable. How did one keep a man like Theodore Chance entertained? More kisses, perhaps?

"I would wrestle wolves for one more taste of your lips. When it comes to kissing, you more than meet the mark."

"You possess the skill," she said, struggling against the weight of his praise. "I am merely a novice."

"You need to learn to accept a compliment."

Heat crept to her cheeks. "It's hard when you have been the constant cause of a man's misery. I feel compliments are undeserved."

He studied her before tucking a stray lock of hair

behind her ear. "There is beauty in your modesty. But when the fire of confidence blazes in your eyes, you're breathtaking."

Breathtaking? She had always believed herself quite plain.

"I—I'm not sure what to say to that."

"You say thank you."

She smiled. "Thank you."

He stepped back. "Now, what is it you'd have me do?"

Watching him prance like a peacock would be wholly amusing. But he had used his forfeit to rouse her desire. While the need to kiss him again was a potent beat in her blood, she wished to know him better.

"Answer one question."

"Which is?"

"What is your greatest fear, Mr Chance?"

He jerked, apparently shocked by the question. Deep furrows marred his brow. No doubt he would rather yap like a Pomeranian than divulge something personal.

"My greatest fear has nothing to do with *my* life," he said, leaving her more than intrigued. "Few things frighten me, but I'm afraid of what will happen to my brother Aaron if he's left to live alone."

It was an answer worthy of the King of Hearts.

It was an answer that caused a flutter in her chest.

"Aaron Chance is the most formidable man in town," she said. He was a dangerous devil who seemed happy his siblings had married. "I imagine nothing fazes him."

"Aaron thrives on solving problems. He lives to protect his family. Every sacrifice he has made has been for us."

"I'm sure he will adapt." Living alone could be daunting. It had taken her months to sleep through the night and not wake thinking every creaking board was an intruder. "Is that the reason you're avoiding female company?"

"I'm not avoiding *your* company." He smiled as his gaze raked over her body. "And you're every bit a woman, Miss Darrow."

"And you're a scoundrel who lives to tease me."

"I'm merely helping you forget your troubles."

He had certainly done that.

"Then there is a more efficient way to spend your time. Gather anything of value. Fill a drawer with gloves. Search for bolts of material. We must take everything we can carry."

Putting distance between them would prevent Eleanor from falling into his arms again. Salvaging the small things might pay for a ticket to Boston. A modiste who had dressed the haute ton would easily find work overseas.

"I shall pack a valise and fetch the villain's book." She gestured to the sprinkling of buttons on the floor. "These will fetch enough to cover a few months' rent."

She didn't linger on the first floor but hurried upstairs.

Mr Chance's soothing scent seemed to follow her, though it did little to prevent the wave of despair when she saw the devastation in her bedchamber. Clothes lay crumpled and scattered everywhere. The bedclothes had been torn from the mattress and now trailed forlornly across the floor. Amidst the chaos, she searched desperately but couldn't find the patchwork blanket her mother had made—the cherished blanket she had clung to all these years.

Suppressing the need to cry, Eleanor dropped to her knees by the loose board. She brushed the mound of clothes aside and raised the plank.

Her heart sank.

The hollow space was empty.

No leather-bound book.

No record of those who had paid her to deliver their missives.

It wasn't enough that the intruder left her feeling violated. He had stolen her only means of putting an end to this nightmare. How could she deliver his note? Mr Pickering knew to accept a specific book.

Eleanor tried to recall the title.

It was something obscure, like *Falkirk or Falkland.*

She could not locate another copy, not in time to deliver it to Mr Pickering. A different book would have to suffice, along with an explanation.

She stuffed garments into a valise and hurried from the room, keen to assist Mr Chance and leave the premises before the silversmith came prying. A quick peek inside the adjacent chamber confirmed it was a shambles, too. It looked like a whirlwind had whipped up the contents.

Stemming her tears, she made for the stairs.

That's when she heard a creak behind her and felt a sudden breeze. A hard shove in the back made her lose her balance. She cried out, her valise slipping from her grasp as she went tumbling down the stairs, hitting her head on a wooden step and landing with a thud.

# Chapter Seven

The thumping sound above stairs had Theo straightening. "Miss Darrow," he called. He thought he'd heard a sharp cry. Perhaps she had stubbed her toe amid the chaos upstairs or kicked the door, annoyed at herself for kissing him again. "If this is part of our game, know I am up to my elbows in ladies' gloves."

Silence.

Not a faint chuckle.

Not a teasing or flirtatious remark.

Theo dropped the bale of gloves onto the glass counter, strode into the hall and gripped the newel post. "If this is a ploy to lure me to your bedchamber, know I would come willingly."

Silence.

Theo might have returned to the mundane task of glove sorting, but a pang in his gut forced him to mount the stairs two at a time. He knew his fears were founded when he reached the landing and saw Miss Darrow lying on the floor.

*Saints, have mercy!*

Theo froze.

Her face was as pale as a cadaver, her legs akimbo.

Her eyes were shut as if the darkness was her solace, too.

A childhood memory assaulted him. A shrill scream had brought his sleepy-eyed brothers racing out of the bedchamber. Four years old and tripping over his nightshirt, Theo had peered around Aaron, desperate to witness the spectacle at the bottom of the stairs. The image of his mother's awkward pose—the blood streaking her golden hair, the bulging whites of her eyes—haunted him to this day.

Gathering his wits, Theo stepped over her heavy valise, dropped to his knees and tried to rouse the lady. Panic assailed him. Blood trickled from a tiny cut on her hairline. Even a minor head wound could have disastrous consequences.

"Miss Darrow." Theo's hands shook as he stroked her limbs to ensure none were broken. He checked her pulse, relieved to feel a gentle pounding beneath his fingers. Gathering her into his arms, he uttered, "I'm going to move you now." He'd been powerless to save his mother, but he'd be damned if he'd let Miss Darrow die. "Hold on to me."

She lay limp in his arms, her breath barely a whisper.

Theo held her close and descended the stairs.

He exited the shop, shouting for his coachman to open the carriage door. "For pity's sake, hurry."

The burly fellow scrambled into action. "Stone the crows. What happened to her, sir?"

"Miss Darrow tripped over the hem of her pelisse and tumbled down the stairs." It was Delphine's pelisse and far too long for her. "Fetch her valise from the first-floor landing and secure the front door. The key is in the lock. Hurry, man. She needs a physician."

Reminiscent of the day Miss Darrow helped bundle him into a vehicle, Theo used brute strength to place her on the seat. Once inside, he drew her onto his lap and continued speaking, willing her to wake.

"There's something to be said for Keats." He stroked her hair from her brow, his stomach twisting into knots. "The line he draws between good and evil is often unclear. Perhaps it's a testament to his humble beginnings."

His hopes of rousing a response came to nought.

Godby reappeared. He threw the valise atop the box, settled on his perch and flicked the reins. The carriage lurched into motion seconds before the nosy silversmith came dashing across the street.

Theo checked his pocket watch. They would miss their appointment with Pickering's mobile library. But all was not lost. They could break the black wax, open the ominous note and force the librarian to confess. They could interview the barrow boy, assuming he was unharmed. Any insignificant detail might be pertinent to the case.

As the carriage raced towards Aldgate, Theo found himself staring at Miss Darrow's lips. They were soft and plump, but that's not what made their kisses unique.

An unknown ingredient had roused a fever in his blood —a secret something entwined with the hypnotic scent of jasmine, the warmth of her lips, and the vibrancy of her adventurous spirit.

He shouldn't have touched her today. He shouldn't have put his mouth to hers and drunk until intoxicated. How was he to solve her problems when every intimate interaction complicated matters? Yet, the need to taste her again was like a silent call from the soul.

Was seduction not part of their game?

Did she not welcome his advances?

His gaze moved over her delicate features. She was as fragile as fine china, yet beneath this dainty exterior was a determined warrior.

Who was she? What had happened to her parents?

Where had she learnt her dressmaking skills?

Had she ever been in love?

The need to know more about her proved compelling. Perhaps she had been plagued by a similar compulsion when saving him from death's door. She had certainly probed his mind as he lay in bed recuperating.

When they arrived at Fortune's Den, Aaron was outside, arms folded and glaring at The Burnished Jade, the ladies' club across the street.

Aaron opened the carriage door, looked at Miss Darrow's lifeless body nestled in Theo's lap and growled, "What the hell happened?"

"Miss Darrow fell down the stairs." Theo shuffled to the edge of the seat, certain Aaron was imagining a horrid scene from their childhood. "Send Sigmund for a physician."

Aaron shouted for Sigmund and barked orders when he came charging out, fists clenched as if expecting trouble. "Fetch Gentry. Tell him it's urgent. Go now."

Sigmund did not dally. Mr Gentry had a private practice in Leadenhall Street. Aaron paid him to attend the monthly boxing bouts in the Den's basement.

"How long has she been unconscious?" Aaron hauled Miss Darrow into his arms like she was as light as a babe.

"Ten, maybe fifteen minutes." He knew the point behind the question. The longer she remained comatose, the more likely she had suffered a lasting injury. "She stirred as we drew into Aldgate Street but didn't open her eyes."

"Let's pray she wakes from this stupor soon." Aaron stepped aside for Theo to alight. That's when he noticed the elegant woman in a green pelisse and matching pillbox hat hurrying towards them. "Lord, give me strength. Just when I thought matters couldn't get any worse."

Miss Lovelace, the delightful owner of The Burnished Jade, came to a crashing halt beside them. "Good heavens. What has happened to Miss Darrow? Is that blood on her forehead?"

"She fell," Theo said as Aaron turned his back on the woman he secretly admired and carried Miss Darrow inside.

"Shall I fetch a doctor?" Miss Lovelace followed Theo into Fortune's Den. "Mr Gentry is an excellent physician. His practice is a two-minute walk away."

"Thank you for your concern, but we have the matter in hand. Sigmund will return with Gentry posthaste." Knowing the woman affected Aaron like no one else, Theo invited her to stay. "You spent time with Miss Darrow at Delphine's wedding. I'm sure she would appreciate seeing a friendly face when she wakes."

"Perhaps I may be of some assistance." Miss Lovelace entered the drawing room—a private place reserved for family—and watched Aaron gently lower Miss Darrow onto the gold brocade sofa. "Though limited, I have some experience of head injuries."

"Of course you do," Aaron mocked, though he seemed determined not to look at her. "Is there anything you cannot turn your hand to, madam? Snake charming? Mapping the stars?"

Miss Lovelace raised her chin. "When a woman lives alone, she must learn to be self-sufficient. If you must know, I invited Mr Gentry to give a lecture on treating common ailments. He proved most popular with the ladies at my club."

Theo suspected Gentry's popularity had more to do with his striking countenance than his admirable profession.

Aaron surely thought so, too, because his strained smile failed to hide a flash of jealousy. "The ladies you serve are wallflowers. The attention of any man would leave them rigid in their seats."

"How parochial, Mr Chance. Never underestimate a wallflower. Just because we do not parade like broodmares at Tattersall's does not mean we are lacking."

Aaron huffed. "You are not a wallflower, madam."

"And how have you reached that conclusion?" Miss Lovelace removed a vinaigrette from her reticule and thrust it into Theo's hand. Unabashed, she raised her skirts and knelt beside Miss Darrow. "See if you can rouse her while I loosen her clothing."

"A wallflower is timid by nature." Aaron's eyes were upon her now that she had her back to him. "You're as bold as a brigadier."

Desperate to see Miss Darrow smile again, Theo pulled the stopper from the dainty bottle.

Miss Lovelace unbuttoned Miss Darrow's pelisse to expose her throat. "Wave the aromatic salts under her nose." She glanced over her shoulder and caught Aaron looking at her ankles. "As you know nothing of my personal struggles, sir, I suggest you keep your opinions to yourself."

Miss Darrow's head jerked the instant she inhaled the potent substance. She coughed, wrinkled her nose and turned her head.

Theo released a deep sigh, relief relaxing every tense muscle. "Miss Darrow? Can you hear me?" He prayed there were no lasting mental effects from the fall. That he'd have every chance to repair the damage he'd done.

Miss Lovelace touched the backs of her fingers to the patient's cheek. "Please pour her a glass of brandy, Mr Chance. It may help to revive her spirits."

Aaron obliged, though muttered something about being a lapdog. He returned and handed Miss Lovelace the glass, careful not to touch her fingers.

The brandy worked wonders. A mere sip brought the colour flooding back to Miss Darrow's cheeks. She opened her eyes, though seemed confused to find herself in a drawing room.

"Where am I?" She winced as she shifted on the sofa.

"You're at Fortune's Den," Miss Lovelace said, gripping Miss Darrow's hand and rubbing the life back into her bones. "Do you remember why? Can you recall what happened?"

"I—I'm not sure." She rambled like a bedlamite while verbally retracing her steps. "I saw Mr Franklin, the silversmith." Then she recalled Theo caressing her cheek while they were collecting gloves. "I think it was part of the forfeit."

"Forfeit?" Aaron snapped, his disapproval evident.

"It's nothing," Theo said. "Just a little game we play to pass the time."

It wasn't nothing. The intimate moments with Miss Darrow fed his newfound craving. Cravings passed, though he would never tire of kissing her.

"Don't you think your games have caused enough trouble?"

"The game is crucial to building trust."

"Yes, I remember we were kissing," Miss Darrow confessed, leaving Theo inwardly groaning. "No, that was before I ventured upstairs and discovered someone had stolen my book and diary."

Stolen! The thief had lifted the floorboards?

Was the villain after the book or the list of Miss Darrow's clients?

Miss Lovelace glanced at Theo like he had committed a mortal sin. "I'm not sure we need to know every detail, Miss Darrow."

Aaron was quick to respond. "With you being a wall-flower, I imagine it unsettles your delicate sensibilities."

"I am hardly delicate. I saw you without your shirt last month and didn't swoon."

The verbal spat left Miss Darrow more confused. "Was this before or after I arrived at Fortune's Den?" She released a weary sigh as her eyes fluttered and closed. "I'm so tired I could sleep for a week."

Gentry arrived promptly, wearing a black coat with fashionable oversized lapels and carrying his bulging leather case.

"You took your time," Aaron said.

Gentry placed his bag on the low table. "I came immediately. I trust this is the lady who fell."

Miss Lovelace rose and offered the physician a beaming smile. "Thank you for coming, Mr Gentry. Miss Darrow has suffered a head injury and has only just regained consciousness."

Gentry spoke to Miss Darrow, observing her speech with keen interest. Then he stared into her beguiling eyes, checked her pulse and touched various parts of her body. "Tell me if this hurts?"

"No, sir, but I fear I must sleep."

"Do you feel nauseous?"

"No."

"Do you recall how you fell?"

Miss Darrow shook her head, though the action pained her. "I kissed Mr Chance," she mumbled. "It is enough to make any woman giddy."

Theo inwardly smiled. He'd found himself equally enthralled, though concern for Miss Darrow had him pestering Gentry for a diagnosis.

Gentry stood. "I suspect a mild concussion. Bedrest for a day or two should suffice. If you find you cannot rouse her, or there is blood from the nasal cavity or ear canal, fetch me at once."

Aaron thanked him and gestured to the door. "I'll show you out. We wouldn't want to keep you from your patients."

"I can show Mr Gentry out." Miss Lovelace straightened her jaunty hat, and her gaze shifted to the doctor. A man who would make any woman swoon. "I hoped you might visit The Burnished Jade to give a lecture on the healing power of the mind. My ladies found your last speech most informative. Miss Moorland has spoken of little else since."

Gentry bowed—though Aaron looked ready to murder someone.

"I would be happy to oblige. I shall check my diary and have my secretary send a list of suitable dates." He raised a stalling hand and a confident smile. "There's no need to see me out. I know the way."

Miss Lovelace did not take her eyes off Gentry until he left the drawing room. Excitement oozed from her pores. Her eyes sparkled like polished sapphires. "Oh, my ladies will be thrilled."

Theo wished it was dark enough to hide the taut lines etched on his brother's brow. He wished he could screw his eyes shut to avoid seeing the signs of Aaron's discomfort. As a child, he had watched Aaron build barricades to shield himself from pain. If those defences came crashing down, there'd be Armageddon.

But he couldn't worry about Aaron now. Miss Darrow needed his help to tackle her problems, problems which were mounting by the day.

"Miss Darrow needs rest." Theo was eager to leave before Aaron said something to chase Miss Lovelace away.

Sadly, Aaron failed to hold his tongue.

"Most women make a fool of themselves over Gentry."

Miss Lovelace shot Aaron a questioning look. "They do?"

"He is married to his work."

"And you think I am searching for a husband?"

"You seem eager for his company."

The lady laughed. "Do you know how hard it is to get professional men to give a lecture to ladies? Practically impossible." She took a step towards Aaron, but his firm stance didn't falter. "I cannot afford to fail, Mr Chance. Encouraging gently bred ladies to visit the club is crucial to my survival."

Aaron did not remind her women lacked the gumption needed to run a club. Nor did he suggest an Aldgate address would deter a certain class of lady.

"Tell me whose services you seek, and I shall ensure they make themselves available to you."

Miss Lovelace stumbled a little. "You will?"

"I'm not in the habit of saying things I don't mean."

That was a lie. Every word spoken to this woman was intended to push her away and keep Aaron's armour intact.

"What would you want in return?"

Aaron did not need time to think. "For you to remain on your side of the street. For you to close your curtains before you undress for bed. For you to pick someone other than Gentry to give a talk on the humours."

While the lady stared at him, dumbfounded, Theo crouched beside Miss Darrow. The need to see her resting comfortably in bed and to talk without interruption had him scooping her into his arms.

"I am taking Miss Darrow upstairs."

Aaron nodded. "Come to my study when she's settled. I want to know what Daventry said today and how you plan to tackle these mounting problems."

"Will you arrange for Mrs Maloney to come and sit with her?" Theo's gaze fell to the woman in his arms. Fate had dealt her a poor hand. It was up to him to shuffle the cards and redress the balance. "Miss Darrow shouldn't be alone, at least not for the next twenty-four hours."

"I'll visit Mrs Maloney and explain the situation."

Aaron was being surprisingly accommodating.

"Thank you."

Theo was about to leave when Aaron called, "You have my full support in all matters. I just ask that you keep me informed of your plans. I'd rather not hear the news from Daventry."

"I trust your counsel." Keen to show Miss Lovelace there was no finer man than Aaron, he added, "You always act in the best interests of this family. No one's opinion matters more." Aaron was the anchor that kept them all grounded.

A silent look passed between them.

The unbreakable bond of brotherhood.

"Whatever you need, it's yours," Aaron said.

Theo thanked him again but was conscious of the woman

in his arms—the only woman he had ever held like this—
and so made his excuses and withdrew.

Miss Darrow's eyes fluttered open when he reached the
stairs, and she smiled, albeit weakly. "I think you enjoy
playing the knight errant. Perhaps that's why you stole my
sewing box. So you might display the qualities of a hero."

"I'm hardly a hero. I'm the scoundrel who stole your box
so I had something to trade for your arousing kisses."

Her hand came to rest on his heart. "You owe me a
forfeit," she uttered as he mounted the stairs. "That's not
why you stole my box."

"No, but you do have the mouth of Venus." And he was
more than happy to pay a penance if it pleased her. "Kissing
you is like drinking the nectar of the gods. And don't challenge me on that. I mean every word."

"I believe I'm supposed to say thank you." Her smile
faded, and he felt her strength seep from every muscle as she
nestled into his chest and closed her eyes.

Fear crept into his heart.

What if this was their last conversation?

What if he never got to truly make amends?

What if guilt would forever be his companion?

# Chapter Eight

Eleanor woke to find herself in a dark bedchamber—Mr Chance's bedchamber. The midnight blue curtains were drawn, though she could hear the hustle and bustle of daily life outside on the street. Dogs barked. Carriages clattered over the cobblestones. A costermonger proclaimed his apples were the juiciest this side of the Thames.

Inside the opulent chamber, all was quiet.

Someone had tucked in the bedsheets. Sheets that smelled of *his* cologne. Sheets that were warm and smooth against her bare legs.

*Merciful Lord, her legs were bare.*

Someone had stripped off her clothes.

Eleanor came up on her elbows, wincing because her head throbbed and every muscle ached. Her mouth was as dry as old parchment, though that was the least of her concerns.

Panicked, she peered under the covers. Her gaze settled on the delicate muslin nightgown clinging to her curves and the silk ribbons fastened into a bow under her bust. The pretty garment did not belong to her, yet wearing another woman's gown was not what played havoc with her insides.

Seeing her bare thighs resting on Theodore Chance's bedsheets caused a strange fluttering in her belly. Being cocooned in his intimate space brought a profound sense of closeness to a man she should keep at bay.

Her gaze shot to the pillows.

Had he slept beside her?

Had his leg stroked hers in the night?

Had his hand skimmed her hip?

She should be glad she could not remember. Mr Chance had a way of slipping under a woman's skin and taking command of her senses. Yet the weight of disappointment was prevalent. She had missed another chance to feel something beautiful, something other than loneliness and fear.

She might have buried her face in his pillow, but the muttering voices on the landing drew her attention to the door. As the knob turned slowly, Eleanor fell back on the pillows and feigned sleep.

She recognised Mr Chance's rich baritone before he stepped into the room. The timbre of his voice was permanently etched in her memory.

He turned to the elderly woman accompanying him and said quietly, "Stay with her. I shall be two hours unless Pickering needs a hard lesson in integrity."

Pickering?

Mr Chance was to visit the travelling librarian without her?

Surely they had missed their six o'clock appointment.

"Take as long as you need," the woman said, a gentle softness to her voice. "I bought a healing tincture from the apothecary in Cornhill. It's meant to restore one's vigour. Let's pray it has some effect."

Eleanor peered through narrowed eyes and saw it was Mrs Maloney. They had met at Delphine's wedding. The woman had given the family lodgings when they were children and was like a mother to them all.

Mr Chance hung his head. "This is my fault. Miss Darrow wouldn't be in this predicament were it not for my foolish antics."

"And you're doing everything you can to make amends." Mrs Maloney rubbed the man's arm like he'd just come in from the cold. "You weren't to know the poor girl was in trouble. Just as she didn't know that helping Delphine would see you shot."

"But what if she never recovers?"

"She will. She needs rest, that's all. Happen she's barely slept these last few weeks. And I expect you're basing the theory on past memories."

"Perhaps." His sad sigh tugged at Eleanor's heartstrings.

Mrs Maloney moved to the washstand and filled the porcelain bowl with water from the pitcher. "Aaron said you refused to leave this room last night. Have you slept?"

"A little. Though I have a crick in my neck from that darned chair."

The woman looked at the offending article. "I'll stay here tonight." She swished a linen square in the water and wrung it out. "When you return from visiting that Pickering fellow, I suggest you rest, too."

Mr Chance stepped closer to the bed. "Gentry said it's normal for someone with a head injury to sleep for three days, but I find it hard to be optimistic."

*Three days!*

Eleanor had spent three days in Theodore Chance's impressive bed? During sleepless nights, she had imagined climbing into bed beside him, but she was always a lucid participant in her dreams.

"I never meant to hurt her." He sat on the edge of the bed, resting his head in his hands. "I pray she will understand why I've taken it upon myself to attend to the issues at her modiste shop."

Eleanor's heart missed a beat.

What had he done? Boarded the windows? Sold everything of value? Given the landlord her notice?

She didn't need him riding roughshod over her ambitions. After a lifetime of subservience, she'd sworn never to be anyone's puppet. And yet, that's precisely what she had become. A pawn for the *ton*'s amusement.

Mrs Maloney came to join him at Eleanor's bedside. "I'm sure Miss Darrow will be most grateful, especially when she learns how hard you've worked."

The press of cold linen on her forehead tore a gasp from her dry lips. "Good Lord." She was so parched the words were barely audible.

Mr Chance jumped like he'd sat on a pin. "Miss Darrow?" he panted, his voice laced with relief. He reached for her hand and clasped it tightly. "Can you hear me?"

Eleanor lifted her eyelids and gazed into his magnificent blue eyes. "Y-yes."

Mrs Maloney hurried to the chest of drawers, pulled the stopper from a green bottle and poured water into a glass. "Have a sip of this, dear. It's boiled, and I added a sprig of rosemary. It's said to aid the memory."

Mr Chance helped her to sit and propped the pillows.

The brief touch of his fingers on her back sent a delightful shiver to her toes.

After taking a long drink of water, Eleanor clutched the glass and tried to gain some clarity. "How long have I been sleeping?" It couldn't have been three days, but to her dismay, Mr Chance confirmed as much.

"You woke a few times but were not always coherent." A weak smile touched his lips. Was he recalling something she had said while in a stupor? "Let's just say I may have new information to trade."

He was teasing her, playing the jester to settle both their fears. Nothing about her mundane life was worth trading for one of his heart-stopping kisses. Still, the desire to see his smile broaden left her keen to reply.

"As this is a gaming hell, perhaps we might take command of the tables and make a proper wager."

"Ah, you refer to the piquet and claret evening you mentioned at the Olympic. Once the lords desert the tables, we might command the card room and indulge in a midnight game of chance."

"Having slept for three days, I think I can cope with one late night." Bantering with Mr Chance made her forget her woes. "Does that mean you accept the challenge?"

He hesitated, pursing his lips as his gaze moved over her face. "Of course I accept, but only when I'm certain you're on the road to recovery. I feared you would never wake."

Mrs Maloney had a grasp of the situation. The pressure to deliver the notes had taken its toll. Trying to prevent her life from crumbling around her was exhausting. Emily had stolen the silk. Someone had taken the books hidden beneath the boards. And someone had pushed her down the stairs.

No wonder she'd not woken for days.

"You're to blame, sir. This is a comfortable mattress."

"I only sleep on the best." One look at the delicate lace neckline of her nightgown and his smile returned. "I trust you found the nightwear just as comfortable and approve of fine muslin from Bengal."

"Indeed." Her cheeks grew hot beneath the weight of his gaze. "Though I must question who this sumptuous gown belongs to."

As if wishing to give them a little privacy, Mrs Maloney busied herself with tidying the washstand.

"I bought it for you. When I unpacked your valise, you had nothing suitable for bed. I walked to Nightingale's, and Mrs Maloney undressed you upon my return."

She wore a nightgown Theodore Chance had purchased? One bought specifically for her? The gesture was borne out of necessity, but that didn't stop the coil of intimacy tightening in her belly.

Eleanor swallowed deeply. "Thank you. My father forced me to make my own clothes. No one has ever bought me anything new."

His smile faded. "Forced you?"

"Encouraged me in such a way I could not refuse."

"Your talent for dressmaking must have been apparent from an early age. Did your mother teach you to sew with such skill?"

Eleanor closed her eyes briefly, her heart pounding with remorse. She breathed against the churning in her gut. "My mother died in childbirth. I never knew her. My father raised me."

"Oh." His Adam's apple bobbed in his throat. "I'm sorry. It must have been difficult."

"Too difficult to explain in words."

Something passed between them. A sense of empathy that came from shared suffering. A silent look of solidarity. The need to lose themselves in another soul-deep kiss.

He must have sensed she wished to change the subject. "Daventry sent word this morning. Pickering's mobile library will be in Hart Street at noon. We plan to accost him and drag a confession from his devious lips."

"Excellent. I'm coming with you." Before she engaged her brain, she pulled back the sheets and eased herself out of bed. "Give me a moment to dress."

A strained hum rumbled in his throat as he studied her nightgown. "You seem intent on punishing me, Miss Darrow. All things considered, it's no less than I deserve."

She could have stood there, stone-still, his eyes devouring her all day. Men had admired her before, but no one had ever made her feel the way he did—like she was the most desirable woman in the world.

"Oh, you'll catch your death in that flimsy thing." Mrs Maloney appeared, draping a wool blanket over Eleanor's shoulders and drawing the edges across her bust. "I don't know what possessed him to buy something so impractical."

"A man is never practical when buying a lady nightwear."

"You're lucky she didn't catch a chill." Mrs Maloney wrapped a motherly arm around Eleanor's shoulders and drew her to the washstand. "I'll help you dress and tidy your hair, dear. You shouldn't be left alone. Not until we're sure you're fit and well."

Mr Chance took that as his cue to leave. "I'll wait downstairs. During the journey to Hart Street, I shall explain all that's occurred since your accident."

Was it an accident?

Had she imagined seeing a shadow?

Had she felt the spectre's hands on her back?

"Is Jules well? Did he offer any useful information?"

"He's well but refuses to speak to anyone but you. I'll take you to see him once we've finished with Pickering." And with that, he closed the door, leaving her alone with Mrs Maloney.

There was something comforting about having an older woman brush her hair. Mrs Maloney's soothing strokes were enough to lull Eleanor back to sleep.

"I know Theo is partly to blame for your troubles, but he's a good man at heart." She took a pin and pushed it gently into Eleanor's hair. "I know he plays the fool but he would die for his family."

Eleanor smiled. "You love him a great deal."

"What's not to love?"

His pranks, for one thing. Yet with a power akin to gravity, he drew Eleanor into his orbit, the invisible tug impossible to ignore.

"There have been times lately when I could have whacked him with a skillet." There were times when she could have locked lips with him until dawn. "But you're right. There's something endearing about him."

Mrs Maloney patted Eleanor's chignon. "He'll light up your life if you let him, though his battle with his conscience will be his downfall. He's chained to this place and will never leave Aaron here alone."

Eleanor remembered him confessing his greatest fear. He didn't worry about his own future. He would happily push his dreams aside out of love for his eldest brother.

Mrs Maloney gave a weary sigh. "Do you know my first

thought when I saw those poor mites on my doorstep, faces dirty, eyes sad with lost dreams?"

"That you were desperate to take care of them?"

"I thought, Maura, it will take a strong woman to fix this family. I was the first to help set them on the right path, but I'll not be the last."

Mrs Maloney did not elaborate but helped Eleanor into the bottle-green dress and matching pelisse she had shoved into her valise three days ago.

"Thank you for your help, Mrs Maloney, for pressing my clothes and caring for me these last three days." If Eleanor's mother had lived, would she have been someone Eleanor could depend upon? "I'm unused to such kindness."

"Then guard your heart, dear," Mrs Maloney said with a chuckle. "When you see what my boy has done with your shop, it will be like a hit from Cupid's arrow."

One question burned in Eleanor's mind as she sat opposite Mr Chance in his family's elegant equipage. Well, maybe more than one. But she did not want to know how long he'd sat watching her sleep. She would rather not think about him stripping to his shirtsleeves and padding about barefooted.

"Mrs Maloney said you spent time at my modiste shop."

Mr Chance relaxed back against the squab. His confident grin could move mountains, yet she sensed his unease. "I wasn't sure you would recover from your fall and feared—"

"I didn't take you for a pessimist."

He held her gaze. "I prayed I wouldn't lose a worthy

opponent, not halfway through the game. And something told me it wasn't the end of our friendship. I only wish I had been there to prevent the accident."

Her shoulders tensed. "It wasn't an accident."

He paused, tilting his head. "Not an accident?"

"Someone or something pushed me."

Mr Chance sat bolt upright. "Are you certain? The door was locked. We were the only people on the premises."

She had replayed the chilling moment in her mind a thousand times. Those few seconds were still a blur. "No, I'm not certain. I saw a shadow before someone shoved me in the back."

He shuffled to the edge of the seat, his knees a fraction from hers. "You said someone or something. Surely you're not speaking about a ghost. I credit you with more sense than that."

"I don't know what to think. Emily is the only person with a key, so why would she not show herself?" She had given Emily a door key weeks ago and had not thought to ask for it back.

Mr Chance gave a mocking snort. "Because she stole your silk and returned to take whatever else she could carry."

Had she stolen the silk or simply taken it for safe-keeping?

"Emily is barely five feet tall and so petite people mistake her for a child. Surely the person who pushed me was much stronger."

"Then one of your devious clients entered the premises intending to steal back their note." He shoved his hand through his mop of golden hair. "Daventry was right. Only the dead keep secrets. Perhaps someone means to silence you, Miss Darrow."

His remark forced her to face a truth she had been avoiding. But what did she know that was so damning? She knew the identity of those sending secrets but nothing incriminating.

"Thankfully, I had the foresight to hire someone to guard your shop," he said, alluding to his mysterious machinations. "Daventry's man Gibbs has taken residence. It's the only way to protect your property."

Eleanor's heart softened. He was determined to restore her reputation, determined to keep her in London. Did his motivation stem from guilt?

"Perhaps me being incapacitated was a blessing," she said. "I would have insisted on returning home and tackling the problem myself." In the process, she might have paid the ultimate price. "You chose well. Mr Gibbs has the strength of three men. I know Delphine valued his help when searching for the truth about her parents."

"I had the locks changed yesterday," he confessed.

"Oh." She was unused to a man taking care of things. "Another wise decision."

"And I supervised the cleaning of the shop yesterday. You would hardly know the place was ransacked a few days ago."

Eleanor swallowed past a lump in her throat. The thought of tidying the rooms had filled her with dread. "You didn't need to do that."

"Miss Darrow," he began firmly, "I'll not rest until things are as they were before the day of the shooting."

The pang in her chest proved confounding.

Shouldn't she be happy he wanted to put things right?

And yet she didn't want things to be as they were. The empty compliments and endless teasing. The feeling they were worlds apart, practically strangers who knew nothing about each other at all.

"So much has changed since then."

One kiss at the theatre had altered the course of fate. They'd grown closer. She was slowly learning to trust him and enjoyed his company. But nothing about this situation was permanent. Guarding her heart should be her only priority.

"I need to know you're happy," he clarified.

A moment of inward reflection confirmed what she already knew. Happiness eluded her. She had been living someone else's life. Fulfilling her parents' dream.

"I'm not your responsibility, Mr Chance. You've offered to help me and need do no more. Your conscience is clear. Once we've gained the information we need from Mr Pickering, our partnership will end."

She hoped the librarian confessed and they had the vandal in custody by nightfall. There'd be no more threats. No more sudden attacks. No more sleepless nights spent wishing for a peaceful life. No more kisses from the only man who had ever made her soul sing. No fears of heartbreak.

She would return to the shop and her silent companion, the ever-present figure of loneliness lingering over her shoulder.

"You sound keen to get rid of me, Miss Darrow."

"The arrangement was always temporary."

"When I trust someone enough to call them a friend, is it wrong to hope the relationship might last a lifetime?"

A lady could not be friends with a man like Theodore Chance. He was like a well-honed blade, powerful enough to slice through her defences. While his masculine prowess had her gawping in awe, his chivalrous deed left her an emotional wreck. Any thoughts of urging him to be realistic vanished when he played his ace card.

"I have never had a friend outside of my family circle," he said. "There has never been a need until now. But I have a feeling you need a friend, too."

She might have melted into a puddle of tears had the carriage not stopped outside Mr Daventry's premises in Hart Street. Her heart hurt more than the dreadful bruise on her back, but the need to comfort him overrode common sense.

"We make an unlikely duo, but I can be myself with you. That's important in any alliance."

Pleased with her answer, he smiled. "Honesty above all else. That will be our motto." His gaze fell to her mouth, his eyes turning an attractive shade of blue. "The odd little lie won't hurt. How else can I claim a kiss when we play cards tonight?"

"Friends do not kiss like we do."

"We're scoundrels and friends. We make our own rules." He alighted and offered his hand. "Besides, you need something valuable to wager. I'll not accept pearl buttons."

*This will end in tears*, she told herself as he handed her down to the pavement. But the brush of his fingers made everything feel right.

The housekeeper led them into Mr Daventry's study. The gentleman stood and rounded the desk, keen to ask about her health.

"I wasn't expecting you, Miss Darrow. Are you sure you're well enough to tackle Pickering? When cornered, all men have a propensity for violence."

Eleanor smiled, banishing the memory of the only time she had challenged her father. "Finding the wretch who destroyed my home is all that matters. He said I would die if I failed to deliver the note, and I believed him. Mr Pickering is the only person who knows the villain's identity."

"It's a pity you don't have the book." Suspicion clouded Mr Daventry's gaze. "Had we played along and hidden the note inside, Pickering would have led us directly to his source."

Did he think she'd lied about it being stolen?

"Emily must have taken it along with my diary." Had the girl panicked and fought to save what she could? Had she taken the opportunity to line her pockets instead? "We will visit her at her parents' home later today."

Mr Daventry perched on his desk. "Why would Emily want your book or diary?" he mused. "None of this makes sense."

"Unless the devil who ransacked the shop stole them," Mr Chance suggested. "He came for the book or the diary and took both."

Unsure why the man had targeted her to begin with, Eleanor sighed. "Why use me and not deal with Mr Pickering himself? Hopefully, the librarian will provide us with the answer."

A timely knock on the door brought the housekeeper, Mrs Gunning. "You asked to be notified when Mr Pickering arrived, sir. He's outside, opening the doors of his fancy caravan."

"Thank you, Mrs Gunning." Mr Daventry waited for his housekeeper to leave before asking Eleanor, "Did you bring the sealed note?"

Mr Chance reached into his coat pocket. He turned the tiny missive over in his hand. "Amongst other things, the desire to break the wax and read the message kept me awake most of the night."

"Read it now. I have black wax to reseal it."

Eleanor looked at Mr Daventry, fear holding her rigid. "But what if the villain knows we've tampered with the note? What if he knows we've read his message?"

"I suspect he will come looking for you to carry out his threat," he said in the calm tone of a man who fought crooks for a living. "Mr Chance will be your protector as we draw the rogue out."

Mr Chance smiled like a cat in a room full of mice. "I'd like nothing more than to wring the blighter's neck."

"Then it's settled." Mr Daventry waved his hand to hurry Mr Chance along. "We need something we can use to scare Pickering. Let's read the damning words that have caused Miss Darrow such misery."

Mr Chance turned to her, his tone softening. "What do you want to do, Miss Darrow? I shall abide by whatever decision you make."

Oh, this man was dangerous.

In a world of patriarchal dominance, he knew how to make a woman feel valued.

"I trust you will support me, whatever happens." She was tired of hiding, tired of running, and meant to fight for what was right. "I say you open it, sir, regardless of the consequences."

Her stomach churned as he broke the seal and peeled back the tiny folds. He studied the paper, shaking his head, a deep frown marring his brow.

"Well?" she prompted as he stared open-mouthed. "Is there mention of a name or a time and place?"

Was she about to learn the identity of her persecutor?

"No." Mr Chance showed Daventry the note before handing it to her. "There is no message. The paper is blank."

# Chapter Nine

"Might he have used a process to conceal the message?" Miss Darrow said, her brows drawn together in consternation.

"Lemon juice on paper leaves a brown mark when held to the heat of a flame." Theo knew because Lady Lucille had once sent him a similar message to evade her father's detection.

Miss Darrow sniffed the paper and wrinkled her nose. "Surely I would be able to smell lemons."

Theo couldn't help but smile. Miss Darrow's hidden innocence heightened her appeal, as did her enthusiasm for solving mysteries. "I doubt it. The note has been in your box for over two weeks."

Daventry lit a candle. He took the paper from Miss Darrow and wafted it back and forth over the flame. When that proved pointless, he held it up to the light streaming through the study window.

"I'll need a chemist to confirm my suspicion," Daventry

began, "but I'm confident there's nothing written on this note."

Miss Darrow shook her head in confusion. "How can that be? I've risked my life to deliver those messages."

Keen to determine the facts, Theo said, "So, the villain is the only person who asked you to deliver the notes personally? The barrow boy never dealt with Pickering?"

"No. I hid the notes beneath the bookplates and delivered them myself. Mr Pickering took receipt of them and I went on my way."

"Then let's see what the man has to say." Daventry gestured to the door and they followed him outside to Pickering's library.

The wooden wagon resembled a spectacle from the Bartholomew Fair. Intricate gold and red scrollwork adorned its sides, and its bow roof was painted a deep forest green. It looked more like a mobile palace than a library on wheels.

Pickering had propped wooden steps against the back porch and opened the wagon's doors. Rows of oak bookcases lined the interior walls.

"Pickering." Daventry stood at the entrance, keen to get the stout fellow's attention.

The wagon rocked as Pickering swiftly turned within. "Mr Daventry. Good afternoon. There's no need to leave your office. I would have brought your order inside." Pickering chuckled as he retrieved a book and looked at the gold-embossed title. "You don't strike me as a man who would read *Memoirs of an Heiress*. Though those brutes plotting to control Cecilia's wealth provide a lesson in criminal machinations."

Daventry smiled. "The book is for my wife, but I confess to having a selfish motive for ordering the first volume."

Pickering's hearty laugh shook the vehicle again. "There's no need to be bashful, sir. I delivered all three volumes of *Evelina* to Lord Marshall only last week. Though between us, I'm told he is giving his new maid private reading lessons."

Theo's attention sharpened. Lord Marshall owed Fortune's Den eight hundred pounds. Using a secret scandal as leverage, they could force the lord to pay.

"You misunderstand. I summoned you here because you've been named as a witness in a criminal case." Daventry gestured to Miss Darrow. "Someone blackmailed and coerced the lady into delivering secret notes to you on three occasions, notes hidden inside books. We need to know the recipient's identity and why you agreed to play the middleman."

Shocked and utterly confused by the allegations, Pickering gripped the doorframe. "A criminal case? Sir, I live to bring pleasure to the masses. I deliver books and know nothing about these strange notes."

"Do you not recognise me?" Miss Darrow stepped forward. "I returned a book by Voltaire, though the title eludes me. I handed it to you personally. You thanked me and told me to hurry home because we were expecting rain."

"Voltaire?" Pickering brushed his greying locks over his bald pate and gave a curious hum. "When was this?"

"Six weeks ago."

The man pulled a ledger off the shelf and rifled through the crisp pages. He found what he was looking for and pointed to an entry. "I remember now. You borrowed the first volume of *Candide*. I have one copy, and it was already on my library shelf. The volume you returned did not belong to me."

"But you took receipt of the book."

"Yes, you'd left before I realised it wasn't mine."

"Do you still have the book?" Theo asked. If Pickering was innocent, the note would still be hidden behind the plate.

Pickering blinked and stuttered, "W-well, yes. I kept it in the hope the lady would realise her error."

"Find it," Theo snapped. "The book is evidence in a case of assault, blackmail, theft and housebreaking."

The ledger shook in Pickering's large hands. "Good grief. You can't think I was involved in these nefarious deeds."

"Find the book, Pickering." Theo was quickly losing his patience.

"Just a moment." The fellow returned to the shelves in his wagon and spent an age scanning the spines. "It's here somewhere."

Theo resisted the urge to climb inside and see to the task himself. "What about the other two books Miss Darrow gave you?"

Pickering continued his search. "Other books?"

"Polidori's *The Vampyre*," Miss Darrow said. "I recall the name because it sounded quite terrifying. The other was the first volume of Radcliffe's *The Italian*."

The latter was a story of happy endings, marriage and the death of the villains. Had she ever read the entire novel? Did she hope for a similar outcome to her tale? Indeed, it bore similarities to the Chance family's saga.

It was apparent that Pickering could not locate the books. He fumbled about and offered one excuse after another.

Theo lost his temper. "You'll tell me where those books are, or I shall take you to Bow Street and have you charged with conspiracy."

"I'm sure you have the information in your ledger," Miss Darrow added, sounding just as annoyed at Pickering's dallying. "You will hand it to me, sir, so I may inspect it myself."

What man could resist the fire in her eyes? Certainly not Pickering. He gave her the ledger before clasping his chubby hands together in prayer.

"I confess. I kept the books. You seemed convinced they were mine, madam, and I thought it better to put them to good use." A whimper escaped him. "I know nothing about the secret notes or any of the charges you claim."

"Did anyone ask to borrow those particular books?" Daventry said.

Miss Darrow flicked through the pages, scanning the entries.

"Yes, *The Vampyre*," Pickering admitted. "Within days of the lady handing me the book, a customer requested two copies. The solution to my problem seemed simple."

Theo cursed under his breath. "That doesn't explain why you stole the books Miss Darrow delivered."

"It wasn't stealing. The lady thought they were mine."

Miss Darrow gasped as she peered at the writing in Pickering's ledger. "Good heavens. You won't believe this. Mrs Dunwoody requested two copies of *The Vampyre*. Is that not the name of the woman who insulted you at the theatre?"

Dunwoody was an unusual surname. "Is there an address listed?" Theo tried to stem his excitement, but the prospect of accusing the hag of a crime had his heart pumping wildly.

"Not in the ledger."

Pickering piped up. "I keep a separate record of customers' details." He rummaged about in his small wagon before appearing at the door. "Mrs Dunwoody lives in

Caroline Street. She's the only Dunwoody with membership."

Aware of the relevance, Daventry grinned. "I'll give you a letter granting permission to interview her concerning the crimes against Miss Darrow. She'll not refuse you when she sees the Home Secretary's seal."

Theo could barely contain his elation. "It seems fate has granted me a boon." He couldn't wait to wipe the smirk off Mrs Dunwoody's face.

Miss Darrow mused over the list of books. "Mr Pickering, according to your records, Mrs Dunwoody returned both copies of *The Vampyre* months ago. They were loaned out again a week later but should be in your wagon."

As luck would have it, the man found the items they required.

Theo snatched one copy and turned to the bookplate—an image of two turtle doves decorated the inner board. Someone had peeled back the plate and taken the note.

"I am submitting this copy as evidence." Theo showed it to Miss Darrow. "Is that the plate you were given?"

Her eyes widened. "Yes. A pretty picture of two doves."

The design was an odd choice for a devilish fiend. But if there was no message or recipient, why go to the trouble of having Miss Darrow hide notes and bring them to Pickering's library?

Did the person who borrowed the books know of the plan?

It was a possibility.

They would know more once they had interrogated Mrs Dunwoody.

However, after another scan of the ledger, Miss Darrow

said, "*The Vampyre* is the only one Mrs Dunwoody borrowed. There's no pattern here."

"Perhaps the rogue had another motive," Daventry said, though offered no further insight.

"What other motive is there for sending blank letters to no one?" Miss Darrow challenged.

That's when Theo saw there was indeed a pattern. "Perhaps the villain's motive was to ensure you left your shop." Hence the demand she deliver them personally. "Where did you meet Pickering's wagon? And how did you know where to find him?"

"I was told to deliver them at a particular time and location. Always after his last visit in Mayfair."

"Mayfair? But that's three miles from the shop."

"Yes, I took a hackney, though often had to wait up to an hour for Mr Pickering to arrive. He was never there at the agreed time."

"My customers can be most demanding," Pickering said, mopping his brow with his handkerchief. "Some request books that are difficult to locate, then are dissatisfied with the copies."

Skilled at detecting liars, Daventry scanned the librarian with a critical eye. "Bring your ledgers into my study. I wish to record the names of those who borrowed those specific books."

As one did not negotiate with the devil, Pickering agreed.

Keen to ensure he did not treat Miss Darrow like a hapless female, Theo let her choose their next destination. "Where to now? Do you wish to see Jules, visit Mrs Dunwoody or interrogate your shifty seamstress?"

Miss Darrow nibbled her bottom lip, debating the dilemma. "Logic says we should follow the notes. I cannot think why Mrs Dunwoody would want to lure me away from the shop, but we should confirm she had no part to play before I question Emily."

They would do more than question Emily.

According to Gibbs, she had tried to access the shop late last night and had left abruptly when she couldn't unlock the door.

"Come to the study," Daventry said. "You'll need an official document if you hope to see Mrs Dunwoody at home." He glanced at Theo and arched a brow. "Unless you would prefer I accompany Miss Darrow. The woman despises you more than she does her wayward husband."

"And miss an opportunity to threaten her with arrest?" One look at the Home Secretary's official seal and Mrs Dunwoody would choke on her own vitriol. "Nothing would give me greater pleasure than to watch that harpy squirm."

*Caroline Street*
*Bloomsbury*

Theo did not give Mrs Dunwoody's doddery butler a second chance to refuse them entry. The evil hag was at home. Her loud cackle might be heard as far afield as Gloucester.

"Step aside." The fire of vengeance burned in Theo's blood. He would forever blame the Berridge clan for abandoning them when their father died. "It isn't a request."

He gripped Miss Darrow's hand, pulling her across the

threshold as he marched into Mrs Dunwoody's Bloomsbury abode.

"Wait," she whispered, tugging his hand to halt his progress. "You're like a wolf baying for blood. You must keep a tight rein on your temper. As an intelligent man, you know this situation calls for brains, not brawn."

The gentle squeeze of her hand settled his thundering pulse. Theo cast her a sidelong glance, wondering how someone so dainty had the power to calm his restless spirit.

"A few week ago, you said I had the brains of a donkey."

"Because you're stubborn and calculating. Donkeys have good survival instincts. All things considered, they're clever animals."

"You're saying I should be pleased I'm an ass?" He wasn't sure why, but the need to see her laugh was as compelling as the need to kiss her again.

Her chuckle did something strange to his insides. "You should be ecstatic. A donkey's ability to adapt to its environment is a quality to be admired. So, the goal today is to be assertive, not aggressive."

He bowed his head. "I thank you for your counsel. I shall remain composed in the face of adversity."

It should have been easy, but Mrs Dunwoody was having tea with Lady Lucille and Theo's estranged cousin, the insipid Viscount Wrotham.

Wrotham nearly slipped off the French bergere chair when he saw them. "What the devil are you doing here, Chance? Perhaps you got lost on your way to a bordello."

"Why would I be in need of a bordello? I am betrothed to Miss Darrow. No woman alive possesses her allure."

Lady Lucille inhaled sharply.

Mrs Dunwoody sucked in her cheeks. "Tribbings!" she

yelled, shooing the Persian cat off her lap. "I said you were to turn this thankless wretch away."

Theo withdrew a letter from his pocket and handed it to Mrs Dunwoody. "I'm here on a matter of national security." They did not need to know the letter Daventry gave him related to a different case. "As you can see, I come at the behest of the Home Secretary."

Wrotham snorted. "Obviously it's a forgery. What would a respectable man like Melbourne want with a gaming hell owner?"

Retrieving the eyeglass dangling from a chain around her neck, Mrs Dunwoody scrutinised the seal. "It's a crime to impersonate a peer. Not that anyone would believe you were of good stock. You're like windfall in an orchard—rotten to the core."

Theo kept his cool reserve.

Miss Darrow was right. Calmness brought clarity. Yet the lady had trouble following her own advice.

"And you're the fruit picked first," Miss Darrow said, albeit with some eloquence. "You're hard and so dreadfully bitter."

Theo chuckled. He couldn't help but admire her insight.

"Says the nobody dressmaker. Though once my friends learn of your shoddy taste, the only ladies you'll dress are those walking the streets at night."

"Why would anyone trust your word?" Miss Darrow countered. "You say your husband is in Boston on business when everyone knows he's living in Hastings with an opera singer half his age."

Lady Lucille gasped.

Mrs Dunwoody dropped her eyeglass and stared in

stupefied silence. Twice, she opened her mouth, but only air came out.

"What is it you want?" Lady Lucille asked in a haughty tone. "Be warned, my father will speak to Lord Melbourne to confirm your claim."

"Your father, not your betrothed?" Theo glanced at his pathetic cousin. "What do you say, Wrotham? Are you happy to play the docile pug? Will you roll over at the lady's command?"

Lady Lucille answered for him. "I shall be Lord Wrotham's responsibility once we wed next spring. Until then, I trust my father to act in my stead."

"How strange," Miss Darrow mused, looking at Theo like he was a god amongst men. "I'm quite confident Mr Chance would fight an army to protect me and I don't even have a dowry."

Wrotham snorted. "Why would Chance need a dowry? He fleeces the lords of the *ton* six nights a week."

Theo firmed his stance, his amusement dissipating. "Are you accusing me of cheating, Wrotham? Have a care. I'll be glad of an excuse to call you out."

Mrs Dunwoody was quick to avert disaster. "Good grief! I am being violated in my own home." She waved the letter at Theo. "Explain what you want then get out."

Theo snatched the letter and slipped it into his pocket. "You requested two copies of *The Vampyre* from Pickering's library."

Mrs Dunwoody's face was a masterpiece of disbelief. "What on earth has my taste in literature got to do with the Home Secretary?"

Wrotham tittered. "I told you the letter was a forgery."

"A secret message lay concealed beneath the bookplate,"

Theo continued, unperturbed by their tittering. "The sender is wanted in connection with serious offences. He may be a spy passing messages to an operative in London." It was not a lie. The villain could be a foreign agent using Miss Darrow to deliver his communications.

"A spy?" Lucille Bowman frowned. "For whom?"

"We're not at liberty to say. But we need to know why you requested two copies of that book. The London operative would have known the note was hidden inside."

Mrs Dunwoody chuckled like the notion was farcical. "For goodness' sake, you really are your father's son. Always looking to bring others down to your level. I ask you. Do I look like a woman who would entertain a spy?"

While Theo battled to keep his temper—finding answers was the priority—Miss Darrow jumped to his defence.

"You don't look like a woman who would lie to her friends. You're hardly in a position to accuse others of dishonesty."

Cheeks aflame, Mrs Dunwoody scowled. "Mind your tongue, gal. Get out. Get out before I have Tribbings throw you out."

"Tribbings hasn't the strength to hang a coat on the stand," Miss Darrow countered. "If you insist on us leaving, we must place you under arrest. The Home Secretary granted us the power to take any suspects into custody. And you have not answered our questions sufficiently."

Theo looked at the woman whose kisses could start a war. It was good to see Miss Darrow's confidence return. He admired her tenacity. Most women would still be abed, nursing a head injury.

"I'm to blame," Lucille Bowman confessed. "I suggested we all read the same book and compare notes. After borrowing one copy of *The Vampyre* from the Minerva Press, I asked Mrs Dunwoody if Pickering had two copies. We were surprised he did, but the man has his sources."

Theo glanced at the lady who turned his stomach. "Did you slice through the bookplate and remove the hidden letter?"

"I wouldn't dream of defacing another person's property."

He wasn't sure he believed her.

Hadn't she proved to be false-hearted?

"What was your opinion of the book?" Miss Darrow asked. "I'm surprised you would want to read about a monster who preys on the upper classes. But then the fiend is a member of the aristocracy."

All three suspects turned as pale as the vampire in the tale.

It was apparent none had read past the introduction.

"It's utter twaddle," the viscount said.

"It's against the laws of nature," Mrs Dunwoody was quick to add. "Who's ever heard of a man thirsting for blood? Well, except for that barbarian you call a brother. Aaron Chance is like a rabid dog. I hear his body is littered with scars."

A heavy silence descended.

Theo could barely see through anger's red mist.

Every muscle tensed, primed to attack.

No one criticised Aaron, not in Theo's company.

"None of us tampered with the silly book," Lady Lucille said in a panic. "None of us intercepted this hidden letter. Surely someone borrowed the book after us. Speak to them. Now, I think you should leave."

The devil's own fury burned in Theo's veins.

Had a man slandered Aaron, he'd be picking his teeth off the floor. As much as he despised Mrs Dunwoody, he would not threaten a woman.

He didn't need to.

Miss Darrow leapt to his aid.

"Connections are everything, are they not?" Miss Darrow said, glaring at the matron who possessed Lucifer's tongue.

"What would a modiste know about connections?"

"You would be surprised what secrets ladies share with their modiste. I know the identity of the person who writes the *Scandal Sheet*. Do purchase next week's copy. There will be a delicious story about a cad who left his wife to live in Hastings with an opera singer half his age."

Mrs Dunwoody's cheeks ballooned and her eyes bulged like saucers. "Spread lies about me, gal, and I'll have you hauled to court."

"You should spend less time making idle threats and more on your appearance." Like a goddess of war, she pointed at Theo's cowardly cousin. "Perhaps consult with Lord Wrotham's valet and have him demonstrate the use of a blade. You have more whiskers than your Persian cat."

Miss Darrow did not bid them good day but took Theo's arm and marched through the hall before exiting onto Caroline Street.

"That woman would drive a priest to murder," she growled, releasing her frustration. "If I made her a gown, I would sew fleas into the hem. They'd bite her whenever she sat down."

That's when Theo laughed.

He laughed so hard his sides ached. "Fleas into the hem?"

She started laughing, too, and they had to hold on to each other lest they fell to the pavement, giggling wrecks. "Or lice to the inside of a bonnet."

He was crying now. Tears of joy streamed down his face.

Miss Darrow brought light to the darkness. She was a source of strength in trying times. A muse that stirred his passions. She was utterly unique.

# Chapter Ten

The corners of Mr Chance's eyes crinkled. He put his hand to his chest and laughed again. He couldn't seem to stop. "You've got more whiskers than your Persian cat," he said, mimicking Eleanor's voice. "I swear, the look on Mrs Dunwoody's face was priceless."

Eleanor watched him from the opposite side of the carriage. She liked the sound of his laugh. The rich, resonant notes spoke of mischief and raw masculinity. She liked that his eyes shone bluer than a tropical sea. Never had she wanted to dive inside a man and explore his hidden depths.

"What happened to remaining calm?" he chuckled.

"Mrs Dunwoody insulted you and your family. After all you have been through, I couldn't leave without putting her in her place."

She despised bullies. They hid behind words or the weight of their fists. Vile comments were their weapons of choice, blades sharpened to slay anyone who discovered their dirty little secret—that a weakling lived beneath the mask of aggression.

"Well, I am in your debt. You used your brains while I was seconds away from unleashing a tempest." His amused expression faded. "I'm built to withstand insults unless they're aimed at my family."

"Your love for your family is to be commended. It's clear they mean a lot to you."

"They're all I have."

She nodded, but the vast emptiness inside reminded her she had no one special. "If I loved someone, I would tell them every day. I wouldn't leave them doubting the depth of my affection."

His gaze softened. "Did you tell your father every day?"

The question took her by surprise. "No. He was a hard man to like." She had pitied her father and blamed herself for his misery. How could she love someone who made her feel worthless? "I have never loved anyone, Mr Chance."

A look passed between them.

A silent communication neither dared to voice.

He breathed a heavy sigh. "When you do, I expect your love will radiate in every honest word and deed. The beauty of it will leave the recipient in no doubt of your devotion."

Tears threatened to gather behind her eyes.

Mr Chance's tender words were as arousing as his ardent kisses.

"Bad things happen for good reasons." She told herself that all the time. "Perhaps I might meet a dashing American when I'm forced to flee to Boston."

He shifted with obvious unease despite her attempt to make light of her situation. "There's no need to leave town. Troubling times always pass. I promise you, ladies will queue the length of New Bridge Street to purchase your gowns."

"I wish I had your optimism. But you saw the way Lady Lucille looked at me." Like she might stab Eleanor through the heart with a poker. "A jealous woman is as dangerous as a loon with a crossbow. She will drive me out of town by foul means or fair."

He fell silent as he relaxed against the squab.

Was he thinking about the woman he admired?

"Do you still love her?" Eleanor said, though it pained her to think of him kissing anyone else. She had been so caught up in her own problems, she had not considered how difficult this must be for him.

"No. I admired her. It was never love." He paused, his expression pensive. "Have you ever tricked yourself into believing something is true?"

Her heart grew heavy. "Many times."

She had told herself countless lies. If she became a successful modiste, her guilt would dissipate as swiftly as a morning mist. Her father's anger stemmed from love, not resentment. Loneliness was a state of mind one could overcome.

"Have you ever convinced yourself you could right the wrongs of the past?" he asked. "That if you did, you might feel whole again?"

Eleanor looked at her clasped hands resting in her lap. "Being a modiste was my mother's dream. Trust me. Making her wish come true did nothing to banish the emptiness."

He reached for her hand and clasped it tightly, and she loved him a little for the kind gesture. "How can the youngest of four brothers help his kin? Not with his fists. Not with his business acumen. But perhaps by elevating them to the life they were born to."

"What are you saying?"

"Should anything happen to Wrotham, Aaron is heir to the title. If I were to marry well, he might be restored to his rightful position. I convinced myself I could love Lucille Bowman. But she used me to force Wrotham's hand. She reminded me I will always carry the stench of the rookeries."

He did not smell like the impoverished.

He smelled like a thunderstorm—fresh and earthy, a man with the power to control the heavens. A voice determined to be heard.

Eleanor gripped his hand. "You used her, too. Surely life has taught you that love is the path through the darkness."

He did not avert his gaze in shame but gave a humourless snort. "That's why I like you, Miss Darrow. You always hold me to account. In truth, I thought romantic love was a fallacy. Then my brother Christian married, and the power of his love for Isabella was almost blinding. Not even Aaron could have prevented their union."

"Love is not something you decide. It chooses you."

He frowned. "You speak from experience?"

"Of course not. I have spent years working myself to the bone." She had never even kissed a man until she had locked lips with him at the theatre. "When would I have had the time to fall in love?"

"Franklin would have you in a heartbeat."

"For a lady of modest means, it would be a good match." Though he did not light a fire in her blood. He did not steal the breath from her lungs or make her giddy. "Perhaps I would come to love him in time, but I would rather love sweep me up in a storm."

"Franklin isn't right for you," he said, his tone sabre-sharp.

"He is undeniably handsome."

135

"It's not enough for a woman with your wild spirit. He wouldn't make you happy. Your arousing kisses would be wasted on him."

She smiled. "Are they not wasted on you?"

"We're kindred spirits. Two passionate people seeking solace in each other's company." His voice was as rich as velvet as his eyes trailed a slow path over her body. "I must be honest. No other man would make love to you like I would. You'd come hard for me. Too many times to count."

She stared at him, stunned and quite desperate to know if he spoke the truth. But Theodore Chance would take more than her virginity. He would carve out a piece of her soul. She could survive losing her business, but she would not survive that.

"You seem so sure of yourself."

"The kiss we shared at your shop told me all I needed to know. I'll wager Franklin kisses like a panicked fish."

The thought of locking lips with Mr Franklin chilled her blood. "He would make a respectable woman of me." Mr Franklin was a good man, kind to his sister, hardworking and pious.

"You value your independence and would rather live like a spinster than have a man tell you what to do."

He was not wrong. Her biggest fear was marrying a man with her father's harsh tongue and critical eye. Tyrants often hid behind affable masks.

"Perhaps." She wasn't sure how they'd gone from discussing Lady Lucille to her marrying Mr Franklin, but they should focus on the case. "What do you make of their story? Do you believe Viscount Wrotham wanted to read *The Vampyre*?"

Mr Chance sat back in the seat, his arms folded across his broad chest. "It was obvious none of them had read the tale. There's no way of knowing if they found the sealed message or if the note was blank."

"No," Eleanor mused, gazing out the window. "Let's pray Mr Daventry has luck finding those who borrowed the other two books."

Still, there was one glaring coincidence Eleanor could not ignore. Lady Lucille had been sending secret notes for months. Did she request *The Vampyre* because it contained a reply?

"We must examine every piece of evidence, regardless of how insignificant," Mr Chance said. "I've heard Daventry say the same thing to his agents. Follow the leads, ask the right questions, and the truth will prevail."

"We need to know who lives in Finch Lane, Cornhill. That's where the recipient of Lady Lucille's note lives, the one I failed to send."

Mr Chance nodded. "We'll add it to the list. The barrow boy may have vital information. Once we've heard from Jules, we will decide our next line of enquiry."

Jules and his family occupied a first-floor apartment on Lombard Street, Cheapside, with an excellent view of the Mansion House. His mother, Alice, was in bed when Eleanor arrived, though she'd heard the woman's hacking cough as she mounted the stairs.

Mr Daventry's man—a mean-looking fellow with a squashed nose—ushered them inside, shouting for Jules from the doorway.

Jules' eight-year-old sister, Hope, came charging into the living room, her face as warm as a sunbeam. "Mr O'Hare. Have you come to play marbles? I knocked Jules out of the circle twice last night. He ain't stopped sulking since."

The hulking fellow smiled and patted Hope on the head. "You know I'm paid to stand guard at the door," he said in a broad Irish accent. "Go to your mammy and give her the medicine. You remember what I said now. She's to take the tincture and eat that broth if she's to gain her strength."

The girl wiped her nose with her hand, wrapped her arms around Mr O'Hare's waist and hugged him. "Tell me you ain't leaving."

The man gulped. His body might have been made of stone but his heart certainly wasn't. "I'll be right outside the door. Now, fetch Jules and tend to your mammy."

Hope released him and skipped out of the room, calling for Jules.

Mr O'Hare turned to them. "Ah, that child kills me, so she does."

Mr Chance laughed. "I suspect Daventry knew what he was doing when he ordered you to guard their door."

"The longer it goes on, the harder it will be to leave."

"You may be here for another week," Eleanor said.

Pursuing all lines of enquiry would take time. Indeed, her heart echoed Mr O'Hare's sentiment. The more time she spent in Mr Chance's company, the more it would hurt to let him go.

"I have a feeling I'll be taking this home," Mr O'Hare said, smiling at the empty doorway. "Father

138

Branagan says when a man feels the glory of heaven on earth, he knows that's his calling."

"All things happen for a reason," Eleanor said, feeling the heat of Mr Chance's gaze upon her face. Had he not stolen her box, she never would have kissed him. "Though during times of trouble, it's hard to be optimistic. Perhaps this is your life's purpose."

Jules appeared. His face was clean, his brown hair combed and tucked behind his ears. He eyed Mr O'Hare cautiously. "Daventry pays you to mind the door. I don't need you here. Wait outside while I speak to Miss Darrow."

Mr O'Hare did not clip the insolent boy's head but nodded. "You call if you need me."

As soon as the Irishman closed the door, Jules grumbled, "I'm sick of him sticking his nose where it ain't wanted. I ain't no fool and can take care of my family. When can we leave this place?"

"When we know your life is not in danger." Eleanor motioned to the chairs beside the hearth, and they all sat. "You're safe here. Mr Daventry told you what happened at my shop. Stock ruined. Cupboards broken. The devil will stop at nothing to keep his secret."

Jules noticed the minor cut on Eleanor's forehead. "Mr Daventry said you tripped down the stairs, but I know you ain't that clumsy."

"Someone pushed me. I hit my head and remember very little. Mr Chance thought I had fallen and didn't know to check the rooms upstairs." If he had, they'd be closer to discovering the truth.

Jules set his distrusting eyes on her companion. "You're that gent what was shot outside the shop. You're the devil who stole her box and left her sobbing for days."

139

"I am," Mr Chance said with some remorse. "But I am doing everything in my power to make amends."

"I ain't never seen her so afraid." The bite of anger in Jules' voice was unmistakable. "Do you know how hard she works? Sometimes she ain't got time to eat and sleep. Then you bring trouble to her door."

"Mr Chance is not entirely to blame," she said.

Mr Chance exhaled deeply. "I give you my word. I'll not hurt her again." He looked at Eleanor and added, "When this is over, I'll cook dinner and sort buttons. I'll take care of all the menial tasks until you're back on your feet."

"Can you cook?" She tried not to picture him sitting beside her hearth, drinking wine and reading poetry, a kiss leading to a passionate romp on the fireside rug.

"I could rustle up a simple bill of fare."

"I bet he ain't never cooked a thing in his life," Jules mocked.

"I was younger than you when I slept on the streets," Mr Chance said, giving Jules a lesson in how not to judge by appearances. "Have you ever roasted a rat over a brazier?" He waited for Jules to wince. "Neither have I, but I have witnessed such desperation. Let me offer you some advice. Never refuse a helping hand when it's offered."

Jules glanced at the closed door. "I ain't good at trusting folk."

"Daventry would never hire an untrustworthy man. Besides, Miss Darrow can sniff out a liar from twenty yards. I think she'd know if O'Hare was a scoundrel."

A brief silence ensued.

Eleanor avoided meeting Mr Chance's gaze. After hearing his thoughtful words, the kindness in his eyes would overwhelm her tender heart.

"We need to ask you about the notes you delivered for me." Eleanor had lost count of how many she had sent. Without her diary, she had no way of remembering the different locations. "To your knowledge, have you ever been followed?"

Jules scratched his head. "I don't wait around long enough to notice. Not when the jobs are across town."

"Have you ever been curious enough to wait and discover who came to collect them?" He had been curious enough to open one. Surely he had lingered in the vicinity, spying.

Jules did not reply.

"You're not in trouble." Mr Chance spoke like a concerned parent. "If it were me, I would want to learn everything I could. It's the only way to protect Miss Darrow."

Jules looked at him with a sense of camaraderie. "Miss Darrow helped put food on our table. The extra work she gave me paid our rent. It's only right I look out for her welfare."

Mr Chance agreed. "A man cares for those who matter most. You wanted to know she wasn't unwittingly involved in criminal activity." When Jules looked blankly, Mr Chance said, "That she wasn't helping thieves and crooks."

Jules puffed out his chest. "She shouldn't have to deal with them things, not on her own. A lady needs someone to take care of her."

Eleanor's heart swelled. It explained why Jules asked her to dine with his family. Not wanting to waste their precious food, she'd used work as an excuse to decline his invitation.

"And so you watched to see who claimed the notes."

Jules nodded. "Wait here." He left the room and returned

with a bent silver notebook. "I found this tossed in the gutter. There ain't no name inside, or I'd have given it to a constable. I couldn't sell it else I'd be dragged off to Newgate, so I used it to record what I saw."

Jules sat and flicked to the first page. Eleanor could see no words written inside, only small pencil drawings.

"What did you discover?" Eleanor said, feeling a rush of pride. Jules couldn't read but had overcome his disadvantage.

"I delivered the letters with the leaf seal to a doctor in St Martin's Lane, hidden in a pair of nice new gloves. I followed him to a coffee house in Long Acre. He spoke to a woman sitting alone, and they both disappeared upstairs."

"Yes. That would be Mrs Langdon. Hers is the laurel seal."

"I asked about," Jules continued. "They say the doctor cures mad women by looking under their skirts. He makes 'em scream till they can't scream no more."

Mr Chance looked at her and grinned. "He's paid to banish the devil and leave her in a state of bliss."

"Whatever he's doing, the manager said he does it on the first Wednesday of every month," Jules informed them before moving swiftly on. "I leave the notes with the rose seal with the landlord of the New Inn." He consulted the odd array of drawings in his book. "A respectable gent from Berwick and Masters Land Agents collects them, though I don't know more than that."

The rose meant it was the letter the Duke of Farnborough's daughter sent. The land agent likely worked for the duke.

Suspecting her other clients were doing nothing more than conducting illicit affairs, Eleanor was keen to discover more about Lady Lucille. "What about the notes with the green seal?"

Jules flicked through the dirty pages of his notebook. "That's an odd one. I've sent four notes, but all to different places."

"Yes, I recall one was to a baker's shop on The Strand." That had been the first note Eleanor had agreed to deliver. Lady Lucille had stressed the need for secrecy.

"I've delivered to a bookshop in Highgate, a perfume shop in Covent Garden. The last one was to the coffeehouse in the Bull and Mouth coaching inn. It's always too busy to see who collects them. When I went back and asked the baker, he gave me a clip around the ear."

Being a man who always rose to a challenge, Mr Chance rubbed his muscular thighs and said, "Then the baker's shop will be our next call."

"And we must visit Emily." Eleanor wouldn't rest until she knew why the girl had helped herself to the material. She turned to Jules. "Emily arrived with her father and removed bolts of silk from the shop. I pray her actions were not self-serving."

The corners of Jules' mouth sagged. "It ain't her father. He's dead. I saw Emily at the burial ground on Shoemakers Row, weeping at her mother's grave. She said her father fell off a barge and drowned in the Thames."

"When?"

"A year back."

How odd. Emily spoke about her parents often. A few weeks ago, she took work home so she could have supper with them. Why would she lie?

"Who does she live with?"

And who had helped her remove the silk from the shop?

Jules shrugged. "I asked her as she walked away, though she mumbled something. I ain't sure I heard right."

Eleanor sat forward, unable to shake a deep sense of trepidation. "What do you think she said?"

Jules paled. "I thought she said she lived with the devil."

# Chapter Eleven

Breadwell's was the prominent bakery Jules had mentioned. Located on The Strand, its reputation for excellence meant the place was thriving. The queue was out the door, and an impatient crowd hogged the oak counter.

Many were servants sent to procure sweet treats: Chelsea buns, Belgian buns, Eccles cakes and scrumptious fruit tarts.

Miss Darrow licked her lips as she gazed upon the plum pies with lattice crusts. "Do you think I might purchase a pie before you harass the baker? Instinct tells me this won't end well."

"You may have whatever your heart desires." Theo bent his head and whispered, "In some cultures, plums are an aphrodisiac. Though if you need to eat a pie to find me phys-ically pleasing, I shall have to join a monastery."

She laughed but didn't look at him. "An aphrodisiac indeed. It seems you're desperate to flap your wings and cluck like a chicken. You already owe me one forfeit. Now it's two."

Had they been in the privacy of his bedchamber, he

would have willed her to turn her head. Their lips would touch, and like a spark to a hay barn, a fierce passion would ignite.

"It's the truth. Have you never read Greek Mythology? Aphrodite invented the plum tree as a symbol of passion and pleasure."

"I know the story of the golden apple," she said in quiet challenge. "Paris gave Aphrodite his apple in exchange for Helen of Sparta. And I know the pomegranate is sacred to her because it represents—"

"A woman losing her virginity," he said, his mouth brushing the shell of her ear. He imagined her sprawled naked in his bed, the pretty nightgown tossed to the floor. "Shall we ask for a pomegranate pastry?"

She turned to face him, a little gasp escaping when she realised they were inches away from kissing. "It represents the consummation of marriage. As we're not marrying, we have no need to ask." She glanced at the other patrons. "People are staring."

"At the pastries, not at us."

She looked flustered, unnerved by their close proximity. "This is a terrible idea. We should have come first thing in the morning. The baker won't speak to us in a shop full of people."

"He'll oblige us. I can be quite persuasive."

"As well I know." She was referring to their *intimate* interactions. "It's that devilish grin of yours. Is it something they teach at Scoundrel School?"

"The way you wrap me around your little finger, you must have attended every lesson."

She laughed, her eyes sparkling like the dance of

sunlight on the ocean. She was so beautiful when unburdened. He made a silent vow to see her smile every day.

"I'm sorry," the words left him without thought.

She blinked in surprise. "Sorry for what?"

"For robbing you of that smile. For stealing the light from your eyes. For those wasted hours when you lay awake hating me."

Miss Darrow stared at him, an intense look that seemed to penetrate his soul. "I could never hate you."

She had every reason to despise him.

Her noble spirit had him gawping in awe.

"I was rude to you."

"At the theatre?"

"No. The day I found Delphine in the yard with Dorian. The day you lied to me." He was the fool they'd deceived so easily. "I wasn't angry with you. I was angry with myself for being blind. For failing my family."

She touched his arm, sending an unknown force charging through his veins. A sudden need to feel close to her.

"You did nothing wrong. Delphine was determined to keep the meeting a secret. You were honourable throughout." Her fingers firmed around his forearm. "The kind way you spoke to her, the concessions you made, never have I respected a man more than I did in that moment."

The compliment touched him deeply. "Then I ruined everything by stealing your box."

"You ruined nothing. Are we not good friends now?"

They were more than friends.

It was only a matter of time before they were lovers.

"Are you deaf?" The maid beside him nudged his arm. "Three times he's asked you to step forward and place your

147

order. Can't you see there's a queue? I ain't got time to waste."

The crowd grumbled in agreement.

Theo grinned, their annoyance playing into his hands.

He approached the counter and addressed the man with a beer barrel for a belly. "I'll take the largest plum pie in the cabinet." He presented the Home Secretary's letter. "You have been named as a witness in an official investigation. You're required to close the shop so we can speak privately."

"Did you hear that?" a customer cried. "He's closing the shop."

Like a run on the bank, the crowd pushed forward, waving their hands and shouting their orders. Amid the cacophony, the baker raised the wooden countertop and beckoned Theo and Miss Darrow forward.

"We're not closing," the baker reassured his patrons, gesturing to the woman in a white pinny. "Gertrude will serve you. Form an orderly queue." Then he turned and ushered them through a door at the back.

Two women were busy rolling pastry on a long oak table in the large kitchen. The heat hit Theo the second he entered. The poor boy stoking the ovens had a face as red as a berry.

"What's this about?" The baker stood with his folded arms resting on his paunch. "What am I supposed to have witnessed?"

"A barrow boy brought a letter here some months ago," Miss Darrow said. "It was a small letter, an inch square. It was so tiny it would be memorable. We need to know if the recipient works here or if someone came to collect the note. It was sealed with green wax."

The baker remembered the incident clearly. "Yes, the boy

handed me the note. I asked who it was for, and he said he didn't know."

"Did you open it?" Theo said, daring him to lie.

"Yes, the writing was so small that the wife had to use a magnifying glass." He jerked his head to the buxom woman behind him. "It was the oddest thing."

"But she read it?" Miss Darrow asked.

That's when the baker winced in obvious discomfort. "It's private business. Nothing that should concern anyone else."

Theo showed the baker the letter again. "You don't need a hand lens to see the official seal. You'll answer our questions here or at Bow Street."

After exchanging odd expressions with his wife, the baker confessed. "It said I was to appeal to Thatcher's & Sons solicitors in Fetter Lane, and a certain debt would be settled in full."

"We were glad of it, sir," the wife blurted. "The debts were mounting, and all requests went unanswered. Getting the note was like a blessing from heaven. Within days, all the bills were paid."

"We will need the name of your debtor." Theo mentally scratched his head. Why would Lucille Bowman have debts at a baker's shop? And why had her father not settled her account?

"Does it matter?" the baker said, raising his voice to compensate for the rowdy noise in the shop. "It would be wrong to reveal the name of such a prestigious client."

"It matters," he snapped. "We know Lady Lucille Bowman sent the note. We need you to confirm it was the case."

The baker's brow creased in confusion. "There must be some mistake. The debt belonged to a gentleman, sir."

"A gentleman?" Miss Darrow tapped her finger to her lips. It took her mere seconds to make sense of the conundrum. "Then the debt belonged to her father, or her affianced? I would guess Lord Wrotham ran up the debt."

While the baker remained tight-lipped, his wife said, "He ordered cakes by the dozen most days. He spent ten pounds one week."

"Ten pounds? On cake?" Theo had to laugh. The lanky fop was all skin and bone. "How much did he owe in total?"

Bowing his head in shame, the baker said, "Almost a hundred and fifty pounds. It's been a problem for over a year."

"Since settling his account, he's not been back," the wife added.

So, Lady Lucille was secretly paying Lord Wrotham's debts. Theo would wager the bookshop owner and perfumer told a similar tale. A visit to the solicitor's office would confirm as much.

But who lived at Finch Lane, Cornhill? Another creditor? And how was it linked to the damage at Miss Darrow's shop?

"We'll ask Daventry to find out why Wrotham cannot settle his own accounts," Theo muttered in Miss Darrow's ear. "We can visit the office tomorrow."

She looked at him and nodded. Plagued by a sudden tiredness, she failed to stifle a yawn. "Forgive me. It's been such a long day. I'm not sure I have the strength to visit anyone else."

"We should go home. Nothing is so important it cannot wait until tomorrow." He thanked the baker and led Miss

Darrow through the crowded shop and onto The Strand. "You've not eaten all day. Perhaps that accounts for your flagging spirits. We'll dine with Aaron before the club opens at eight. Then you should rest upstairs."

She glanced at him through tired eyes. "What about our game of piquet? You have debts to pay. You owe two forfeits."

He resisted the urge to stroke her cheek and say something wicked. "They'll be your stake in the game tonight. I shall do my best to win them back. Assuming you're well enough to meet me for a midnight liaison."

She smiled before yawning again. "What might I claim if I win? I shall have to give the matter a great deal of thought."

"I'm a man of many talents. I suggest you choose wisely."

"Hello!" The baker's assistant came hurrying out of the shop, something wrapped in parchment in her hands. "You forgot your plum pie. Your wife seemed keen to take one home."

His wife?

Theo did not correct the misconception. He thrust a few shillings into the woman's hand despite her insisting it was a gift. He did not take advantage of the hardworking classes. He was not his cousin Wrotham.

They settled into the carriage, Miss Darrow cradling the wrapped pie in her lap. "We should have it with our claret at the card table tonight."

He didn't care for gaming or plum pie but longed for their secret rendezvous.

"It occurs to me I need to win back one forfeit, not two.

You thought I'd lied about plums being an aphrodisiac. Perhaps tonight, I shall prove I'm right."

Aaron held his chin between his thumb and forefinger, his expression a mix of contemplation and concentration. "Everyone knows money runs like water through Wrotham's fingers. But to have Lady Lucille mop up his mess is downright embarrassing."

Theo swallowed a tender piece of beef and dabbed his mouth with his napkin. "Why order *The Vampyre* from Pickering's library? What are the odds she would innocently pick the villain's book?"

"Extremely poor." Aaron reached for his wine, took a sip and looked at Miss Darrow, seated to his left. "Are you sure you've told us everything?"

Appearing quite revived, she nodded. "I have no need to lie or keep secrets." Her gaze drifted to Theo. "Honesty above all else. That is our motto."

Aaron's mocking snort rang through the dining room. "There is no such thing, Miss Darrow. Everyone manipulates the truth for their own advantage."

Theo did not challenge Aaron's opinion. He had professed to be Miss Darrow's friend when he wanted to be her lover. "You should know. You're an expert. You ask Miss Scrumptious to close her curtains, then grumble to yourself when she does."

Aaron shot Theo a murderous look.

"Miss Scrumptious?" Miss Darrow said.

"It's Miss Lovelace's moniker," Aaron snapped. "My brothers find childish games amusing. I ask that you refrain from repeating it outside these walls. As competitors, our relationship is often strained."

Miss Darrow's playful shrug mirrored her teasing smile. "I'm sure Miss Lovelace would see it as a compliment. What lady wouldn't want to be considered scrumptious?"

Aaron downed his wine. "An intelligent woman wants a man to worship her mind, not her physical attributes. I would hate for her to think I encouraged my brothers' juvenile banter."

"All women like to feel attractive. I'm sure men are the same, too." The glint in her emerald eyes said she had mischief in mind. "You're an incredibly handsome man, sir. I'm sure Miss Lovelace has a similar moniker for you. I've seen her admiring your physique on numerous occasions."

Aaron placed his cutlery on his plate and pushed out of the chair. "I suspect she was looking for ways to weaken my resolve. If you'll excuse me. I must change before we open the club." He glanced at Theo. "I'll require your assistance tonight. Pendleton has a death wish, and Rothley won't rest until every lord in London is declared bankrupt."

"I shall forsake dessert and meet you in the card room. Miss Darrow kindly offered to share her plum pie later." While Aaron wasn't looking, Theo smiled at her and winked. "We'll devour it while attempting to solve a puzzling theory."

"A theory?" Aaron said. "About the case?"

"No, about Greek Mythology and foreign cultures."

Miss Darrow was quick to add, "Though I will devise a plan of action for tomorrow. We have many lines of enquiry.

Above all, I must discover why Emily removed the bolts of silk."

Tomorrow would be another tiring day, following pointless leads and listening to endless lies. Miss Darrow would suffer another disappointment. Her trusted seamstress was a sly thief.

"I took the liberty of having your things moved to Delphine's old room, Miss Darrow." Aaron glanced at Theo, a silent warning that he was tired of having a woman living under their roof. "With Gibbs installed at your shop, you may want to return home soon. Theo has gone to great lengths to ensure you can accept clients again."

Though Miss Darrow smiled, she had clearly heard the veiled message. "And I am grateful beyond words. I shall visit the shop in the morning and speak to Mr Gibbs. If he agrees, I see no reason to delay."

Theo shot daggers at his brother. A deep sense of loss settled in his chest at the thought of her leaving. "Miss Darrow, you may stay at Fortune's Den until we've caught the villain."

"I'm sure Miss Darrow knows her own mind," Aaron said, determined to have the last word before withdrawing from the room.

They finished their meal, though the potatoes were cold.

Theo glanced at the mantel clock. "You should retire upstairs before the first patrons arrive. Aaron fears he cannot protect you when the house is teaming with degenerates."

Miss Darrow arched a brow. "Oh, dear. That lie left your lips with such ease, Mr Chance. Your brother is afraid of nothing or no one."

Aaron was afraid of being alone.

He was scared of being thought inadequate.

He was terrified to lower his guard and love a woman.

Still, Theo laughed and raised his hands. "Another penalty for me, then. At this rate, I shall be your servant for an eternity."

"I rather like the idea of having you at my beck and call."

"Some ladies hire handsome servants to bring them the bliss Mrs Langdon seeks. I shall do whatever it takes to please my mistress."

Miss Darrow gave a curious hum. "I see a problem. You'll want one who's willing, and we only have one plum pie."

The card room smelled of smoke and sweat and spilled liquor. A veritable den of vice. An undercurrent of tension still rippled through the air. Rothley had come with one mission in mind—humiliation. Much to Aaron's annoyance, and having won a small fortune, the marquess had gone outside to smoke his cheroot and spent ten minutes studying The Burnished Jade.

While they needed to discover Rothley's motive for frequenting Fortune's Den, his attendance worked to Theo's advantage.

Aaron had retired to his study. The gamblers had left long before the stroke of midnight, leaving Theo free to partake in a game of high stakes.

He lit the censer, filling the room with the sensual smell of frankincense, rose and myrrh. He shuffled the cards, opened the wine, poured two glasses and waited.

He lounged in a chair, a primal hunger simmering in his blood. A vision of Miss Darrow slipped into his mind. What was it he found so appealing? What was it that spoke to his soul?

The answer came when she pushed open the door and peered into the candlelit room. It was everything. Eyes with the healing power of malachite. Hair a vibrant cascade of copper. A body he'd glimpsed only once beneath the fine nightgown yet had pictured every second since. A sharp mind he wanted to explore and unravel.

"Welcome." He crossed the room, a stirring in his loins. They were to play cards and eat pie, not fornicate on the tables. "I feared you'd fallen asleep."

To endure another day without a kiss would have killed him.

"I was waiting for the chime of the tall-case clock, but then the house fell quiet, and I came to investigate."

He beckoned her inside. "You were impatient. Desperate to beat me at cards and prove I lied about that plum pie you're holding."

"I can't see how a plum could stir a lady's passions."

He was quick to enlighten her. "A plum drawn over the mouth would raise the required response. A plum stolen from between your lips would have the desired effect." He closed the door and turned the key in the lock. Plum juice licked from her breasts would have her writhing in pleasure. "We can test the theory if you think I'm lying."

"Perhaps." She stepped farther into the room, inhaling the aromatic scent from the Orient. "I expected it to smell like cheroots in here."

"It did, but I thought oil of frankincense might soothe your aching muscles." He took the pie from her and placed it on the walnut console table, next to the silver cutlery, napkins and two china plates.

"Are you always so thoughtful?" She ran her fingers over the green baize, noting the neat deck of cards and poured wine.

"The occasion calls for a concerted effort."

"Are we not to play a simple game of piquet?"

"Yes, but I mean to win back my forfeits and prove a point."

She faced him, her eyes sparkling in the candlelight. "Is that the only reason you asked me here? Do you not have another motive for wanting time alone together?"

"What other motive could I have?"

A sweet hum escaped her soft lips. "Perhaps you seek to explore this strange energy that flows between us." Her gaze dipped to his mouth. "Whatever the reason, consider our motto before you answer."

The minx knew how to lure a man into a trap.

"The truth would have you fleeing the room. I'll not ruin a wonderful evening before it's begun."

Something he'd said made her smile. "Very well. We'll play for confessions. Let's make a wonderful evening a magnificent one."

Miss Darrow had a siren's allure. The enchanting timbre of her voice promised a night of pleasure. The sensual haze in her eyes spoke of a slow, subtle seduction.

He drew out a chair. "Shall we begin, Miss Darrow?"

"Eleanor. Friends use their given names."

Lovers did, too.

"Would you care to sit, Eleanor?" Saying her name tightened the muscles in his abdomen. "Drink some wine. Relax."

"Are you trying to get me drunk, Theo?"

"Not at all. I want you awake and alert when we kiss again."

She chuckled. "You seem so sure we will."

"If you want a confession, you must earn it." A thought struck him. Based on her inexperience, a round of piquet could take up to an hour. Why waste precious time when he had a different game in mind?

He sat beside her, shuffled the cards and dealt four each.

"Highest card wins," he said, before sipping his wine. "Look at your hand. Decide which one will win a confession."

The urge to win would see her using her best cards first.

Like a miser clutching gold, she held them close to her chest, giggling with excitement as she scanned them twice.

"Place your card face down on the table." He threw down his lowest card, the four of clubs. "Remember what you're playing for. You want to know why I'm sure we'll kiss again."

She pursed her lips as she studied the cards. Then she drew one and slapped it on the baize. "Who will turn first?"

"A lady always goes first."

She turned over her card, an eight of spades. Interesting. He suspected that wasn't her highest card. This woman knew how to mess with his mind.

"You beat my four of clubs." He held her gaze and hit her with the truth. "Something happened the first time we kissed. Something indescribable. The second kiss ignited a blazing fire of passion between us. We're both longing to see what would happen a third time."

The lady gulped. "Yes, it's like a terrible addiction."

"Terrible?" he scoffed. "Your mouth is glorious."

"Terrible in that we might ruin a friendship if we pursue these romantic urges."

"Not if we're honest about our feelings." It sounded simple, yet he grew more needy by the day. "It's my turn to play for a confession. Why come if you know I had an ulterior motive for inviting you?"

They placed their cards.

He won, his nine of hearts beating her seven.

"Confess, Eleanor."

"Because I want to kiss you, but you'll have to earn it. You need to give me a reason why I should."

He relaxed back in the chair. He had solid reasons for every decision he'd ever made, until he kissed her at the Olympic. His mind had not been his own since.

"The truth is, you should avoid me. I cannot leave Aaron here alone." The thought was more than he could bear. "I can offer companionship and stolen moments of pleasure. You deserve more than I could ever give."

He expected to witness the chill of recognition in her eyes, to watch her physically withdraw. To feel the ache of loss. The opposite was true. She smiled as if he'd given her the greatest compliment.

"Don't underestimate the attraction of stolen moments. No one can say what tomorrow will bring. One should live for today."

"Are they not the words of a scoundrel?" he teased.

"We're kindred spirits. Two people trying to escape the pain of the past. Life is precarious. We both know that."

The words hit a nerve. But the body he pictured at the bottom of the stairs wasn't his mother's. Miss Darrow might not have woken from her stupor. Was that the reason for her

ADELE CLEE

devil-may-care attitude? Did it account for his urgent need to bed her, too?

"The next question is yours," he said.

She reached for her wine and took a large gulp, shaking visibly from its potency. "It's late. Shall we skip to dessert? I know you're keen to prove your point."

His pulse rose more than a notch. "Perhaps you'll permit me to pay my forfeit and act your servant. Let me feed you, Eleanor."

He moved to the console table to retrieve the plum pie, his cock already swelling in his trousers, lust drumming a potent beat in his blood.

Eleanor stood, taking the napkins and cutlery from him. "Where shall we eat? I wouldn't want to get plum juice on the green baize."

"Here. Stand still. Close your eyes." The pie was cold, but it didn't matter. He scooped a tiny amount of stewed plum onto a spoon. "Open your mouth, Eleanor."

Clasping her hands in front of her body, she did as he asked.

The first touch of the spoon on her lips made her quiver. Her chest rose rapidly, but Theo kept his attention on her mouth.

"Lick the spoon, love."

The rapid flick of her tongue was almost his undoing. She lapped every drop of sweetness and sighed.

"Given the chance, I'd devour you in much the same way. Are you not aroused, Eleanor?" Hell, he was so hard he was about to split the seam of his trousers.

"What's next?" said his willing protege.

"Now you must take a whole plum and suck it gently." He spooned one out and placed it between her lips. "Don't

160

let it fall. Don't eat it yet. Don't be greedy." He watched the juice trickle down her chin. "Do you need your servant to mop up the mess?"

She nodded, peeking at him through narrowed lids.

He gripped her hips with both hands and sucked her chin clean. "That plum is too big to eat by yourself," he whispered. "There's more than enough for two. Are you good at sharing, Eleanor?"

She nodded, threading her arms around his neck.

He wanted to crush his mouth to hers, but first he needed to get rid of the damn plum. One bite, and he swallowed his half whole.

Eleanor did the same. She licked her lips. "What now?"

"Now I beg for a kiss from—"

Her mouth was on his, hot and insistent—a kiss like wildfire, untamed and unbridled. Heat infused him, turning his blood molten, every muscle as hard as stone. His heartbeat quickened.

God, he wanted her, here on the table.

Later, in bed. Tomorrow, in the carriage.

Anywhere the next day and the one after that.

But not before he'd plundered her senseless.

He cupped her face in his hands, sliding his tongue between her lips, smiling as she moaned into his mouth. She wanted him just as badly.

A point she proved when their tongues mated with an urgency that defied logic. The strokes were fast and deep. Arousal pumped so hard through his body he could scarcely stand still.

He didn't want the kiss to end.

He didn't want the case to end, yet he knew they would find the culprit who'd ruined her stock. Everything would change. He would lose her, lose this beautiful, unexplainable thing that flowed between them. He needed no one but his family, but he was beginning to think he might need her.

"Tell me, Eleanor, are plums an aphrodisiac?" He cupped her neck, brushed his lips over hers, pressed a tender kiss to her temple.

Her breath came quickly. Her eyes were the most vibrant shade of green he had ever seen. "I concede. I have never been so aroused." Driven by the same urgent need for physical contact, her hand glided over his chest in slow, caressing strokes. "Is that the end of the lesson, Theo?"

How could it be?

There was no end to what he would do with her.

"No, love. It's only the beginning."

# Chapter Twelve

Eleanor looked at him, this fallen angel, as handsome as a celestial being consumed by earthly desires. "You have made your point. What else is there to learn?"

She wished it would take a lifetime of kissing to prove he was right. Damp between her thighs, her sex ached for his touch. Never had she been so reckless. Never had she experienced the potent power of lust.

"How can a lady judge the quality of shoes if she doesn't wear them?" he replied cryptically. "How can she know if a bonnet fits without trying it on?"

Eleanor narrowed her gaze. The way he wrapped his tongue around every syllable said he had mischief in mind. "What have hats and shoes to do with pleasure?"

"Every experiment needs a conclusion." His devilish grin said they would kiss again soon. "How can you judge if plums are an aphrodisiac unless you reach the pinnacle of desire?"

"The pinnacle?" she stuttered.

"I need to make you come, Eleanor."

Her breath caught in her throat.

Shock should have been her first reaction, yet she couldn't help but admire his honesty. It wasn't the only thing she admired. She liked how his new coat clung to his biceps, a wrapper for a tempting package. She liked the way candle-light flickered over his chiselled jaw, a sculptor's masterpiece.

"As an unmarried lady, I attend to my pleasure in the privacy of my chamber." Two could play his game. "I don't need a lesson in that."

The admission had a strange effect on him, a growl rumbling in his throat. "Next time you indulge in wicked-ness, I hope I'm watching from a chair in a shadowy corner. A whisky in one hand, something hot and hard in the other." His tongue skimmed the seam of his lips. "Tonight, I have a different goal in mind, something in keeping with the theme of food."

Eleanor laughed, or else she might faint from a lack of oxygen. "Are you so drunk with desire you cannot form a coherent word? I confess, you have me at a loss."

"I'm hungry, Eleanor."

He sounded ravenous.

"Have a piece of plum pie."

He stepped closer, pressing her back against the card table, their thighs touching. His breath mingled with hers, warm and intoxicating, as his fingers gently brushed a strand of hair from her face. "You're the only thing I want. Indulge me." He gestured to the cards on the green baize. "Let's make a wager. The highest card wins."

"What are we playing for?" she dared to ask.

"For you. If I'm victorious, you'll be my personal feast."

"And if you lose?" She prayed he didn't.

"You'll go to bed tense. Restless. Spend a sleepless night wondering what I planned to do." He bent his head, his mouth brushing hers softly. "Trust me. Turn over a card, love."

She hesitated.

Her virtue was the only thing she truly owned. Hers to give to a man of her choosing. No one affected her the way he did. No one made her heart thunder like a tempest, wild and unrestrained.

"We're playing for kisses," he whispered against her lips. "Intimate kisses. Nothing more. You have my word."

Curiosity and a deep-rooted need to feel close to this man had her turning over the ten of diamonds. "It will be hard to beat," she said, trying not to sound deflated.

Theo reached for his card, his confident grin causing a flutter in her belly. "I always play to win. I'd never risk losing something I want so badly."

With the flick of one finger, he flipped over his card.

The King of Hearts.

Why was she not surprised?

He stole hearts and broke them; that's what the gossips said. He held hers in the palm of his hand. It was too late to claim it back. And so she would do what she'd sworn to do initially. Trust him.

"I imagine you want to claim your winnings now."

"Only if you want me to."

"As you said, a conclusion is crucial to this particular study. Though I fear the effects of the plums have worn off."

"Allow me to rectify the problem." He reached behind her and stuck his thumb into the pie before coating her lips with juice and sucking the residue. "Now, where were we?"

He was quick to remind her.

The kiss was slow, hypnotic, so deep it had her core muscles clenching. He tasted of claret and plums and an indefinable male essence. He kissed like the dangerous devil men feared. Like he meant to own her. Like he meant to ruin her for every other man.

Theo tangled his fingers in her hair, tilting her head back and baring her throat. He was panting when he spoke. "I want you to lie on the table, Eleanor. I'm desperate to claim my winnings."

"On the table?" She shivered when he pressed his lips to the sensitive spot below her ear, arousal heating her blood. "Is it safe?"

"How many times must I tell you to trust me?" Setting his hands to her waist, he lifted her with ease and sat her on the table's edge. "I've won an intimate kiss. I'm sure you know what that means."

"Theo, every kiss we've shared has been deeply passionate."

His subtle smile said he agreed. "I'm going to kiss you everywhere. Let me show you. Tell me to stop if you feel uncomfortable."

She breathed through a pang of excitement. When it came to this man, the word *stop* wasn't in her vocabulary.

He locked eyes with her, the intensity of his stare holding her spellbound. His lips parted as he gathered her skirts and slid them slowly up to her thighs.

A sweet hum escaped him, followed by a curse when he glanced at the ugly purple bruise marring her skin. "I'll kill that devil when I catch him. As God is my witness—"

"Hush." She touched his hand. She had more bruises on her back and bottom. "Let's not think about that now." These moments with him were precious. "Perhaps your kisses can heal wounds." Perhaps they could chase away ghosts or fill the inner emptiness.

Like always, Theo was quick to find out.

The feather-light touch of his lips sent heat coursing through her. He kissed the bruise once, then twice, his tongue lightly tracing the tender skin as if he possessed a magical elixir.

"Lie down for me, love," he said, his voice husky as he eased her back onto the baize. "Men take their pleasure at the tables. That's how I intend to take mine. You look good enough to eat."

Then he dropped to his knees, ready to worship her. He hooked her legs over his shoulders, pressed his mouth to her thigh and kissed a path to her forbidden place.

It was shocking.

It was heavenly.

It was the most thrilling experience of her life.

Every slide of his hot tongue over her bud had her gasping and gripping the table. He knew where to stroke her. Every sweep of her sensitive flesh had tremors shooting to her toes.

"Theo!"

He continued his wicked torment, the pleasure so intense her head felt light while her body quivered. The need to climax was so profound she arched her back and rocked her hips against his mouth.

It took the slide of one finger into her sex to make her come, her whole body shuddering as she moaned and panted his name.

When he rose between her legs, licking his lips and grinning sinfully, she didn't want this night to end. She wanted more hours of mindless pleasure. More hours spent in his arms. She wanted to see his face aglow with the effects of his own release. To hold him inside her and never let go.

*Don't stop!*

Those words danced on her tongue.

The sudden knock on the door dragged Eleanor from her reverie. She had been a moment away from offering herself to the man she couldn't resist. Lust had the power to banish inhibitions. Having spent a lifetime stifled and denied a voice, lust brought a sense of liberation.

"Theo?" Aaron called, his voice hard, his timing abysmal.

"Just a second." Theo straightened. He groaned in frustration as he scanned her bare thighs. "Perhaps you should return to your shop. At least there, we would have some privacy." He reached for her hands. "Let me help you."

Another loud rap had them straightening their clothes and gathering their wits. The knob turned, but thankfully the door was locked.

Eleanor sat in a chair and snatched her wine glass, though her body was still aglow from her dazzling release.

Theo unlocked the door and opened it wide. "There'd better be a fire," he said through gritted teeth. "Or a bloody good reason for the disturbance."

The air turned decidedly chilly when Aaron Chance strode into the room. He did not hide his emotions out of politeness.

"This room is reserved for gambling." Aaron glanced at her attire, appearing more irritated by her lack of dishevelment. He did not like to be proved wrong.

Theo gestured to the table. "Which is why we're playing cards and drinking wine. We're on our fourth wager."

Aaron inhaled deeply. Hopefully, the aromatic smell of frankincense filled his nostrils, not the scent of arousal.

"When I allowed Miss Darrow to stay here, I asked for one thing." Aaron's eyes were as hard as obsidian in the candlelight. "Keep me informed. Don't let Daventry make me look foolish."

Theo shrugged. "I told you everything during dinner tonight."

"You omitted one minor detail."

Eleanor stared at him blankly. "I assure you. Theo trusts you more than anyone. He would never keep you in the dark." *He would sacrifice his own happiness to ensure you're not alone*, she said silently.

Aaron snorted. "Are you saying the gossiping lords are lying? Sigmund just told me the news gained from witnesses at the Olympic."

"What news, sir?"

"The news that you're betrothed."

A laugh escaped her. "But we're not really betrothed. Theo said it in the heat of the moment while threatening Lord Wrotham. He has no intention of ever leaving Fortune's Den."

Theo looked at her with obvious admiration. Most people were terrified of Aaron and seldom voiced their opinions. Yet she knew when a man's temper stemmed from love and concern and when it was borne from his own selfish interests.

"I'm afraid you're stuck with me," Theo said, his smile failing to reach his eyes. "We made a pact to be bachelors until we're old and grey."

Aaron contemplated the remark for lengthy seconds. A frown marred his brow, and when he sighed, it was long and weary. "As I said, you don't need to hide anything from me. Your happiness has always been a priority." He stepped back and motioned to the door. "It's late, Miss Darrow. I suggest you retire before you lose your most prized possession in a game of chance."

It was a demand, not a suggestion.

Eleanor stood and made for the door. "I thank you for your hospitality." She had outstayed her welcome. "I shall return to my modiste shop in the morning." Mr Gibbs would tackle the villain if he dared to attack her again. "Hiding is only delaying our progress. Perhaps it's time I lured the blackguard into a trap."

Theo made to speak, but Aaron replied first. "I admire your courage and tenacity, madam. In the face of adversity, true emotions are often revealed."

True emotions?

Eleanor sensed he was referring to her relationship with Theo, not the devious ransacker's motives. She also suspected Theo would object to her leaving but understood the logic of Aaron's suggestion.

"I mean to bring this matter to a swift conclusion." She turned to Theo, hoping her smile did not convey the true depth of her affection. Anything more than a brief affair was out of the question. "Thank you for an entertaining evening, Mr Chance. As to our game of trivia, you were right. Aphrodite is the goddess of plums."

# Chapter Thirteen

"You left the card room last night like you were late for an appointment." Theo studied her in the confines of his carriage, his eyes a smouldering azure. "Do you regret our experiment?"

Regret feeling a passion she did not know existed?

Regret feeling close to a man for the first time in her life?

Regret this delicious obsession?

Heaven help her, she should.

She should be cursing her stupidity.

"No. I'm only sorry we were interrupted. I suspect Aaron rode in on his metaphorical white charger intending to save my virtue."

"He wished to prevent us both from making a mistake. He told me so when he ordered me into his study and dragged me over hot coals."

Did Aaron fear living alone at Fortune's Den? Did he hope Theo would set his sights on a lady, not a lowly modiste? Despite their upbringing, the men had an aristocrat's blood.

"For what? Seducing me on a card table?"

His slow smile became a confident grin. "You've been seducing me since you stormed into the theatre box, threatening to hound me night and day until I give you what you want."

That seemed like a lifetime ago.

So much had changed since then.

"Did you get what you wanted, Eleanor?"

"Did you?"

He laughed. "I left the card room feeling like I'd emptied the Marquess of Rothley's purse."

"Is that a good thing?" She knew her clients found the marquess to be an enigma. The largest dowry in all Christendom would not convince him to marry. According to gossip, he was amoral. A hedonist.

"An exceptionally good thing. After our amorous interlude, I'm obsessed with plums. I'm obsessed with you, Eleanor."

Any woman would melt upon hearing his declaration. Every heart longed to hear sweet whispers of affection. But would these intense emotions fade with time? Would their friendship survive when lust released them from its talon-like grip?

"What happened to the pie?" she said, changing the subject.

"Aaron wanted a piece but declined, saying it looked like it had been ravaged by wolves." His voice took on a husky gravel. "I didn't tell him it's because we ate it without cutlery. Shall I send Sigmund to Breadwell's and order another for tonight?"

Her pulse raced.

Last night had been magnificent, but she would be a fool to believe this affair would end well. Despite her donning steel armour, this man had stolen her heart. What hope had she of reclaiming it now?

"I meant what I said to Aaron. I must return home today." The thought filled her with dread. "Working to find the villain must be my priority."

He said nothing for a moment and simply stared as if she'd spoken a foreign language. "I would rather you remained at Fortune's Den until the culprit is in custody."

"There's no need. Mr Gibbs will guard my premises." She swallowed past a lump in her throat. This was harder than expected. "Perhaps we might dine together at the Pheasant once we've visited Emily."

He smiled. "I'd like that."

Pleasing Theo Chance was like waking to a beautiful day. It left every part of her being infused in a warm glow.

Theo asked his coachman to park on Water Lane so they might access the premises via the yard. Mr Franklin and the other shopkeepers doubtless had a myriad of questions, but she hadn't the strength to deal with their interference today.

There wasn't a shard of glass in the yard, not one weed growing between the cracks in the paving. The back door did not swing ominously back and forth in the wind. It was new and painted dark green.

Theo removed a key from his pocket and unlocked the door. "Some cultures believe green is lucky."

She smiled though she felt like crying. How had he fixed things so quickly? "I always thought green was the colour of envy."

"Perhaps that's true. Every modiste in London wishes

173

they had your talent." He looked at her and winked. "When a man gives you a compliment, you're allowed to say thank you."

She drank in his handsome countenance. "Thank you." She would be the envy of every woman in London because she had kissed him.

They were walking past the fitting rooms when Mr Gibbs yanked back the curtain at the end of the corridor and growled like a bear. "Who goes there?" He met Theo's gaze and glanced heavenward. "Only thieves and beggars sneak in through the back door. You should have said you were coming. I might have shot first and asked questions later."

"You're not holding a pistol," Theo countered.

Mr Gibbs whipped a pistol out of his greatcoat pocket. "I could put a lead ball in your shoulder before you take your next breath."

Although Theo laughed, Eleanor took umbrage. "How insensitive, Mr Gibbs. You might recall Mr Chance was shot in the shoulder outside my premises."

"Aye, and like a ninny, he lay in bed moaning for days."

"Have you ever taken a bullet, sir?" The man might be built like a marble effigy of Goliath but was he experienced enough to comment?

"Twice, miss. My scars make Aaron Chance's look like cat scratches. Now, have you locked the back door?"

"I'm not an imbecile." Theo ushered the fellow into the shop. "Do you have any information to share? Has anyone else tried to gain entrance since we last spoke?"

"A few nosy shopkeepers came knocking, wanting to know if the peelers had caught the intruder. Seems they think those sailors on the merchant ships are out to cause trouble."

Eleanor entered the shop, her breath catching in her

throat. What was once a scene of chaos and destruction now gleamed with meticulous order. The polished oak floor sparkled. Pretty combs and kidskin gloves filled the fixed drawers and cabinets. Large vases of silk flowers stood on two plinths near the doorway. There was a new gilt mirror and plush velvet chairs.

It was like stepping into a dream, a heavenly dream.

Her throat tightened. She looked at Theo, who was busy quizzing Mr Gibbs and felt the pierce of Cupid's arrow. He had done this. He had not boasted or sought praise or tried to claim a reward.

She moved past them into the hall and climbed the stairs, desperate to see what he'd done with the other rooms. She had to grip the storeroom door before her knees buckled in shock. Bolts of colourful fabrics filled the shelves. Silk and satins. Linen and lace. There were boxes of buttons, rolls of ribbon. A new mannequin and expensive walnut drawers.

Tears filled her eyes.

She was done for.

There was no coming back from this. Love had taken command of her heart and soul. Theo owned her now. No other man could ever compare.

But what of her bedchamber?

Her whole body shook when she reached the upper floor.

The door creaked as she pushed it open. A peek inside brought tears of gratitude to her eyes. The room was immaculate, her clothes removed to the armoire, her bed made without a crease in the sheets. Her mother's blanket was folded neatly on the chair. He'd bought her a new diary and pencil and left them on the nightstand, next to a single pink rose in a bud vase.

It wasn't the endless expense that left her sobbing like a

babe. This act of kindness was beyond anything she had ever encountered.

"Is everything all right?" Theo entered the room, his masculine presence commanding the space. "You're crying. Have I overstepped the mark? I know how you value your independence. I know you're quite capable of dealing with this on your own, but I had to put things right, Eleanor."

She dashed tears from her cheeks but more fell. "You didn't steal my diary," she said, gesturing to the nightstand. "I've never had a flower by my bed. You've done more than tidy the shop, Theo."

There were too many thoughtful gestures to mention.

He closed the gap between them, his large hands resting on her shoulders. "Forgive me. I'm a bold brigadier and insisted the jobs were done with military precision." His gaze softened. "And I thought you might like to have a flower by your bed. There's beauty in this world. We'd both do well to remember that."

The rose paled next to him.

He was so beautiful he stole her breath.

Another sob escaped her, but he cupped her cheeks and pressed a tender kiss to her lips. "You'll be the most famous modiste in London. I swear they'll be queueing all the way to St Paul's just to wear your exclusive designs."

The thought brought no surge of joy or pang of happiness. "Being a famous modiste was never my dream."

"What is your dream?" he whispered.

She looked at his mouth. He was a dream come true. A friend she could trust. A valued confidant. Someone to love. "I have never given it much thought."

"Perhaps you should."

Their gazes locked for a heartbeat.

Their lips met as if pulled by a magnetic force. The kiss was soft and slow and achingly sensual, and when their mouths parted, they were panting.

"Gibbs left to visit Daventry and to fetch provisions. Apparently, he eats enough for three men. He won't be back for two hours. I thought you might take advantage of his absence to wash and change your clothes. I can heat the water if you want to bathe."

She smiled. They were alone, without interruption. It was time to reward him for his efforts. "So you're done playing the brigadier and now wish to be my footman."

His gaze dipped to her chin, then a little lower. "I'd rather be your maid than your footman. I've wanted to strip you out of your clothes for as long as I can remember."

The air between them crackled with unsated desire. The need for physical contact was as compelling as the need to breathe.

"Perhaps I would make a good valet," she said, sliding her hands up his chest to open the top button on his waistcoat.

Theo clasped her hands to stall her. "Have a care. You know where this will lead. Do you want me inside you? Do you want to lose something precious? I suggest you consider those points carefully before you unfasten another button."

She took a moment to do as he asked. She didn't hear her father's stern voice berating her decisions, insisting he knew best. For once, she was a master of her own destiny. And Theodore Chance was the only thing she wanted.

"I'm not about to lose anything," she said, prompting him to release her hands. "I'm about to make a trade."

"A trade?" he said, intrigued.

"My virginity for a memory that will last a lifetime." She

gripped his waistcoat and tore it open. The expensive buttons went skittering across the floor. "I want you, Theo, and I mean to have you."

He wasn't angry or shocked but glanced at his torn waistcoat and grinned. "I always said you were my kind of scoundrel." His voice had a husky quality, each word laced with raw intensity. "Now you must finish what you started."

Nerves assailed her, but she'd not stop now.

Gathering every ounce of courage she possessed, she pushed his coat off his shoulders. It hit the floor, quickly followed by his waistcoat and cravat.

"We agreed to be truthful," he said, watching her tug his shirt from his trousers. "I must tell you, I have never been so aroused."

To prove his point, he took her hand and smoothed it over the solid ridge in his trousers. It was long and thick, a veritable weapon. She should have been terrified, but knowing she affected him this deeply was more of an aphrodisiac than plum pie.

"You still owe me a forfeit," she said, loving the way he felt beneath her fingers. Touching him was addictive. "Remove all your clothes."

"I'm sure I paid that forfeit, but I'll not quibble." He dragged his shirt over his head and tossed it aside. "Not when it plays to my advantage."

Eleanor stared in awe. His shoulders were broad, his chest muscular with a dusting of golden hair. His skin was smooth and stretched tight over his bulging biceps. Her heart sank as she looked upon the scar just below his shoulder, a haunting reminder of the bullet that had nearly taken his life.

"Does it still pain you?" she said, guilt tightening her throat.

"Sometimes." He unbuttoned his trousers and palmed his erection as soon as it sprang free. "Though the ache to be inside you is more than I can bear."

She gulped. Never had she been so out of her depth. And yet, the softness of his gaze put her fears to rest.

"I know what you're thinking," he teased. "You're wondering how you'll take me. Be assured, in the throes of passion we'll fit together perfectly."

"Actually, I was wondering when you might remove your shoes. Time is of the essence, and Mr Gibbs is likely to storm upstairs if he hears odd sounds."

Theo laughed. "Then I suggest you undress, too. Gibbs may fire before he asks questions." His eyes trailed a path along her curves, a hungry anticipation lurking in his gaze. "I'm panting at the prospect of seeing you naked."

Despite her shaky hands, she undid the buttons and was out of her dress before he'd finished removing his socks and shoes.

A low hum vibrated in his throat when he noticed her undergarments. "Allow me to help you." He closed the gap between them, stalking her like a panther hunting prey. He tugged the front ties on her corset, pulling her into his hard body. "Perhaps I might savour this moment and take my time."

She gripped his muscular arms to steady her balance, the feel of his bare skin beneath her fingers sending her pulse soaring. Her whole body ached for something she could not define.

His mouth was on hers, moving in slow, hypnotic strokes, kissing her the way he had at the theatre. It was beautiful and gentle, each delicate caress of their lips tugging at her heart.

179

He broke contact and stared into her eyes. "If we'd been alone at the theatre, this is how our kiss would have progressed."

He didn't give her time to catch her breath. His hands slid down over her buttocks while his tongue slipped into her mouth. The world around her blurred. He was everywhere. Consuming her with his touch, his taste, his smell.

Passion's glowing embers ignited into an inferno.

"Eleanor," he growled, devouring her lips once more before kissing every inch of exposed flesh. He was sucking her earlobe, kissing her neck, holding her so close the ridge of his erection pushed against her belly.

"Theo. Don't stop."

*Don't ever stop loving me.*

Was this how it felt to be adored?

To be treasured beyond compare?

He kissed her collarbone, kissed the swell of her breasts rising out of her corset. His fingers traced the curve of her buttocks, dipping between them to stroke the entrance of her sex.

Merciful Lord! It was too much.

"Get me out of these clothes," she demanded.

With the same urgency, he removed her corset, stopping to bury his face between her breasts, cupping them in his hands and kissing her nipples through the fine fabric.

Then he stripped her naked, his eyes burning with desire until they dipped to the bruises on her hip and thigh. "As God is my witness, no one will ever hurt you again."

She didn't want to think about the terrible things that had happened, only about this perfect moment with him. "I need you." She took his hand and smoothed it over her breast. "Make me feel like I did at Fortune's Den last night."

His thumb grazed her nipple. "It would be my pleasure."

He was on her in a heartbeat, kissing her wildly before turning her around, his erection pressing against her buttocks.

"Everything about you is spectacular," he said against her neck as he slid his hand down between the apex of her thighs. His fingers teased her entrance before gliding over her bud. "You're so beautiful."

She almost cried.

No one had ever said such wonderful things.

No one had ever made her feel special.

But his fingers moved in enticing circles over her flesh, his other hand caressing her breast, anchoring her to him. She moaned aloud, each cry getting louder as her body shuddered and she came so hard her knees buckled.

Theo swept her up into his arms and lowered her onto the mattress. "I'm so hard, love. I'll try not to hurt you. You're certain you want to continue?"

"I've never been more certain of anything in my life."

He smiled. "You came so splendidly you've earned a confession."

"I have?"

He rose above her, his powerful arms bearing his weight, a golden lock of hair hanging over his brow. "I volunteered to escort Delphine to her modiste appointment. I didn't care to read the newspaper. I came only to watch you."

Her heart was racing. "Why?"

"Because I have always found you enchanting." He nudged her legs open with his knee and settled between them. "I've imagined this moment many times. It hurt to think that you hated me. Know I never meant to hurt you."

He kissed her again, his body pressing her into the

mattress, the feel of his warm skin on hers like a dream come true.

She wrapped her legs around him as he entered her slowly, each gentle nudge tearing a gasp from her lips. She stared into his eyes, relishing the feeling of having him inside her.

"Are you ready to take all of me, Eleanor?"

She wet her lips and nodded.

He didn't thrust to the hilt straight away. He withdrew, rubbing his manhood over her slick folds until he drove her mad with need. When he entered her, she couldn't help but express her pleasure.

"Yes. Don't wait."

"Forgive me," he uttered as one sharp thrust left him buried deep inside her. "You feel so damn good. Take a minute to get used to me."

A minute?

She could stay like this for a lifetime.

Never in her wildest dreams did she think this was possible.

Then he started moving, sliding out, then sinking deep. Filling her. The rhythm was so intoxicating she was breathless with desire. They couldn't get enough of each other. The tempo changed. She begged him not to stop. He angled his hips, rubbing against her as he pumped so hard the bed creaked and took a chunk out of the plaster.

"Theo!" She came again, a wave of euphoria rippling to her toes. She gripped his tight buttocks, holding him inside her, not wanting to let go.

"Love, I'll spill inside you if I don't withdraw."

He came over her belly, a deep groan rumbling in his throat.

She watched, loving the glint of passion in his eyes, how he uttered her name when he lost control, gawping at his toned physique when he retrieved a handkerchief from his coat pocket.

He lay in bed beside her, cleaning her belly. "I've barely had time to recover, yet I need you again." He hauled her on top of him.

She rested her head on his chest, his hair tickling her face, his heartbeat thumping loudly in her ear. "Is that a good sign?"

He chuckled as he stroked her hair. "An extremely good sign. I'm yours whenever you want me. I can't get enough of you, Eleanor."

Men were fickle. That's what Lady Summers professed. One minute, a lady is his diamond of the first water; the next, she's a pebble beneath his feet.

A wise woman would guard her heart.

But Eleanor knew it was too late to save herself.

Theo had taken a piece the night he'd kissed her at the theatre. Stole another with all the thoughtful things he had done at the shop. He had claimed the rest while making love to her in bed. No matter what happened in her life, nothing would ever be this perfect.

# Chapter Fourteen

It was late afternoon when they crawled out of bed, dressed, and began the half-mile walk to Emily's house on Great Eastcheap. Lovemaking had left them exhausted and sated to their bones, but Eleanor wanted the exercise.

"My head throbs a little, and exertion is good for the blood."

Theo regarded her with some amusement. "After our romp in bed, I imagine your blood was coursing faster than the Rhine." He brushed her hip with his hand, relishing her little shiver.

A pretty blush stained her cheeks. "I hadn't expected it to be so vigorous. Lady Mulberry said she often naps during her husband's conjugal visits."

Theo laughed. "Do ladies tell their modistes all their personal secrets?" He reached for her hand, wrapping it around his arm as they walked. Since leaving the shop, she seemed unsure whether to touch him.

He couldn't get enough of her.

"Yes, mostly tales of how they avoid marital relations. One lady, who shall remain nameless, drinks a tincture to bring on nausea."

He sensed her relaxing now and asked the question they had been avoiding. "Do you regret what happened between us earlier?"

Despite the crowded pavement, she brought him to a halt on Watling Street. "Don't feel guilty. I seduced you." She looked at him as if remembering the pleasure they'd shared. "You didn't hurl me over your shoulder and throw me onto the bed."

"I can play the Neanderthal if you'd prefer, though I rather like it when you ravish me." A man knew a lady desired him when she couldn't keep her hands to herself. "Next time, I shall act the scoundrel."

She bit down on her lip. "There'll be a next time?"

"We're lovers, Eleanor. I'm yours until you tire of me."

A long sigh escaped her. "I have spent my whole life planning for the future. Spent every day fulfilling my parents' dream. There's no need for us to think beyond today."

As the only brother left keeping Aaron company, he should have felt relieved. Yet he experienced an odd tug of regret.

"Now, let us concentrate on the case," she said, gripping his arm as they walked. "Mr Daventry will expect an update tomorrow."

Based on the evidence, there was only one suspect. "If I had to hazard a guess, I'd say the man Emily lives with is the beast who attacked you in the yard. They wanted you out of the way so they could steal your supplies."

Eleanor was quick to make excuses for her seamstress. "I would have noticed if bolts of material had gone missing. And I had no reason to doubt Emily's loyalty."

"When did you last take an inventory of your stock?"

She muttered to herself while trying to remember. "A while ago. I've been busy and never needed to do more than a rough count."

He paused, unsure whether to tell her what he'd found, but they had made a pact to be truthful. "Gibbs said Emily came late at night and tried to unlock the door. She ran away before he had time to question her. And according to your ledger, you should have four silver hat pins in your cabinet. I could only find three."

"What?" The word carried the weight of surprise and the pain of betrayal. "Are you sure?"

"I'm certain." He'd hurt her once before and wouldn't deliver upsetting news without justification. "If I'm right, we will have the culprit in custody before nightfall."

A flicker of dread shot through him. It wasn't that he enjoyed playing the detective, but he enjoyed spending time in her company. And something told him that solving her problems wouldn't be that simple.

Eleanor spent the rest of the journey trying to find a valid reason for Emily's duplicity. "She's kind and as gentle as a lamb. I'm sure there'll be a valid reason for her actions."

Theo smiled to himself. Eleanor Darrow had a good heart. She did not belittle others—only Mrs Dunwoody, but he was grateful for that. She liked to believe the best in people. One would think a woman who had never felt loved would be bitter.

"I hope you're right," he said, fearing how she would cope with more bad news. Emily would not have stolen the silk if he had not taken the sewing box. "You do not deserve to suffer."

"My father would disagree," was her sad response.

The narrow terrace house on Great Eastcheap did not look like a slum or a den for thieves. The windows were clean, the door newly painted. A swift rap on the polished brass knocker yielded no response. Despite further attempts to rouse the occupants, no one came to the door.

In the street, an older boy stopped chasing a stray dog and called to them. "There ain't no one home. For a penny, I can tell you where to find them. Who you looking for? Mr Rogers? Emily?"

Theo considered the boy's torn trousers. He drew a sovereign from his waistcoat pocket and twirled it around his fingers. "Are they the only people who live here?"

"No." The boy stared at the gold coin as if it were a piece of plum pie. "Mrs Rogers cooks and cleans for the vicar of St Clement's and won't be home for hours. You'll find Jack Rogers at the Red Lion down Billingsgate docks." Disdain coated his words. "He won't be home till they throw him out."

"Where might we find Emily?" Eleanor said.

The boy held out his grubby hand. "Cross my palm, and I'll tell you what I heard this morning."

"I'll chase you if you run," Theo warned before dropping the coin into the child's hand. "What did you hear this morning?"

Clutching the sovereign as one did their purse in Covent Garden, the boy said, "He took Emily with him, told her she can't come home until she's earned two shillings. Said she's a burden, and he'll put her out on the street if she ain't found a job by Monday."

ADELE CLEE

Theo glanced at Eleanor. Her lips were pressed into a solemn line, and her eyes carried a haunted look as if disturbed by ghosts from the past.

She gulped before speaking. "I understand the pressure to please one's kin. Is he hurting Emily? Is he forcing her to do criminal things against her will?"

The boy shrugged. "He don't care what she does as long as she pays her way. He treats her no better than his mangy dog. Says they're both pains in the rear."

Lining the boy's palm with another coin, Theo sought to clarify an important point. "Are they related? We were told Emily's parents were dead."

Beaming like he'd been touched by Midas, the lad said, "The other Mr Rogers drowned and left the house to his brother. Jack Rogers moved here a year ago with his wife."

"What about Emily's mother?" Eleanor's tone carried a desperation Theo didn't quite understand.

Glancing over his shoulder, the lad lowered his voice. "Mrs Crane said Ivy went off with the captain of a merchant ship when Emily was eight. She came back but died of a fever five years ago."

Eleanor paled. "Ivy?" The tremble in her voice mirrored the panic evident beneath her pretty visage. "Ivy was Emily's mother's name?"

The answer was a curt nod. "Mrs Crane said the name suited her, said she clung to any man with two legs and would choke the life out of him if she could."

Confused about the relevance and why Eleanor inhaled sharply, Theo suggested they visit the Red Lion to confirm the facts. "We must speak to Emily and her uncle."

"Happen you've got a death wish, mister." The boy sized

Theo's muscular frame. "Rogers has the devil in him when he's had a skinful of rum."

"I can rouse the devil without downing liquor." Knowing the boy would welcome another coin, Theo made a request. "Should you see anything untoward at the Rogers' house, send word to Miss Darrow's shop in New Bridge Street. Should the news prove accurate, I'll reward you for your time and trouble."

Hope shone in the lad's eyes like a lone star in the darkness. "You've a kind heart, mister. Happen the Lord will send a chariot to take you to the pearly gates."

"Not everyone would agree," Theo said. Some lords called him the devil's spawn. Some said his heart was as black as coal dust. He handed the boy his calling card. "In case anyone should question how you came by the sovereigns."

They left Eastcheap and headed towards Billingsgate.

Eleanor hugged Theo's arm and walked as if swamped by the weight of a burden. Each trudge seemed an effort. What had brought about this melancholic mood? Her spirits flagged at the mention of the name Ivy.

"Perhaps you should tell me what's wrong before we find Emily." He felt her body shiver against his. "Is it that Emily lied about her parents?"

Eleanor took a deep breath, but her voice quivered when she said, "It's probably nothing more than a coincidence. My mother was called Ivy. It's funny how something as simple as a name can stir painful memories."

Not just a name. The catch of sunlight in golden hair often brought his mother's image crashing into his mind. The smell of violets tugged at his heart. He could not eat a macaroon without seeing her popping one into her mouth. The memories were few but frequent. A bittersweet pill that was hard to swallow.

Eleanor was not so fortunate.

"Doubtless you feel responsible for Emily. You may see something of yourself in her. Her skill as a seamstress. Her troubled family life."

"Emily has suffered far more than I have. She lost her mother twice. I wish she had spoken to me about it. I understand how grief can rule one's life."

They walked in silence, past the Monument and the church of St Magnus, towards the Red Lion tavern. The hanging sign creaked back and forth in the wind like an omen warning them away. One did not enter a public house full of drunkards and hurl accusations.

"We'll sit and order drinks. Hopefully, Emily will serve us." Theo stopped outside the oak door and faced her. It was barely five o'clock, yet the noise of rowdy conversation and boisterous song spilled onto the street. "Promise me something."

She blinked in surprise. "Anything."

The answer sent his mind spinning in a different direction, but their lives depended upon focusing on the task. "Should there be an altercation, you must consider your own safety, not mine."

A frown marred her brow. "I would rather meet my maker than see you hurt because of me. Should we encounter trouble, we will deal with it together."

Most men would stamp their feet in protest, their tempers frayed, eyes wide with alarm. Yet he understood the need to fight for one's survival. He didn't think she was foolish, just wonderful and brave.

"Promise me something else," he said, stroking her arm.

"Yes?"

"If you hit anyone, tuck your thumb over your middle finger when making a fist." He demonstrated. "I don't want you to break your hand."

Her mouth curled into a smile, her eyes sparkling with an irresistible blend of mischief and determination. "If only I had an iron skillet. There's no danger of breaking one of those."

In awe of her resilience, he cupped her cheek. "Once we've gained a confession and this is over, I shall take you to the Olympic to watch Madame Vestris' parody of Macbeth. Instead of witches, Macbeth stumbles upon gossiping matrons."

"Does one go by the name Mrs Dunwoody?"

"I hope not. The matron enjoys predicting my downfall, and the witches' prophecies tend to come true."

They laughed again.

Now she was more at ease Theo cricked his neck, straightened his spine and led Eleanor into the Red Lion tavern.

Three unkempt sailors occupied the first table, clouding the air with pipe smoke. Their tanned, leathery skin suggested they'd returned from the West Indies, not a port in Hamburg or Rotterdam. The men watched Eleanor as if starved of female company.

More men stood around the oak counter, a distinct odour of fish wafting from the vicinity. An older fellow used his tankard to keep a map open on the table next to the hearth.

Theo met the landlord's gaze and gestured to an empty table by the bow window. They'd barely sat down when a petite woman with auburn hair hurried towards them, wiping her hands on her pinny.

"What can I get for you good folks?" Emily said, not bothering to look at them properly until Eleanor whispered her name.

"Emily." Eleanor glanced covertly around the taproom. "Is your uncle here? We were told we could find you both at the Red Lion."

"Miss Darrow," Emily said just as quietly. She stiffened as if to move might alert Satan's minion. "What are you doing here?"

"Looking for you. We're leading an investigation into a theft at my shop." Speaking from her head, not her heart, Eleanor mentioned the Home Secretary. "I'm sorry, but we've come to arrest you for stealing a bolt of silk and a silver hat pin. You need to come to Bow Street and answer our questions."

"Bow Street?" Emily's chin hit the floor. The flare of guilt in her eyes confirmed her motives were immoral. "Please, Miss Darrow. Whatever I've done, it ain't my fault." Tears filled the young woman's eyes. "I had no choice."

Eleanor's shoulders sagged with the weight of betrayal. "I trusted you. I tried to convince Mr Chance that he was mistaken. You've made me look a fool. You lied, lied about your parents. We know about Ivy."

Emily's knees buckled, and she grabbed the chair rail for support. "Who told you about Ivy? No one knows but Uncle Jack. Did he visit you? Did he break his promise? Did he tell you the secret?"

Eleanor looked baffled. "What secret?"

Theo intervened. "We seem to be at cross purposes. Why would Miss Darrow be interested in a secret about your mother?"

The woman stared at him like she had nothing in her head but straw. Her mouth gaped, her breath falling in ragged pants. "You said you knew about Ivy."

"We know she was not the perfect mother," Eleanor explained.

"Emily!" the landlord called from behind the oak counter. "What do these fine people want to drink?"

They ordered ale.

Emily hurried away and returned with two mugs. Her hands shook as she placed them on the crude table. "We can't talk here. Don't arrest me, miss. I'll pay for the silk I took. A shilling a week once I find work as a seamstress. Now you've changed the locks, he'll look for other ways to line his purse."

"You're referring to your uncle?" Theo's blood simmered. He despised men who used children and women to do wicked deeds.

"Don't look, but he's sitting at the table behind me. The man with the red waistcoat who thinks he's a gent. Down your drinks and leave. He likes to start trouble when he's pickled."

Theo did look.

Rogers had sunken eyes and a perpetual sneer that showed his crooked teeth. His bloated belly was incongruous with his thin frame. He had a cruel glint in his eyes, typical of most bullies.

"Perhaps I might persuade him to find employment," Theo said through gritted teeth. "A legitimate way to fill his coffers."

Emily clutched her chest. "No, sir. Best you leave now. I'll come to the shop tomorrow while I'm out looking for work. I'll find the funds to pay for what he took. I swear."

Eleanor did not try to placate her and seemed determined to get answers. "Were you hiding at the shop the other day? Did you push me down the stairs, fearing I'd discover what you'd stolen?"

"Push you down the stairs? Good heavens, no." Emily's brow furrowed. "I could never hurt you, Miss Darrow. You're the only person who's ever believed in me."

"Yet you stole from me the minute I turned my back."

"It weren't my fault. He made me do it. I told him there'd been thieves in the shop and it was in a dreadful state. He said no one would know if we helped ourself to a few things."

Theo made to stand, but Eleanor touched his arm to stall him. "Wait. We'll tackle Mr Rogers in a moment." Her gaze sharpened on Emily. "You came to steal the silk at dawn. Hours after the incident. How did you know what had happened at the shop?"

Theo watched Emily intently, looking for signs of discomfort or anything that suggested she was about to lie. She seemed calm and rational.

"Uncle Jack sent me to beg for more work," Emily uttered. "He said I wasn't to come home until you'd agreed. I saw the mess when I arrived, and ran home and told him."

Theo wondered why she'd not called a constable, but after taking a deep breath, Emily answered the question.

"I was too scared to fetch a watchman in case he thought I'd done it. Then Uncle Jack made me return with the cart and take the silk. When Mr Franklin saw me out his window, my uncle said it would look like I was saving your stock."

Indeed, Eleanor may have been none the wiser had the silversmith not kept a close watch on the street.

"It's time I had a word with Uncle Jack." Theo spoke

loud enough for the buffoon to hear. There'd be hell to pay if Jack had attacked Eleanor in the yard.

"Please don't," Emily begged.

But Uncle Jack pushed out of the seat and strode towards them, swaying like he was on deck in a storm. "They pay the girl to serve, not to keep you entertained."

Some syllables were slurred, and his pronunciation was anything but precise. He reminded Theo of his father. A pathetic fool who thought gambling and liquor could solve life's problems.

"This is Miss Darrow," Emily blurted. "She's come to offer me more work. Says I can have two full days next week."

Jack looked at Eleanor, his beady eyes narrowing. "So you're the dressmaker Emily's so fond of. My niece thinks the sun shines out of your arse, but I reckon—"

Theo shot to his feet. "You'll mind your tone and language, or else I'll wrap your tongue around your scrawny neck."

Jack's head pitched left, then right. "What did you say?"

"I said I'll knock your crooked teeth down your throat." Theo rounded the table, hoping the fool would throw a punch. "Then I'll have you arrested for theft. You stole silk and a silver hat pin from Miss Darrow's shop. We have a witness statement placing you at the scene."

Jack laughed, then burped, releasing a waft of rum. "I ain't stolen a thing. I went to the shop with Emily because she had to collect work to bring home. As far as I know, the silk is in her room."

Eleanor stood, keen to join the fray. "You sold the silk, or did you force Emily to do that too? I suspect her father is

195

turning in his grave, angered by your mistreatment. I'll be keen to hear what your wife says on the matter."

That's when the drink got the better of Jack, and he raised his clenched fist. "You keep my Daisy out of this. If you—"

Theo grabbed the drunkard's arm and twisted it behind his back. "I've warned you once. Let's take this conversation outside."

Men at the bar stared.

One stepped forward, debating whether to intervene.

A scuffle ensued as Jack tried to tug his arm free. He was in no shape to fight and fell on his backside when Theo released him.

Much to Theo's horror, Eleanor rushed over, planting her foot firmly on Jack's chest, pinning him to the ground, a ferocious look in her eyes.

"You'll confess in front of these men," she said in a thunder of anger. "You'll admit you forced Emily to act unlawfully. You're supposed to protect the women in your family, not treat them like slaves and dogs."

As Theo watched Eleanor's cheeks turn red with rage, a painful truth was revealed. Her sudden outburst was more than just anger. It was a raw wound from her past. She was not merely shouting; she was confronting her father, berating him for the hurt he had caused her.

"Is it not enough that Emily has lost her parents? Must you continue to make her life miserable just for a few coins?"

Jack didn't grab her foot and twist until she cried in pain. Perhaps he knew Theo would throttle him if he dared lay a hand on her.

Instead, Jack looked at Emily as if he meant to punish

her and said, "Happen you inherited your mother's gumption, Miss Darrow. You got a hearty plate of courage while poor Emily was left with the scraps."

While Eleanor frowned, Emily cried, "Don't say another word, or I'll report you to Bow Street myself."

Jack cackled. "And you'll hang with me unless your sister here takes pity on you. I suspect she'll be mad you've kept your mother's dirty secret."

It was as if time stilled.

Sailors stopped talking.

Shady figures froze.

A silence as heavy as a storm cloud descended.

"I—I beg your pardon?" Eleanor's face turned a deathly shade of pale. "Whose sister? What secret?"

She looked so lost that Theo closed the gap between them and gently touched her back. "Emily will explain." He beckoned the seamstress to offer some insight and prayed this wasn't a cruel trick.

Emily wrung her hands and struggled to stand still. "I'm sorry. When I took the job at your shop I didn't know we were related. The more you told me about your life in Eynsford, the more things slotted into place. I wanted to tell you. But I know how bad it felt when she ran away. I couldn't put you through that, Miss Darrow."

Eleanor swayed. She pressed her fingers to her brow. "But my mother died in childbirth. I have borne the guilt all these years."

"I'm sorry," Emily repeated. "She told me about you on her deathbed. She told me your name and about your house in Eynsford. That your father Henry was a bitter man. You were a babe in arms when she left."

Theo slid his arm around Eleanor's waist, and she sagged

against him. He would have taken fifty lashes to ease her suffering. He would give everything he owned to make time move forward. For her to wake up months from now, free from pain.

Silent seconds passed. Eleanor did not ask about Ivy. She didn't flinch when Jack Rogers scrambled to his feet. She turned to Theo, tears trickling down her cheeks, and whispered, "Please take me home."

# Chapter Fifteen

Eleanor walked a mile without uttering a word. Memories of the past flooded her mind, her father's refusal to attend village fetes and church services, his constant demand for privacy. Was he afraid she would discover the truth? Had she feared she would run away like her mother?

Things might have been different if he'd been honest. It would have explained his behaviour and shown his anger stemmed from shame. He might have mellowed, taken a wife and had more children. The house might have been filled with love, not been as grim as a mausoleum.

She gripped Theo's arm tightly, her fingers settling over his bicep. He was a pillar of strength. He did not speak or attempt to ease her pain. He instinctively knew she needed time to process what she had learnt.

"Thank you," she said as they entered New Bridge Street and met the familiar smell of the river and coal smoke. "For not telling me what to think or feel. For not bombarding me with mindless questions."

He touched her hand and smiled. "The remedy for chaos is peace. When the mind is quiet, a way forward emerges. You need to deal with this in your own way, in your own time."

"I don't know if what Emily said is true." Why would Eleanor's father play such a cruel trick? To lie, to deceive her for all these years. It beggared belief.

"If it's not true, then Emily is not the kind person you championed. If it is, I would offer you one piece of advice."

She looked into his calming blue eyes. "Yes?"

"Focus on what you've gained, not what you've lost." He released a deep sigh, one carrying the weight of experience. "Loss ties you to the past. Trust me, there is nothing but misery there."

Guilt had tied her to the past, too.

Every thought and deed stemmed from seeds sewn years ago.

"Life moves forward with or without you," he added. "Don't waste time trying to understand a person's motives. It brings nothing but heartache. I've had to accept that my father was a rotten scoundrel."

Talk of scoundrels made her think of Jack Rogers.

The man was a leech who lived off the hard work of others.

"Do you think Emily will be safe at home?" She'd heard the shocking revelation half an hour ago but was already thinking like an elder sister. "What did Mr Rogers say when you took him outside?"

Theo's satisfied grin said the men had exchanged more than words. "He agreed to take her home and play the loving uncle. Should I hear otherwise, he knows I'll be waiting for him outside the Red Lion on a misty night."

His confidence was contagious.

He had a way of lifting her spirits.

A means of making everything right.

"What would I do without you?" she teased, but there was a resounding truth to her remark. She was in love with him. It was hard to imagine life alone. She'd miss the warmth of his smile, the mischief in his eyes, his kind words, his tender touch.

"I'm merely fixing the problems I helped to create."

"Is that why you're so kind to me, out of guilt?"

He brought her to a halt outside the shop, his eyes meeting hers. "Did I look guilty when I kissed every inch of your naked body? Did guilt have me losing my mind when I pushed deep inside you? Is it guilt that leaves me desperate to make love to you again?"

The feverish look in his eyes said he spoke in earnest.

"That is lust," she said, wishing he loved her, too.

"And yet the word barely defines what happened between us in bed. It doesn't explain why we remained in each other's arms for hours."

She swallowed hard. "I'm certainly no expert, but perhaps that's what happens when friends make love."

His gaze dipped to her mouth. "Perhaps."

"Miss Darrow! Miss Darrow!"

Theo grumbled at the interruption. "Devil take it. What now?"

Eleanor turned to see Miss Franklin hurrying across the road, clutching her plain bonnet to her head while waving to get Eleanor's attention. The poor woman was breathless, her cheeks berry red.

"Thank heavens I've caught you." Miss Franklin, a young woman of twenty with a pleasant countenance, clasped her chest and took a deep breath. "Have you heard what happened at Mr Walker's premises last night? My brother has spent most of the day helping him clear broken glass. An intruder smashed all his medicines and tinctures. Who would do such a thing?"

Eleanor waited for Miss Franklin to pause so she might introduce Theo, but the woman barely stopped for breath.

"What's most peculiar is that the criminal took nothing. Not even Mr Walker's silver mantel clock he inherited from his grandmother. The lady hailed from York but left her Roman coins to Mr Walker's sister. She sold them and left him heartbroken. But no matter. I ask you, how can we protect ourselves from these miscreants who walk the streets at night?"

Eleanor opened her mouth and closed it again.

"My brother hasn't slept properly in months. He's up all hours of the night, peering out of the window. It's beginning to take its toll. Only yesterday, he wrote the wrong date on a customer's receipt."

Theo put his hand to his mouth and coughed to disguise a chuckle. Never in the history of oratory had a person crammed so many words into a minute.

"It's undoubtedly the same person who caused the damage in your shop. How do you propose we catch him? The devil gets a thrill from ruining lives and reputations."

"That's why I hired a guard to watch the shop in my absence," Eleanor said, grateful for a chance to speak. "And my friend, Mr Chance, is leading an enquiry into the matter. We're sure to find answers soon."

Miss Franklin looked at Theo as if she'd not noticed he was there. Her brown eyes widened, and she dabbed her fingers to her brow.

"Mr Chance, good ... good afternoon." Miss Franklin took time to appreciate Theo's broad shoulders. "You're exactly what we need. A capable man to take charge of the matter. You should both dine with us this evening. My brother is quite protective of Miss Darrow. He will be pleased to know someone is considering her welfare. Yes, I'm sure it will be a splendid evening all round."

Dine with the Franklins?

Eleanor would rather listen to a lecture on the history of lint.

"Sadly, we have a previous engagement." She tried to look a little downcast. "Perhaps some other time. Once we've caught this blackguard and can all rest a little easier in our beds."

"Yes, I suppose it's hard to strike up an appetite when we might be attacked at any moment." Miss Franklin fluttered her lashes. "Perhaps a stroll in the park might suit us better. We might—"

The lady stopped abruptly when she noticed Mr Franklin approaching. Her smile died, and she grumbled under her breath.

Mr Franklin had Eleanor in his sights. He greeted her with the warmth of a man who had more than friendship in mind. "Miss Darrow. I trust you've heard the dreadful news about Mr Walker's apothecary."

"Yes, though I find it strange nothing was stolen."

Theo agreed. "If the culprit arrived by barge or merchant ship, as you previously claimed, surely he would have stolen the mantel clock."

Mr Franklin brushed a hand through his wavy brown hair. "Then it must have been the vagabond who broke into Miss Darrow's shop. The whole business is confounding."

"Have you spoken to the warden at Bridewell?" Theo gestured to the entrance of the correction facility a hundred yards along the street. "Perhaps an inmate escaped and went on the rampage."

Eleanor might have thought so, too, had the villain not lifted the floorboards and stolen her diary. Had he not threatened to kill her if she failed to deliver his notes—his blank notes.

"I spoke to the warden after the raid in the cobbler's yard," Mr Franklin said. "He assured me all prisoners were accounted for. Besides, the incidents occurred over a period of weeks. I doubt the villain escaped on three separate occasions."

Miss Franklin hadn't uttered a word since her brother's arrival. Perhaps that's why she gabbled in his absence.

"Well, I am glad you have returned to the shop, Miss Darrow." Miss Franklin sounded relieved rather than glad. "We cannot let these dreadful beggars scare us from our homes. Will you be accepting clients soon?"

After hearing Emily's shocking revelation, Eleanor's head was as heavy as lead. Everything she had believed was a lie. Her mother's death was not a tragedy. Her father was not a grieving widower. Ivy's dream was to amass lovers, not become a famed modiste.

"Perhaps I shall have a grand reopening."

She might not open at all. She would be on the first boat to Boston had she not fallen in love. A new life abroad would see an end to her problems. But things were different now.

"How wonderful." Miss Franklin clapped her hands together in glee. "I will be delighted to attend."

It was another odd reaction. Miss Franklin could not afford Eleanor's prices, though she often came to the shop to stare doe-eyed at the gowns on display. She commented on the designs, sat on the sofa and spoke to waiting relatives. Once, Eleanor had caught Miss Franklin showing Lady Lucille the array of pretty combs in the cabinet.

Maybe she hoped to work as a modiste.

Maybe she found excuses to stay out of her brother's way.

"A talent like yours should not go to waste," Mr Franklin said, fixing Eleanor with his admiring stare. "I would be most disheartened if you were to move your business elsewhere."

"Yes, we cannot let these ruffians defeat us." Miss Franklin shook her gloved fist, though it was obvious she would break her wrist if she hit anyone. "We'll protect you, Miss Darrow. We'll watch your premises night and day."

A little embarrassed, her brother coughed to clear his throat. "Miss Darrow has employed Mr Gibbs as a deterrent. He seems like a capable man. I wouldn't want to encounter him in the yard at night."

"Only a fool would tackle Gibbs," Theo said, his voice carrying a note of caution. "He's far more dangerous than he looks."

"He looks terrifying," Miss Franklin agreed.

"Let's hope he's a permanent presence," Mr Franklin managed to say before his sister interrupted.

"Yes, it pains me to see your hard work reduced to rubble and scattered about the floor. I do admire your resilience. Your stock was ruined. You've taken a terrible tumble down the stairs, and still, you're smiling and making plans to reopen." Miss Franklin turned to her brother. "Is she not a remarkable woman, Geoffrey?"

"Utterly remarkable." Mr Franklin's gaze was a clear message of adoration. "Though a woman should have someone to depend upon. A man she can confide in and trust."

Good heavens. Mr Franklin had never been so frank. He looked at Theo like the word *rogue* was engraved on his forehead.

"Miss Darrow *has* a man to depend upon." Theo's devilish grin exuded self-assurance. "I am her closest friend. The person she turns to in times of crisis. A man who would defend her with his last breath."

He might have said they were lovers.

The fact couldn't be plainer.

"I'm friends with Mr Chance's sister," Eleanor explained. She would not have the Franklins spreading malicious gossip. "And have known the family for some time." Keen to leave before the men flexed their muscles to prove a point, she said, "If you'll excuse me. Since I fell, I've been suffering from headaches and need rest."

Eleanor winced and pressed her fingers to her temples to make her plea look convincing. That's when an odd thought struck her. One that had her reaching for Theo's arm and bidding the Franklins good day.

They entered the shop, and Eleanor locked the door.

"I'm not happy about leaving you here alone tonight," Theo said after informing Mr Gibbs they were home. "Franklin is besotted. He might start a fire so he can come to your rescue."

She might have accused him of being jealous but had something more important to convey. "Did you tell Mr

Franklin I fell down the stairs? I'm wondering how Miss Franklin knew."

Theo frowned. "No. I've not spoken to him, but I believe he saw me carrying you to the carriage. My sister-in-law helped to tidy the shop. Perhaps Franklin questioned her while I was out."

"Yes, that's probably it."

And yet the gnawing sense of unease did not abate. Had Miss Franklin entered the shop and started snooping upstairs? If so, where did she get the key? Was she a thief? Had she taken the villain's book and Eleanor's diary? Had she pushed Eleanor down the stairs?

The notion seemed ridiculous.

The firm shove in the back had been deliberate. Miss Franklin was as fragile as a fledgling sparrow. And if she did have a mean streak, what was her motive? Eleanor had not exchanged a cross word with her these last five years.

Not wanting to worry Theo, she forced a smile. "It's probably better you return to Fortune's Den. Miss Franklin couldn't take her eyes off you. She'll find an excuse to visit if she thinks you're here."

Theo glanced over his shoulder before capturing her hand. "I'm yours until you tire of me." He held her gaze and pressed a lingering kiss to her knuckles. "Let me assure you, I'll never tire of you."

"You seem keen to pay another forfeit."

He took umbrage at her comment. "After all you've been through, do you think I would lie?"

Her heart clenched. He must be confusing lust with something more permanent. "I'm not used to men saying nice things."

"This man has plenty of nice things to say about you,

Eleanor Darrow." He gave a cheeky wink. "And some he wishes to keep to himself, as they're too scandalous to repeat aloud."

"Perhaps you might whisper them in the carriage tomorrow. We must visit the solicitor as part of our ongoing investigation."

"Perhaps I'll whisper them tonight," he teased. "Will you not consider returning with me to Fortune's Den? I can't leave you here."

It was a tempting offer, but she could not escape her problems. And she was safe in Mr Gibbs' care.

"I cannot live with you indefinitely." Yet the thought roused an ache in her chest, a deep and persistent longing. "I must get used to staying here alone. I must solve the mystery and return to work before I find myself in the Marshalsea."

A muscle in his jaw twitched and his eyes conveyed an inner torment. "Then let me stay here tonight. Aaron can manage without me. He'll understand the importance of me remaining with you."

After a quick tussle between her head and her heart, she said, "I'm not sure he would. Besides, we both need a good night's sleep. I shall see you in the morning. If you can rise before noon."

Her jest did not bring the desired result.

His mouth remained a taut line. "You don't want me to stay?"

Oh, this man could break hearts. One look at his doleful expression, and she almost surrendered. "Theo, this isn't about what I want." She wanted more than he could give. "I need time to process what I've learned today. And it will be better for us if we spend some time apart."

The conversation went back and forth before he said, "But what will you eat? Gibbs returned with half a pig."

That accounted for the delicious smell wafting from the kitchen.

She chuckled. "I shall find something in the larder."

He stayed for another hour while Mr Gibbs showed his arsenal of weapons and made a blood oath to protect her until he heaved his last breath.

The sun was setting as Theo lingered in the doorway, a towering silhouette against a mellow orange sky.

"I would kiss you goodnight, but I can feel Franklin's gaze burning a hole in my back." His mouth curled into a slow smile. "Your kisses are worth dying for, but I'll sacrifice one in the hope of gaining more tomorrow."

She might have joked or lied but delivered a resounding truth instead. "I shall miss your company tonight. I shall miss you."

"It's not too late to reconsider."

A vision of his sweat-soaked body burst into her mind. He was the forbidden fruit. The thought of making love to him would tempt anyone to sin. But a small sacrifice now meant less pain later.

"Goodnight, Theo. Shall I see you promptly at ten?"

"More like noon. We have a family meeting at ten every day. If I'm at home, I'm required to attend."

She imagined the scene—a loving gathering around the dining table. "I shall be waiting. Come when you're ready."

"Don't open the door to anyone," he urged her.

"If you hadn't noticed, Mr Gibbs is watching me like a hawk."

He nodded, though looked ill at ease. "Goodnight."

He bid her farewell three times as she closed the door. She turned her back to him before her resolve faltered.

Mr Gibbs had made a pork and apple stew for supper. Eleanor shocked him by asking him to sit with her at the small kitchen table.

"I beg your pardon, but I ain't got a gentleman's manners, miss." Mr Gibbs swamped the small wooden chair and held his cutlery like they were weapons to disable intruders.

"I'm not a gentleman's daughter, though my father rapped my hand with his bible if I slouched."

"He sounds like a brute." Mr Gibbs shovelled a spoonful of stew into his mouth and swallowed with little chewing. "I've met a fair few of them in my time."

Lost in thought, Eleanor took time to eat her next mouthful. Had her father insisted she forge a career in dressmaking so she wouldn't make her mother's mistakes? Were the endless hours of sewing a way of keeping her out of the gossips' way. Or did Emily have a reason to lie?

Mr Gibbs mistook her quietude for worry. He wiped his mouth with his hand and offered every reassurance. "No one will hurt you on my watch, miss. I'll not sleep tonight. I give you my word."

Eleanor wouldn't sleep either, not when her bedsheets smelled of Theodore Chance. "Do you know how to play piquet or whist?"

"Know how to play?" he scoffed. "I've ruined every devil who's played against me at the Grapes tavern."

A game of cards would be the perfect distraction.

Theo had been gone an hour, yet it felt like a lifetime. Thoughts of him would have her tossing and turning all night. Love's ache was like a sickness, a nausea his presence kept at bay.

"Well?" Mr Gibbs asked, whipping a pack of cards from his pocket and shuffling them so fast they merged into one. "Have you the courage to wager with a champion? If you want to play, I'll take no prisoners."

Eleanor smiled. "I've courage abound, Mr Gibbs, though perhaps we should play for buttons."

# Chapter Sixteen

*Fortune's Den*
*Aldgate Street*

Theo sat at the dining table with his brothers, discussing the Den's accounts, their new clients, and those Aaron had barred from the club this week. Aramis was to pursue Lord Blakemore for the two thousand pounds he owed to the house.

"Take Christian with you," Aaron said, closing his ledger. "I'm told Blakemore hired three thugs for protection. They're Crawford's men, so shouldn't pose a problem."

Aramis rubbed his hands together and grinned. "The reprobate has run out of excuses. I shall take pleasure in reminding Blakemore there's a punishment for testing our patience."

"Escort him to the pawnbrokers if necessary. Remind him he does not want a midnight visit from me."

Theo stole a glance at the mantel clock. Fifteen minutes, and he could leave to visit Eleanor. They had a busy day ahead of them—a solicitor to question, Daventry to appease and more kisses to claim. And they should check on Emily.

Aaron noted his lapse in attention. "Where did you go last night? You left at midnight and didn't return until dawn. You've barely slept."

A yawn escaped him at the mention of sleep. "Out."

"To visit Miss Darrow?"

All eyes were upon him now, eager to hear his confession. "I kept Gibbs company while Miss Darrow slept upstairs." She had played cards with Gibbs for hours and lost all but two games. She had darned Gibbs' socks to pay her debts and sewn new buttons on his waistcoat. Gibbs said she cried herself to sleep. "She knew nothing of my visit. I left before she woke."

He had crept upstairs, stood in her doorway and listened to the gentle cadence of her breathing. Knowing she was at peace did odd things to his insides. Never had he felt an overwhelming need to protect a woman.

"Gibbs has the strength of four men," Aaron countered. "He could ward off an army and remain unscathed. I'm confident he didn't need a chaperone."

Christian came to Theo's defence. "It's only natural Theo would feel responsible for Miss Darrow." Christian offered him a sympathetic smile before looking at Aaron. "Knowing she's safe puts his mind at ease. I'm sure we all understand that feeling."

Eleanor's safety had become Theo's primary concern. It came before his own welfare, and dare he say, before his duties at Fortune's Den.

"Guilt can play havoc with a man's emotions," Aramis added. "The wager was my idea. I will manage Theo's responsibilities until he has found Miss Darrow's ransacker."

Aaron sat back in the chair and studied them over steepled fingers. "I understand the reason for Theo's actions. And I'm not his keeper. All I ask is that he considers his own safety when walking the streets at night. Men with a point to prove are unpredictable."

Theo wanted to argue but couldn't. "As always, your points are valid. I was shot protecting Delphine. I may get shot while protecting Miss Darrow. It's the price a man pays for chivalry." He chuckled to allay the tension. "Be assured, when navigating the metropolis, I shall proceed with an air of caution."

Aaron sighed, his silence stretching for what felt like an hour. "You see me as perfect, but I've made countless mistakes."

"When did these freakish events occur?" Theo teased.

A shadow of guilt passed over Aaron's features. He firmed his jaw before saying, "I left you all once. I left Mrs Maloney's bookshop in the dead of night and ran away. Caring for you seemed too great a burden when I was struggling to take care of myself."

Theo's mouth dropped open in shock. He could not recall a day when Aaron wasn't a strong shoulder of support. Aramis looked equally disarmed. Christian was the only one whose eyes swam with recognition.

"I reached the end of Lime Street before I realised I was nothing without my siblings. I have been your protector ever since." He paused, an air of sadness about him. "But we're men now. Each one of us must forge our own way in the world. If you want to visit Miss Darrow, that is your business, not mine."

Amid the stunned silence, Theo observed his eldest brother. Guilt and bitterness had poisoned his spirit, leading him to neglect his own happiness. Was his one mistake the root cause of his misery? Amidst the shadows of his painful past, would he ever find peace?

Aaron stood and gathered his ledger. "A judgement based on fear is a poor one. It's something I shall strive to remember in the difficult months ahead."

With that cryptic comment, Aaron left.

Seconds passed.

"It's impossible to imagine what Aaron has been through," Aramis said. "He had his innocence knocked out of him at a young age. Everything he does is for the good of this family."

"I imagine he feels like he's losing everything," Christian offered, his voice tight with emotion. "He won't know what to do if he's left alone here."

"I'll not leave him," Theo declared, ignoring the pang of remorse in his chest when he thought of Eleanor. To save Aaron, he must relegate his own happiness to a dusty shelf. Aaron had sacrificed his life to secure their future. It was only right Theo made sacrifices, too.

"Yet I suspect leaving him alone will force him to exorcise his demons." Aramis looked Theo's way. "If you're meant to leave, nothing will stop you. My love for Aaron remains unchanged despite my love for Naomi. Yet, I'd rather die than be separated from my wife."

Theo had found it hard to leave Eleanor last night. He'd been unable to stay away. The thought of never holding her in his arms again, of never seeing her smile … it was too painful to bear.

They spoke about Miss Lovelace.

"Women like to feel treasured," Christian said. "Can you see Aaron playing the romantic hero? The doting lover? He's cold and cynical. A woman would need a backbone of steel to tolerate him."

Miss Lovelace was the only woman in the history of the female sex who wasn't afraid of Aaron. Under the right circumstances, it would make for an explosive union. But Aaron's defences were forged in the fires of hell. No mortal woman could bring down his barricades.

"After all he's done for us, he deserves to be happy." The heaviness in Theo's chest returned. As the King of Hearts, he couldn't add to his brother's torment. Yet every waking moment was consumed by thoughts of Eleanor—her image, her voice, her touch—all etched into the fabric of his being. They were friends, lovers, but he wanted more. He needed more. He needed her.

"The outcome is already written in the stars." Christian laughed. "Daventry is up to his matchmaking tricks and won't rest until we're all wed."

When Theo arrived at New Bridge Street, Miss Darrow was waiting at the door, her beaming smile lighting his world. Her pelisse, a deep forest green reminiscent of forbidden forests, enhanced her figure to perfection. The ribbons of her silk bonnet framed her beautiful face. He had missed her, missed her more than he should, more than he dared to admit.

"You're late," she teased.

"I believe it's two minutes to twelve." He removed his

gold watch, flashed the face and returned it to his pocket. "It sounds like you missed me."

"Missed your teasing remarks and fiery kisses?" She chuckled, though he could see the strain behind her smile. "I spent most of the evening fixing Mr Gibbs' clothes and fell asleep as soon as my head hit the pillow."

He had watched her sleeping. She had clutched the bedsheets to her chest as if hugging a lover. Having discarded her pillow, she slept on the one he'd used to rest his head. Had she inhaled the remnants of his scent? Because he had laid face-down in his bed and breathed the essence of her.

"I've barely slept," he admitted. "I'll be useless today."

"Did London's rogues refuse to leave the gaming tables?"

"No, Eleanor. I spent the night thinking about you."

She swallowed deeply. "Thinking about the case and what I discovered about Emily? Now I know why she was so interested in my life in Eynsford."

He moistened his lips. "No, about the dimples in your cheeks when you smile, about the way your voice drops an octave when you're aroused." The way his name fell from her lips with she came. "The list of your charming qualities is endless."

"Oh." Her brows knitted together. "And what did you conclude?"

"That you have me bewitched." He was besotted.

She shifted nervously. "Perhaps I shall see if Madame Vestris is looking for another witch for her parody of Macbeth."

"I'm not joking." He stepped close enough to rest his hand on her waist. "It killed me to leave you last night."

217

She held his gaze. "It killed me to let you go."

"Then we should deal with the solicitor promptly and spend the rest of the day in bed." He bent his head to avoid attracting a passerby's attention. "I've never known desire like this."

He was acting like a lovesick fool, lingering in the shadows just to glimpse his enchantress. Looking for any excuse to touch her.

"We must visit Mr Daventry, and I hoped to check on Emily and ask her more questions. I would also like to ask Miss Franklin how she knew I'd tumbled down the stairs."

*Don't you want me?* he wanted to say.

She was being logical while he could think of nothing but her soft thighs and porcelain skin, how everything felt right when he was buried inside her. Equally, he didn't want her to worry and bringing her the peace she deserved was just as important.

"Then I shall work tirelessly to help you achieve your goals."

"We could speak to Miss Franklin now," she said, her eyes flicking to the silversmith shop and the woman at the window. "But we'll never get away. I cannot help but pity her. It's why I permit her to idle away hours in my shop."

"I suspect she'll be at the window when we return. We can ask then."

Miss Franklin seemed the pious sort who would wash out her mouth with bar soap if she uttered an untruth. She was keen to foster a relationship between Eleanor and her brother, so why push her down the stairs?

The journey to the solicitor's office on Fetter Lane took less than ten minutes by carriage. Thatcher's & Sons occupied a four-storey terrace house next to the grocers. The smooth stucco exterior had recently been painted.

"Will you take the lead?" he asked.

"Me? Professional men rarely take women seriously."

Theo reached into his pocket and retrieved the Home Secretary's letter. "This will force them to take notice. I'll intervene if necessary."

The gesture earned him a sweet smile. "Perhaps if I prove my worth, Mr Daventry will employ me as an enquiry agent."

A chill ran down Theo's spine. "One of his female agents was shot at the observatory some years ago. I'd never sleep a wink if I knew you were tackling murderers and spies."

She looked at him strangely. "My welfare never concerned you before."

"Everything is different now."

"Because we're friends and lovers," she jested.

"Because I care what happens to you." Because he realised as he watched her sleep last night that she owned a piece of him. "You're important to me, Eleanor."

Eleanor's hand fluttered to her chest. "That's the nicest thing anyone has ever said to me. I care about you, Theo. I always have."

They stared at each other, the world around them fading away.

But then a burly fellow stormed out of the solicitor's office, complaining about the extortionate fees. "It's criminal, that's what it is." Spittle flew from his mouth. "I'm the one owed money, yet I have to pay through the nose just to send a letter."

He stormed off, waving his fists and cursing the law.

Eleanor straightened when Theo held the door open. "I'd have a few sovereigns ready," she said. "I suspect information comes at a price."

The clerk, a young fellow whose trousers were too short, brushed a greasy lock of hair off his brow and came to greet them.

Eleanor spoke before the clerk opened his mouth. "We have a meeting with Mr Thatcher. Don't bother checking your diary. We're here on official business." She presented the letter. "If Mr Thatcher fails to grant us an audience, he will be required to answer our questions at Bow Street."

Theo watched with glowing admiration. She would make an excellent enquiry agent, but he couldn't bear the thought of her chasing criminals at night.

The clerk stuttered and eventually said, "Wait here. I'll fetch Mr Crump. He's in charge while Mr Thatcher is in Brighton on business."

Crump, an elderly man thin enough to slip through gaps in the paving, came hobbling out of his office using a walking cane for support. He observed them and frowned. "Mason said there were men from Bow Street."

Eleanor smiled. "We're investigators acting on behalf of Lord Melbourne, the Home Secretary. He asked—"

"I know who Melbourne is, but I haven't the faintest clue why it should concern me. Show me the letter."

Theo presented the document, grateful it was vague. "As you can see, that is Melbourne's official seal. You're required to answer questions about a matter of national security. We're investigating the possibility that a French spy is operating in London."

Crump's bottom lip quivered. "A French spy? Surely you can't think anyone working here is involved."

"May we discuss the matter in your office," Eleanor said. "I'm sure you understand this is a sensitive subject."

The fellow showed them into his office, a cluttered space that smelled of damp coats and old books. They occupied the chairs near the desk and waited for Crump to settle into his worn leather seat before pressing him for answers.

"I trust what we say here shall remain confidential," Eleanor said.

Crump nodded. "Of course."

"You have a client who made an unusual request. Lady Lucille Bowman invited Lord Wrotham's creditors to apply to you to have their bills settled. Can you confirm that is correct, sir?"

The man mumbled, clearly worried about discussing such high-ranking individuals. "A client's personal wishes are confidential."

"I'm sure you'd agree there is nothing criminal about paying one's debts," Theo said. Having one's betrothed pay them was utterly shameful. "Perhaps you require more information."

Eleanor took that as her cue to list the debts that had been paid. She mentioned the bookshop in Highgate and the perfumer in Covent Garden. "The owner of Breadwell's confirms you paid his debts on behalf of Lord Wrotham. As the person who delivered the letters on Lady Lucille's behalf, there is little you can tell me I don't already know."

Crump rubbed his forehead. "Yes, but how is this related to a search for a spy? And if you know this much already, what do you hope to learn from me?"

"Understanding the lady's motives is crucial in our hunt for the spy," Eleanor said, sounding convincing. "You will tell us what she said when she gave you the funds to pay Lord Wrotham's creditors."

"It will give us a better understanding of the situation," Theo pressed. "I see no need to mention your office other than to inform Lord Melbourne we received your full co-operation."

Crump considered them before saying, "The lady dealt with Mr Thatcher, but I was party to their conversation. Lord Wrotham's bills were excessive, amounting to over seven thousand pounds. She said it was a small price to save a lady's reputation."

"How many creditors were there?" Eleanor asked.

"Twenty or more. The viscount has wasteful tendencies."

Theo gave a mocking snort. "I know. He's my cousin."

Crump's cheeks coloured. "Forgive me. I did not mean—"

"Say what you like about him. I despise the ingrate. Any man who makes a woman pay his bills deserves to rot in hell."

Crump jerked in the seat and appeared a bit more lively. "It's odd you say that because Lord Wrotham had no idea who had paid his debts. He came asking questions, complaining he was a laughing stock, and left believing his aunt had secretly made the donations."

A creditor must have mentioned the solicitor's office.

Eleanor sat forward. "You didn't tell him about Lady Lucille?"

"Heavens, no. I said we dealt with a courier. The lady insisted on secrecy. We assumed she had saved her allowance or her father had given her the funds. But she became teary and confessed to parting with precious jewels to pay the baker's bill."

But why?

It made no sense.

Many lords had mounting debts.

It's why they married ladies with large dowries.

Theo sighed. "Is there anything else you can tell us that might explain her motive?" They were missing something. The clue that tied it all together. "What made her settle her betrothed's accounts?"

Crump shrugged. "We all thought it most peculiar." He leaned closer. "I'll deny this if questioned, but I'm inclined to think Lord Wrotham is the spy."

Now they were getting somewhere.

"Why would you say that?" Theo said. Spies needed nerves of steel. Wrotham was as weak as a wilting flower. Moreover, there was no spy. Just a devil out to hurt Eleanor and ruin her business.

"It's fair to say she despises the man. I'm sure her father could find just cause to withdraw from the marriage agreement."

So why pay the debts of a man you detest?

"She cursed him to the devil in a most unladylike manner," Crump continued, "and made us swear not to mention her name should he call. Thatcher thought she looked as frightened as a doe. Before she left, she urged us not to accept his money unless we wanted to meet our maker. It was most perplexing."

Theo's pulse rose. He was a moth drawn to the flame of curiosity. Wrotham had something to hide. Seeing to his downfall was Theo's life ambition. What secret was worth killing a solicitor over?

Having wrung Crump for every snippet of information, they left the office and returned to the carriage.

"Why would Lady Lucille entertain a man like Lord Wrotham?" Frown lines marred Eleanor's brow. "Do you think her father is insisting she marry him?"

Theo relaxed back against the squab. "Nothing matters more to the aristocracy than maintaining appearances. While our visit answered some questions, it brings us no closer to the blackguard who threatened you."

She pursed her lips, her expression grim. "Suspicion falls on Jack Rogers. He fits the profile and wanted me out of the shop."

"When I threatened him outside the tavern, he swore he'd never been in your yard. The man is a drunkard. You'd have smelled liquor on him, and he cannot afford to waste money on books."

Her shoulders slumped. "No one else has a motive. Mr Rogers needed me out of the way so Emily could steal haberdashery."

Lucille Bowman could afford to leave a book in a coal shed. She had a motive for stealing Eleanor's diary, and there was a record of her notes being delivered to Wrotham's creditors. Had she hired a man to do her wicked deeds?

Theo aired his concerns. "Is it a coincidence that Lady Lucille requested the book with the blank note from Pickering's library? She wanted you out of the shop so she could steal your diary."

She pressed her fingers to her eyes to stem her tears. "How did I get myself embroiled in the *ton*'s affairs? I should have known it would end badly."

"Has it ended badly?" Despite every worrisome problem, the moments they shared were the most memorable of his life. "I'm not sorry we're sitting here attempting to solve a mystery."

In truth, he didn't want the day to end.

Then, he would have the dilemma of where to sleep tonight. Did he leave Aaron alone at Fortune's Den and join Eleanor? It shouldn't be a difficult choice as being with her was his only desire.

"I bet you wish you'd never taken my wretched box."

"I was destined to take it." He had been unable to resist, compelled to have something belonging to her. "Fate granted me a boon the night you hid in my bedchamber."

She brushed a tear from her cheek. "Part of me wants an end to the nightmare. Part of me doesn't care what happens as long as I'm with you."

He understood.

He wanted her with a ferocity that defied logic.

"Come here." The need to touch her drummed a powerful beat in his blood. He called to Godby and instructed him to head to Finch Lane. Not because he cared about the recipient of Lady Lucille's note. He wanted more than ten minutes alone with Eleanor. "Sit astride me."

She crossed the carriage, gathered her skirts and straddled his lap. "You'll need to hold me close. If we turn sharply, I'll fall."

"I'll not let you go." He wrapped his arm around her waist. He had no intention of ever letting go. "But I have a confession to make."

Her eyes widened, and she swallowed twice. "You do?"

"I couldn't stay away last night. I came to the shop at midnight and left at dawn. After what happened with Emily, I had to know you were all right."

Her smile spoke of relief. "You didn't wake me."

"Gibbs said you cried yourself to sleep and I didn't want to disturb your peaceful slumber." He'd wanted to climb into bed beside her, hold her close and lose himself in the heat of her body.

Tears welled in her eyes again. "I don't know what to believe anymore. If what Emily says is true, my entire life has been a lie."

"It's not a lie." He drew the backs of his fingers across her cheek. "You're a beautiful person with an extraordinary talent. The past is like a pebble in your shoe. You must discard it, or it will hinder your progress."

She slid her arms around his neck. "My mind is full of other things. I cannot think about Emily or my mother now. The past is too painful to contemplate."

"Is there anything I can do to ease your mind?"

"Yes." Her gaze fell to his mouth. "You can kiss me."

Kissing a passionate woman in a carriage was always a mistake. The moment their mouths met, they were consumed by a savage hunger. He didn't tear his mouth from hers when he fumbled to close the blinds. He pulled her close. Kissed her harder. Though it wasn't enough to satisfy his craving.

"Theo." She pushed off his hat and tangled her fingers in his hair. She tugged a lock, anchoring him to her, as she devoured his mouth in a heart-stopping kiss.

He had never taken a woman in a carriage, but the need to push deep into Eleanor's body had him fiddling with his trousers. "I need to be inside you, love, before I lose my damned mind."

"Hurry," she said, scrambling with her skirts and wiggling on his lap.

He entered her, their loud sighs like the notes of a beautiful symphony. Their gazes locked, the power of unspoken emotions passing between them with every deep thrust.

*I'm in love with you.*

The need to have her went beyond physical desire.

He knew what it meant.

He would have to disappoint someone.

As much as it pained him, that someone would be Aaron.

# Chapter Seventeen

*Finch Lane*
*Cornhill*

By the time the carriage turned into the lane and stopped outside a quaint shop selling ladies' trinkets, Theo had cleaned the evidence of their lovemaking from Eleanor's thigh. They spent a moment straightening their clothes, looking at each other and smiling like they were the only two people in the world.

Were their thoughts aligned? she wondered. Was he imagining how impossible life would be if they did not spend every hour together?

"That's the most scandalous thing I have ever done," she said, tying the ribbons on her bonnet. "You're a bad influence, Mr Chance."

"You asked for a kiss." Eyes a soft, sated blue lingered on her mouth. "I never do anything in half measures, Eleanor. You know that."

No, he'd exceeded all expectations when tidying her shop. He had more than fulfilled his vow to put things right.

"Does this intense euphoria ever fade?" she asked. When would lust's flames stop burning so brightly? Would the inner agony dull over time?

Theo shrugged. "What exists between us is unlike anything I have experienced before. Our relationship is unique."

"Oh." What did that mean? She was too afraid to ask.

When you secretly loved someone, there was still hope.

The pain of shattered dreams was hard to bear.

Seeking a distraction from her wayward thoughts, she glanced at the pretty reticules in the shop window and nearly fell off the leather seat.

She pointed at the sign. "Tell me my eyes deceive me."

He read the name painted in red script on the pale blue background. "Franklin's Emporium? Franklin? Any relation to the silversmith?"

"I don't know. Might it be a coincidence?"

"There's only one way to know for sure."

They alighted. With Finch Lane being a five-minute walk from Fortune's Den, Theo instructed Godby to return home.

"I thought you might appreciate the exercise," he said to her, a teasing glint in his eyes. "Perhaps we might dine with Aaron tonight. He will be glad of the company. You can wait in my room while I assist him at the club."

The thought of dining with Aaron filled her with dread. He didn't want her there, but Theo loved his brother, and so she would smile and be polite.

"While I wait, might I sleep in your comfortable bed?"

His smile turned sinful. "Sleep while you can. When I return, I doubt we'll keep our hands off each other."

A vivid scene entered her mind. Them kissing until breathless.

*I'm so in love with you*, she wanted to say.

"You know how to appeal to a woman's fantasies."

"I know how to appeal to yours. I don't care about anyone else."

They locked gazes for a heartbeat.

No words were needed.

Upon entering the emporium, they were greeted by the tinkling of a tiny bell and an enticing display of costume jewellery filling the glass cases.

A woman of thirty approached them, her dark hair fixed in an elegant coiffure, a pretty lace choker fastened around her neck. "Good afternoon."

Eleanor stepped forward. "Good afternoon. Might I look at the emerald-green reticule in the window? The one with the gold embroidery?"

"Of course." The assistant removed it from the window and placed it on the velvet pad on the counter. "The colour matches your eyes perfectly."

Eleanor could sew something similar in an hour, but she studied the stitches and the tiny glass beads. The design reminded her of something she had made to complement Lady Beckett's new carriage dress.

"It's beautiful."

Theo moved to stand beside her. "It's yours if you want it."

She looked at him, tempted to say yes so she could thank him later. "You've spent enough money already." She turned to the assistant. "Are they made by a local seamstress?"

"They're made by my cousin. She's a budding designer." The lady explained she was the proprietress and introduced herself as Miss Franklin. "Those in the window are the first Anna has had the courage to sell."

"Anna?" Eleanor feigned curiosity. "I'm quite sure I know her, assuming her surname is Franklin. I live in New Bridge Street and taught my neighbour Anna Franklin to sew."

The lady clapped her hands in surprise. "You must be Miss Darrow. How wonderful. Anna speaks so highly of you. You're her inspiration." Her smile faded. "There's been some terrible business in the street lately. Thieves running amok. It's bound to ruin livelihoods."

"Anna believes the men on the merchant ships are to blame."

"I fear it's a problem throughout the city. Anna's friend had me make a paste version of her grandmother's diamond necklace." She gestured to the display of costume jewellery in the cabinet. "The poor lady was terrified to wear the original in case someone snatched it from around her neck."

The cogs in Eleanor's mind began turning. There would be an uproar if Lady Lucille's family knew she'd sold her jewels. The only way to avoid detection was to have copies made.

"Ah, you speak of Anna's friend Lucille."

The proprietor tapped her finger to her lips. "It's supposed to be a secret. Anna is quite protective of her new friend. Different social backgrounds can be a problem. Few members of the aristocracy are accepting of the working classes."

"Of course. Lucille asked me to deliver a letter here for Anna, but a thief stole it when he ransacked my shop." Eleanor slapped her hand to her chest as if she had spoken out of turn. "Forgive me. I swore my involvement would remain a secret."

The lady offered a reassuring smile. "Yes, Anna was expecting the note. Her brother Geoffrey is very protective and would have bombarded her with questions if it had been delivered to the house. He would assume someone of Lucille's standing was mocking Anna and then tear up the missive."

"I'm sure that's not the case," Eleanor said. But how had the women fostered an unlikely friendship? It can only have been when they met at her modiste shop. "But you have my word. I'll not mention our conversation."

The shop bell tinkled, and two women entered.

The proprietor greeted the newcomers before returning to their conversation. "It's hard for Anna, living with her brother. She is keen for Geoffrey to marry in the hope a sensible woman might curb his frivolous ways."

Frivolous ways? Mr Franklin seemed the practical sort.

"Well, I shall not say a word. I'm pleased Anna's sewing is giving her a small income." As the lady had been so help-ful, Eleanor decided to make a purchase. "I don't need a reticule, but might I look at that gold cannetille brooch with the cluster of green stones?"

When the owner went to fetch the brooch, Theo whispered, "I shall buy you one with real emeralds. One with a price tag of more than twelve shillings."

"I like simple things. The cost doesn't matter."

Eleanor made the purchase, although Theo insisted on paying.

He stopped outside the shop and pinned the brooch to her pelisse, his fingers brushing her breast. "The need to see you smile is becoming a compulsion."

She touched his hand, her heart fluttering with the depth of her affection. "Good. You can treat me to coffee and a slab of seed cake. There's a quaint little coffeehouse on Bishopsgate, a short walk from here."

"Remember we're dining with Aaron tonight."

She chuckled and gripped his arm. "Any lady will tell you, cake never spoils one's dinner."

They were about to walk away when the other Miss Franklin burst out of the emporium and thrust a package into Eleanor's hand. "Would you mind giving this to Anna? It will save her the walk here."

Eleanor turned the wrapped item over, confident it was a book. "I might not see her until tomorrow."

"Perfect. I doubt she'll have time to call before the weekend." The lady patted Eleanor's arm. "The brooch looks marvellous on you, Miss Darrow." And then she dashed back to the shop.

They sat in Pickins coffeehouse eating cake and discussing the unlikely friendship between Lady Lucille and Anna Franklin.

"It makes no sense," she said, licking crumbs from her lips. "They met once, maybe twice, while Lady Lucille attended a dress fitting. They couldn't have exchanged more than a few words."

"Yet now they're sending secret missives and arranging assignations." Theo leant forward and brushed her lip with his thumb, though looked like he wanted to eat her.

"Did I miss more crumbs?"

"Just one, but I needed an excuse to touch you." He glanced at the book on the table, wrapped in brown paper and fastened with string. "Will you give Miss Franklin the book? If you do, it's as good as admitting we know about her secret meetings with Lucille Bowman."

Eleanor sipped her coffee as she considered the question. Her patience had worn thin. She was tired of tiptoeing around. It was time to grab the proverbial bull by the horns. Maybe set a trap.

"Theo, what if Lady Lucille used Miss Franklin?"

"For what purpose?"

"To retrieve my diary. To cover her tracks so Lord Wrotham doesn't discover she paid his debts. Perhaps Miss Franklin knew I kept a record of my dealings with the aristocracy." Had she been spying, watching Eleanor's every move? "She might have seen it during our sewing lessons."

Theo relaxed back in the chair. "The woman is as timid as a mouse, though I imagine that serves as an excellent disguise."

"How did Miss Franklin know about my accident?" A chill ran across Eleanor's shoulders. "Maybe she pushed me down the stairs. She stole into the shop to pinch my diary. Heaven knows where she got a key."

Theo thought for a moment. "Why would Miss Franklin risk her neck just to appease Lucille Bowman? Why would either woman want to harm you? I cannot help but think we're missing a vital clue."

Yes, why would two women from different social backgrounds conspire together? "Lady Lucille doesn't want anyone knowing I delivered her letters."

"You're not likely to tell Wrotham."

"She doesn't know that." Eleanor had noticed the unmistakable glint of jealousy in the lady's eyes that night at the Olympic. "Mr Daventry will know how to proceed. We should seek his counsel."

Theo diverted his attention, focusing on the tall, sturdy man standing outside the tobacconists across the street.

"Is something wrong?"

"I'm sure I saw that man in New Bridge Street yesterday. And he entered the Red Lion tavern near the docks when I was wrestling the truth from Jack Rogers."

Eleanor gave a surreptitious glance out the window. "Are you sure? He's the same height and build as most dock-workers."

"Look closely. Though his clothes suggest he's a labourer, he has a gold watch in his pocket." Theo straightened. "Someone hired him to follow us. That, or a debt-ridden lord named me the first to die when he made a bet at White's. Wait here."

Eleanor shot out of the chair. "You're not going alone. I'm coming with you." She snatched the book off the table. "Please, Theo. Don't leave me here."

Theo sighed but made no objection. "You'll do exactly as I say. We need to be certain he's following us. It's a short walk to Fortune's Den. We'll lure him there."

He paid the bill and escorted Eleanor along Bish-opsgate.

"When we reach the street corner, drop the book," Theo said. "Make it look like an accident. As you bend to retrieve it, check if we're being followed."

Though nerves assailed her, she did as he asked, stealing a quick peek before picking up the book. "He's walking behind us at a distance of twenty yards. Two other men have joined him."

"Cursed saints!" He gripped her hand. "Keep walking."

To avoid suspicion, they navigated Leadenhall Street as if in no hurry. They laughed and stopped to look in the milliner's window. Theo kept her close and whispered for her to run should the thugs attack.

With Fortune's Den in their sights, Theo brought her to an abrupt halt at the entrance to the Saracen's Head Inn.

"Wait until they come a little closer, " he said, "then I shall confront them and demand to know who the devil hired them. We can't afford for them to run."

Eleanor could see the men out the corner of her eye. "Should we not call on Aaron first? We're but a stone's throw from the front door."

He'd been itching for a fight ever since he was shot in the shoulder. He couldn't tolerate being seen as weak.

"If these men have nothing to hide, it will be a brief conversation." He made to usher her across the street. "Alert Aaron. Go now. I'll be fine on my own."

Eleanor turned her head, meeting the burly fellow's gaze.

To avoid detection, he led his lackeys into the inn's yard.

"Theo, you're outnumbered."

"I live on this street. I know all the men who work here."

Every instinct said not to leave him. While struggling with her dilemma, the answer to her prayers left the confectioner's shop and walked towards them.

Miss Lovelace noticed them and stopped. "Miss Darrow. How wonderful to see you looking so well." She turned to Theo and inclined her head. "Mr Chance."

Eleanor clutched the lady's arm and whispered, "We desperately need your help. Would you call at Fortune's Den and ask Aaron to join us at the Saracen's Head. Tell him it's urgent and relevant to the case. Go now. Hurry."

Miss Lovelace frowned. "Are you in some sort of trouble?"

"I'll explain later. There's no time to lose."

Eleanor as good as shooed the lady away.

Miss Lovelace raised the hem of her skirts and hurried across the street before hammering on the door of Fortune's Den.

"Eleanor, go with Miss Lovelace."

She gripped Theo's arm. "I'm staying with you."

After a brief exchange, they entered the yard. The men were leaning against the wall near the taproom door. The owner of the gold pocket watch straightened when he saw them.

Keeping her behind him, Theo strode up to the men and addressed their leader. "You've been following us for days. Tell me who hired you, and you can leave with your face intact."

The lackeys gawped at their master.

"I don't know what you mean, governor," the bold brute said.

"Don't lie. You were outside Pickins coffeehouse fifteen minutes ago, watching us drink our beverages."

The thug laughed like Theo was a loon. "You've got me confused with someone else. I'm out for a stroll and to see a man about a dog."

As the King of Hearts, Theo was kind and considerate. As the part-owner of a gaming hell and the brother of Aaron Chance, he could be the devil incarnate.

A darkness passed over his handsome features. He rose to his full height and lunged at the beast who dared to mock him. His fist connected with the man's jaw, a punch that sent the fellow reeling and left his counterparts wondering what on earth to do.

One found the courage to strike. He was about to hit

Theo when Eleanor whacked his hand with Miss Franklin's book. "Touch him, and it will be the last thing you do."

Panic ensued when Aaron Chance burst into the yard, looking like he could flay men alive with his obsidian glare. People hurried indoors and peered through dirty windows. Men scrambled to move carts and horses.

One fled but tripped over Miss Lovelace's extended foot and hit the ground with a thud. The lady looked quite pleased with herself.

Sigmund grabbed the lout by the scruff of his coat and hauled him to his feet. "I'll take this one to the basement," he yelled before dragging the fellow away.

Aaron gripped the other scrawny devil by the throat. Though the man tried to fight, he was no match for one with an arm of steel. "We'll question them in the fighting pit. It's been a while since I flexed my fists."

Theo scowled at the miscreants' leader. "You'll come with me to Fortune's Den, or I'll drag you there myself. As I said in the beginning, save yourself the trouble and tell us who hired you. Was it Berridge?"

The fellow held his hands up in surrender. "I ain't a fighting man. I was paid to follow you about town and keep a list of the places you visited. Duncan and his brother"—he pointed to the man with his neck wedged between Aaron's firm fingers—"are out of work and said they'd help."

"Who hired you?" Theo demanded.

"If I tell you, I won't get paid."

"You'll spend a month in the infirmary if you don't." Theo gave the man a few seconds to reply before adding, "Trust me, you don't want to visit my brother's basement."

Shifting nervously, the beast wrung his hands before

confessing. "She never gave her name. Her maid is friends with Duncan's sister and knew we were men for hire."

"Her maid?" Eleanor said, knowing the culprit was one of two people. "Was the lady young or of middling years?" Was Mrs Dunwoody looking for the means to hurt Theo? Was Lady Lucille worried they'd discover she'd paid her fiancé's debts?

"She was young and pretty. Spoke like she had a peg on her nose. Had hair like spun gold. She spread her hanky out on the chair before she sat down."

"It has to be Lucille Bowman," Theo grumbled. "It's time we confront the woman and demand to know what the hell is happening."

"What, and be fed a pack of lies?" Eleanor said. The lady had something to hide, something that amounted to more than secretly settling Lord Wrotham's accounts. "No, we need to trick her into meeting Miss Franklin. Of the two, the latter is more likely to confess when pressured."

"Confess to what?" Aaron said.

Eleanor shrugged. "We don't know."

With a growl of frustration, Aaron released his prisoner and made for the sturdy brute. "I want to know everything the lady said when she hired you. What information does she seek?"

The craven fellow stepped back. "I was to list the places they visited. And what dealings they had with the man at the silversmith shop."

"Mr Franklin?" Eleanor sought to clarify.

"She got all in a tizzy and said the devil had ruined her life."

How odd.

Had Lady Lucille fallen in love with the silversmith?

Was that why she nurtured a friendship with Miss Franklin? Did she enjoy rubbing shoulders with the lower classes? Or did she have reason to fear him?

"You'll make a statement to that effect," Theo said. "I'll have every word in writing. She'll not worm her way out of this."

With some reluctance, the men for hire accompanied them to Fortune's Den. They stood in Aaron's imposing study and scrawled their names on a document stating why Lady Lucille had hired them.

"You're lucky you're walking out of here," Aaron said, shooing the louts out the front door. "If I see your faces again, you won't be so fortunate." He returned to the study and dropped into his black, throne-like seat. His gaze slid to Miss Lovelace, who sat beside Eleanor. "I'm sure you have much to do before you open tonight."

"Nothing that cannot wait."

"You seem to make a habit of becoming embroiled in my family's affairs. One would think you have enough problems of your own."

The lady raised her chin. "What problems could I have besides an absent father, the threat of bankruptcy and a host of young women who demand I play matchmaker? Surely you've heard their excited screams when the Marquess of Rothley comes to gamble."

Aaron snorted. "I've seen them peering through the window—hardly what one expects from wallflowers. Besides, Rothley would eat them alive."

Before the lady replied, a loud knock on the front door had Sigmund trudging through the hall. Seconds later, Daventry entered the study.

"What the blazes do you want?" Aaron said.

Mr Daventry smiled. "Good afternoon. I've been following the leads on the books Miss Darrow gave to Pickering." His gaze came to rest on Eleanor. "I went to the shop to update you on my progress, but Gibbs said you were out. I came to see what Aaron thought of the information."

"It's about time you considered my opinion," Aaron replied.

Mr Daventry ignored the snipe. He reached into his leather satchel and dropped a book onto Aaron's desk. "The first volume of Radcliffe's *The Italian* left in Miss Darrow's coal shed and delivered to Pickering. You'll see the note is still hidden beneath the bookplate."

Aaron took a paper knife from the drawer. With surprisingly gentle movements for a man with large hands, he cut the plate and retrieved the tiny note. The paper was blank.

Eleanor sighed. "So, the motive was to ensure I left the shop."

"Undoubtedly," Mr Daventry said. "We must ask ourselves for what purpose? Why put on such a dramatic show?" He removed another book and handed it to Aaron. "*Virtue Rewards* by Samuel Richardson. Perhaps you might tell me what the books have in common."

"I did not deliver that book to Mr Pickering," Eleanor interjected.

"No, I acquired it this morning."

Aaron studied both books. "They have the same bookplate."

Eleanor straightened. "Who does the book belong to?"

Daventry found the question amusing. "I confess, I had my agent break into the house to *borrow* it. Therefore, we cannot use the book as evidence." His smile broadened into a grin. "D'Angelo took it from Lord Wrotham's library. He inherited the books from his mother. Hence the image of two turtle doves. In her memory, Wrotham had more plates printed. D'Angelo found a file full of them in the desk drawer."

The room plunged into silence.

While Eleanor tried to imagine Lord Wrotham attacking her in the yard, Aaron gritted his teeth and cried, "That cowardly fop used Miss Darrow because of her connections to this family."

"That's not the motive," Theo said. "How can it be? Until our encounter at the Olympic, Wrotham knew nothing about my relationship with Miss Darrow."

"This case has us going around in circles." Eleanor knew there was but one way to solve the mystery. "We need more information. We should begin by using what we have against Lady Lucille and Miss Franklin."

Everyone remained quiet while considering the point.

"I agree," Mr Daventry eventually said. "We trick them into meeting and apply pressure to get answers."

Eleanor had an idea. "I have a letter Miss Franklin sent thanking me for giving her sewing lessons. I could copy the handwriting and write to Lady Lucille."

"You have a book from Miss Franklin's cousin," Theo added. "Why not say you were given a message as well? Use the term *friend* instead of giving a name. If the plan works, they'll both believe they have been summoned by the other."

It could work.

Providing Eleanor perfected her acting skills.

"Excellent." Mr Daventry clapped his hands together.

"Let's put the plan in motion." He raised his hand. "Just a word of caution. It takes cunning to keep a secret. Men kill for a pocket watch. Remember, nothing is more important than protecting each other."

# Chapter Eighteen

"Thank heavens Rothley is otherwise engaged tonight." Aaron observed the men throwing their fortunes away at the tables. "Many refuse to play with him. I might ask Devon Masters to join a game and see if Rothley is hiding cards up his sleeve."

Theo wondered if Aaron's problem with Rothley had more to do with the marquess' interest in The Burnished Jade. "You're the only man in London who could accuse Rothley of cheating and live to tell the tale."

Theo prayed the marquess hadn't set his sights on Miss Scrumptious. Aaron could handle anything, except watching the woman he secretly admired being courted by another man.

"I'd take great pleasure in wiping the smug grin off his face."

"You should tell Miss Lovelace that Rothley is watching her property. You don't want him to catch her unawares."

Aaron cursed under his breath. "If he hurts her, he's a dead man. I don't care about his damn title." He paused, realising his outburst may have revealed too much. "I cannot abide men who target vulnerable women. The sooner Rothley gets bored with this club, the better."

An argument erupted at the hazard table.

After a few cross words from Aaron, the game resumed peacefully.

"Thank you for letting Eleanor stay," Theo said. They agreed that until they determined how the Franklins were involved, it was safer for Eleanor to stay at Fortune's Den. "I'm sure this dreadful business will be over soon, and we can return to normality."

Aaron held Theo's gaze, a questioning look in his dark eyes. "We don't keep secrets, not from each other. You know I despise being kept in the dark."

Theo should have called him a hypocrite. Aaron was never honest about his own feelings. "I have kept you informed every step of the way."

"I'm not referring to the case, but your feelings for Miss Darrow." Aaron gave a humourless chuckle. "Daventry possesses an otherworldly skill. He knows exactly what a man needs in a woman. He found your ideal mate."

Eleanor was more than his ideal mate.

She completed him.

"Daventry had no part to play in my relationship with Eleanor." Daventry had not encouraged him to steal her sewing box. He had not persuaded them to kiss, make love, or forge an unbreakable bond.

Aaron frowned. "No, he's subtle and manipulates events from behind the scenes. I'll be damned if I know why."

"Perhaps he understands the value of emotional connections. Daventry had a difficult upbringing. Meeting his wife changed his life. He's an example to us all."

Aaron fell silent.

Theo's thoughts turned to Eleanor, sleeping upstairs in his bed. And how he had no choice but to hurt the man he loved most in this world. How he would fail the person he admired and respected above all others.

He pinched the bridge of his nose to stem a swell of emotion. "I'm in love with Eleanor," he said, feeling a dreadful guilt for being happy. "She's everything I could want in a woman—kind, compassionate, intelligent." Beautiful inside and out. "She understands me like no one else."

Aaron kept his gaze on the gameplay. "Does Miss Darrow know how you feel about her? Might your regret over stealing her box account for these temporary feelings?"

"My feelings are not temporary," he said with unwavering conviction. Being with her felt like coming home.

"Are they reciprocated?"

His mind flashed to their interlude in the carriage. She'd missed him. She touched him at every opportunity, made love to him like he was the most desirable man alive. "I can only hope I have not misread the signs. If I'm wrong, I shall be inconsolable."

"Who wouldn't love a man with your kind heart?" Aaron faced him. Shadows of loneliness flickered in his eyes, but he smiled. "Go to her. Tell her how you feel. I can deal with things here. Sigmund will help me throw this rabble out."

Theo's chest tightened. Not because he was afraid to confess his love but because he sensed a gulf opening between him and his brother. They had walked the same path their entire lives. Now, the path had diverged.

"I'll stay until the last patron leaves."

"I'm fine on my own."

If only that were true.

Sensing Theo's discomfort, Aaron gripped his shoulder with brotherly affection. "You don't need to concern yourself with me. I'm renowned for being robust. Follow your heart. It has served your siblings well. You deserve the best life has to offer."

He swallowed past the thump in his throat. "There's no one I admire more than you. I want you to know that I love you, as a brother, as a friend."

Perhaps the smoke from the candles or the patrons' cheroots had made Aaron's eyes water. "I trust my actions always convey my feelings. All I have ever wanted is for you to be happy." There was a sudden shift in Aaron's mood, and he slapped Theo playfully on the back. "Go now. You know where to find me if you need me."

Aaron crossed the room under the guise of speaking to the croupier.

With a heavy heart, Theo mounted the stairs to his chamber.

Perhaps Daventry had a plan for Aaron. The agent was the only person skilled enough to topple Aaron's barricades. The road to love would be rocky. Too arduous for most women. He might help by making Miss Lovelace see Aaron was *almost* everything she would want in a husband— strong, honest, fiercely loyal. If only he could love her with the same fervency.

Theo forgot Aaron's plight the second he walked into the softly lit chamber and found Eleanor in her shift, brushing her hair before the freestanding mirror.

"I thought you'd be asleep." He crossed the room and stood behind her, threading his arms around her waist. Happy just to hold her. "We have a busy day tomorrow. Hopefully, everything will go according to plan."

She leaned back against his chest and gazed at him through the looking glass. "Deception is a complex game. What if I can't convince both ladies to meet in Hyde Park?"

"We'll think of another way to discover the truth."

"What other way is there but kidnapping and torture?"

He laughed. "I imagine you're ruthless when the mood takes you." He moved his hands to her shoulders, gently kneading her tight muscles. "Bed for you, Miss Darrow. You've had a long day."

A soft hum left her lips. She tilted her head, her body swaying to the rhythm of his fingers. "That feels so good." All moral intentions left him when her mouth parted, and she whispered, "Don't stop, Theo. You have such magical hands."

He watched their dancing reflection in the glass. As he stroked her temple with his cheek, their eyes met in a shared moment of intimacy.

She wanted him. He was in no doubt.

Rather than take liberties, he said the gentlemanly thing.

"You need sleep."

Except he didn't want her to sleep. He wanted her writhing beneath him, gripping his buttocks and urging him to thrust deeper.

"I've not seen you for hours. Let's stay up a little longer."

Mesmerised, his gaze dipped to her pert nipples pressing against the lightweight linen. "I can stay up for as long as you like."

She heard the implicit meaning and smiled. "Scoundrel."

"Is that not why you love me?"

She froze, her eyes growing wide like a startled doe.

Had he made a mistake?

Had he misread the signs?

Fearful of rejection, any man would have laughed and played the teasing card, pretending it was said in jest. But he was the King of Hearts, not the King of Liars.

"I'm in love with you, Eleanor." He turned her to face him, wanting to gaze into her eyes when he declared his feelings, not look at a distorted version through the glass. "I love you."

She swallowed hard, her chin trembling. "How do you know?"

He brushed her hair from her brow and pressed a lingering kiss to her forehead. Anything to delay the agony that came with misjudging a situation. Now he knew why Aaron avoided intimacy.

"How do you know it's more than lust?" she added.

"Because I don't need to make love tonight. I care that we're together. I can talk openly about anything, and you'll listen like I'm the most interesting man in the world."

"You are the most interesting man in the world."

He touched her again because he couldn't help himself. "You bring light to every dark moment. Joy when I should feel sadness. I respect how hard you work. Admire your capacity for forgiveness."

"Well, you have certainly given it much consideration."

He waited for the "but"… It never came.

She rose on her tiptoes and kissed him tenderly, the touch of her lips a gift from heaven. "You're my love, my life. I only hesitated because Delphine said men often confuse lust with deeper emotions."

"I know how I feel about you." His arms were around her now, holding her tight. "As I told Aaron, nothing about this is temporary. It's the stuff of dreams and lifelong promises. I never thought I would leave Fortune's Den, but I would leave for you, Eleanor."

"Leave Aaron?" She blinked rapidly. "What will he do here alone? How will he cope when he closes the doors at night?"

"Trust you to think of others." In truth, he didn't know how Aaron would fare. "I hope it will be the impetus he needs to confront the past." He had to believe Aaron would benefit from a time of reflection.

"We must help him," she said. "In any way we can."

He drew her hand to his lips and rained kisses over her palm. "That's why I love you. You're my match in every way."

A coy smile touched her lips. "There's one way we differ."

"Oh?"

She stepped out of his embrace to gather the hem of her shift and draw it over her head. "I really would like to make love tonight, Theo."

The sight of her full breasts made him tremble. "We both know I'd struggle to keep my hands off you. Prepare to be ravished beyond all reason."

"Is that a promise?"

"Damn right it is." He was out of his coat and had thrown it on the floor when she ran from him like a lithe little sprite. It wasn't a question of whether he could catch her but how long he wanted to play this game.

Indeed, he could spend his life watching her bottom shake as she tried to evade him. Where did he want her? That was the question.

He didn't want to take her against the wall or bend her over the bed. He wanted to watch Eleanor as she came, to see pleasure dance in her eyes like sunlight on emerald waters. He wanted to take his time and relish every thrust. He wanted her beneath him in bed.

"Come here, you rapscallion." He caught her and hauled her over his shoulder—though she did not put up a fight— and delighted in gently biting her bottom.

"You devil."

He dropped her onto the bed, though seeing her fiery red hair splayed over his coverlet, her breasts heaving as if begging for his mouth, well, it left him rampant.

While she giggled, he tore off his clothes as if the damn things scorched his skin. "Open your legs. Let me see that glistening jewel."

She panted upon seeing his raging erection. "I thought you didn't need to make love tonight."

"I'm happy to admit I was wrong." She squealed when he grabbed her foot and drew each dainty little toe into his mouth. "I mean to brand every inch of you tonight."

Her breath came short and fast as he kissed his way up her milky-white thigh. A lengthy moan escaped her when he buried his face between her legs and licked her like there was no tomorrow.

"Oh, Oh, Theo … don't … yes."

The brazen woman he would marry bucked against his mouth, shuddering on a keen cry.

He climbed on top of her, his erection an angry-looking thing in need of her love and attention. "Touch me."

She did his bidding without question, her tentative fingers stroking him back and forth until he thought he might go mad.

"I need you now, Theo."

He liked the thought of having her in his bed.

He liked the thought of owning her body, even though her mind would always be her own.

He eased into her, his eyes rolling in his head. She was so sweet, so tight, so wet. "You hug me like a glove. I could bury myself inside you and never leave."

She wrapped her legs around him, taking him deeper. "I love you."

He wasn't prepared for the power of those words. They hit him in his chest, in a distant place he'd not known existed. "I love you."

He angled his hips, quickening the pace, sinking into her as the feeling overcame him again—the need for this soul-deep connection to last a lifetime. He wanted more than her friendship, more than her love. He wanted marriage. He wanted everything this woman had to give.

# Chapter Nineteen

When arranging a meeting in Hyde Park, one prayed for dry weather. The gods were on their side today, a day that defied the season. Sunlight danced through scattered clouds, and the gentle breeze carried the warmth of summer.

Eleanor turned her face to the sky, soaking in the sweet September rays. It was as if the heavens knew she was deeply in love and wanted to celebrate. For the first time in her life, she felt complete and utter bliss.

Treachery was afoot, though she couldn't help but smile as Theo walked beside her, a strong presence in every aspect of her life. She held his arm—touching him an irresistible compulsion.

She should have known fate would test their resolve.

When they reached the silversmith shop, the door was locked, the shutters closed. A heaviness hung in the air, a strange undercurrent of something sinister.

"I have never known Mr Franklin close the shop on a weekday." Eleanor swallowed past her growing apprehension. "Not in all the years I've lived here."

Theo hammered the door with his clenched fist. "Perhaps he's ill."

"Anna is competent enough to deal with the orders."

Eleanor stepped back off the pavement and glanced at the upper windows. She could have sworn she saw a curtain twitch.

Moments later, Mr Franklin appeared at the door, a shadow of stubble darkening his jaw, his crumpled shirt untucked from his trousers. "Miss Darrow." Her name left his lips with a gasp of surprise as he attempted to smooth his unkempt hair. "Thank heavens you're well."

"Is something wrong, sir?"

He looked dreadful. Like he had not slept in weeks.

"Did you not hear the terrible commotion last night? We caught two men breaking into the shop—foreign men, French, I think." He stepped aside to show the floor littered with candlesticks and cutlery and serving platters, the doors on the cabinets smashed, the glass a spiderweb of cracks.

"Good Lord." Eleanor knew how it felt to see one's work tossed aside like yesterday's rubbish. "Did they steal anything?"

Mr Franklin hung his head. "Enough to fill a sack. The fiends had the gall to leave by the front door."

"Speak to Gibbs," Theo said. "He may have witnessed them fleeing and can provide a description."

Mr Franklin nodded as though grateful for the advice, but then he put his hand to his eyes and sobbed.

Eleanor stepped forward and touched his upper arm. "It feels like a punch to the gut when someone treats your work with disrespect. But it will pass." That said, Mr Franklin didn't have a knight in shining armour fighting to make his troubles disappear.

"It's not that," he sniffed, almost embarrassed to look at her. "It's Anna. She heard a noise and was first downstairs. She must have presumed I was working late and had knocked something over."

Eleanor shrank back, clasping her hand to her chest. "Did they hurt her? Please tell me she is well." Despite Miss Franklin's questionable friendship with Lady Lucille, Eleanor wouldn't want her to suffer.

Mr Franklin opened his mouth to speak but choked on the words.

"Is Miss Franklin here?" Theo said, equally concerned.

The silversmith nodded. "One devil hit her with a silver candlestick before making his escape. The doctor said it's likely a concussion, but the next few hours are crucial to her recovery." His voice broke, but he added, "I'm waiting for a constable to return to take a statement."

Having hurt her head recently, Eleanor offered a few encouraging words. "It's best not to rush these things. I slept for three days after I fell down the stairs. Other than the odd headache, I'm fine now."

"Yes, Anna said you'd taken a tumble." He muttered to himself before changing the subject. "Was there something you wanted?"

The question jogged Eleanor's memory. "Yes, I visited your cousin's emporium in Finch Lane. She asked me to deliver a book for Anna." She handed him the parcel, though the paper was torn where she had whacked the lout in the yard of the Saracen's Head.

Mr Franklin accepted the book. "I'll leave it by her bedside."

"If there's anything I can do, don't hesitate to ask." She feared what he might suggest but had to be polite.

The man's eyes brightened. "Once the constable has been, you're welcome to sit with Anna. You might try to wake her from this worrying stupor."

Eleanor forced a smile. "I shall visit tomorrow. Give her a little more time to rest. Mr Chance can help tidy the shop if you require assistance."

Mr Franklin was quick to refuse the offer. "I'll have it cleared by tonight. I'm not one to sit idly by when there's work to be done."

They spoke for another minute before parting ways.

"How awful," she said to Theo as they crossed the street. "Poor Anna. Perhaps we should speak to Mr Gibbs. He may have seen something."

Theo agreed. "Until the police have caught these villains, it's not safe for you here. I find it odd that they're still targeting the area. Thieves rarely hit the same street twice."

"It wasn't thieves who targeted my shop but someone known to me." Someone with a secret to keep. "Maybe Mr Franklin has enemies. Maybe the apothecary prescribed the wrong medicine, and someone sought vengeance."

Mr Gibbs had seen nothing untoward. "That's odd. I barely slept and would have heard a commotion. On another matter, Emily came to the shop last night, wanting to speak to you, Miss Darrow."

"Oh?" If Eleanor had any hope of understanding the past, she needed to speak to Emily, too, but she couldn't think about that now. "If she calls again, tell her I will be in touch soon."

Mr Gibbs nodded and asked for an update on their progress.

Theo told him about their visit to the emporium, and that Lady Lucille had hired men to follow them about town.

"Daventry came here yesterday, looking for you," Mr Gibbs said. "He mentioned Wrotham uses a bookplate with two turtle doves. Though why the lord wants to deliver blank notes around town is a mystery."

"We were hoping Lady Lucille might shed light on the matter." She explained their plan to have Miss Franklin meet the lady in Hyde Park. "We've already sent the note purported to be from Miss Franklin. Lady Lucille should be waiting in Hyde Park at three this afternoon."

"I doubt she will wait around once she sees us," Theo said. "If we visit her at home, her father will ensure she never speaks to us again."

Mr Gibbs scratched his head while observing Eleanor's figure. "Happen you're a similar height and build as Miss Franklin. And I saw a row of wigs upstairs. If you wore a disguise, you could get close enough to speak to her before she scarpers. Give her a reason to hear what you've got to say."

Eleanor looked at Theo. "It might work. If we threaten to reveal her secrets, we might convince her to confess." Confess to what? Eleanor had no clue. "It's worth a try."

Theo's face was a picture of unease. "You're not going alone."

Her heart swelled at his concern for her welfare. "I could dress you in simple clothes and give you a flat cap. Jules could lend you his barrow."

"I'm not pushing a barrow around Hyde Park."

Eleanor chuckled. "If you want to come, you'll have to wear a wig and an oversized greatcoat."

Eleanor arrived at Hyde Park ten minutes early. She stood before the naked statue of Achilles, a grand monument to the Duke of Wellington, praying she looked remotely like Miss Franklin.

Miss Franklin rarely stood still, so Eleanor paced back and forth, wringing her hands and keeping her head slightly bowed. Few women gazed at the statue. Some had swooned before the sculptor covered Achilles' genitals with a bronze fig leaf. But the statue was close to the gate, quite convenient for a lady who did not wish to be seen by the masses.

Theo ambled along the path behind a row of trees, pausing every few steps to ensure all was well. Looking menacing in a black wig and an enormous coat, people saw him and walked the other way.

In the distance, the bells of St George's chimed the hour.

Long minutes passed before Eleanor spotted Lady Lucille Bowman strolling through the gates, her pretty parasol shielding her profile.

Eleanor turned her back, keen to draw the lady closer.

"What do you want, Anna?" Lady Lucille stopped behind Eleanor and tapped her shoulder. "We agreed not to meet again. We cannot be seen together in public. It won't help my case if the inspector from the bank comes knocking."

Taking a calming breath, Eleanor faced the lady hiding beneath the parasol. "I'm afraid Anna couldn't come today. She was hurt in a robbery at the silversmith shop last night."

Lady Lucille jerked in horror. Her pretty eyes darted over Eleanor's dark hair and face in a look of utter disbelief. "Miss Darrow?"

"Forgive the deception, but I had to speak to you and knew you would not meet willingly." When the lady paled and couldn't form an articulate word, Eleanor added, "I know you stole my diary." Anna Franklin lacked the courage to break into a person's home. "I know you pushed me down the stairs to avoid detection. You hired men to follow us. You've been paying Lord Wrotham's debts. We have the solicitor's statement and those of his creditors."

The last comment sparked a reaction. "Now I know you're lying. A solicitor must keep his client's confidence."

"Ordinarily, but the Home Secretary gave me a letter forcing your solicitor to comply." She reached into her reticule and showed Lady Lucille the document. "As you can see, your business dealings are a matter of national interest. Tell me your secret, or I shall have no choice but to visit you at home."

Eleanor expected a verbal attack—the bite of a viper— but the lady's hand shook violently, and her voice broke. "Stop this. You don't know what trouble it will cause. It will be the death of me. I beg you. Walk away. Pretend I never asked you to deliver my silly notes."

Paying a fiancé's debts hardly warranted this reaction. It confirmed what Eleanor already knew, that they were unaware of the real problem.

Eager to ensure no one discovered the truth, Lady Lucille exclaimed, "Has a man ever hurt you, Miss Darrow? Has he ever treated you like your life doesn't matter? If so, I beg you to show mercy and forget everything you have learned."

Bitter memories of her father flooded Eleanor's mind.

The times he had forced her to stay awake all night because her stitches weren't straight. The times she had cried herself to sleep believing she was wicked.

Being kindhearted, Eleanor's resolve faltered. "There are good people in this world. Trust me. Tell me what you've done, and I will help you."

Lady Lucille dabbed tears from her eyes. "No one can help me. The damage is done. I only pray that my actions have prevented a catastrophe."

Good grief. She made it sound like the world was ending.

Whatever her troubles, Lord Wrotham had caused them.

"A man attacked me in my yard and forced me to deliver secret messages." Eleanor shivered at the memory. The fiend's grip had left bruises. "I was given books and told to hide notes behind the bookplates. Every volume in Lord Wrotham's library bears the same plates." She went on to tell a harmless lie. "I enquired at the printers. It's an exclusive design."

The lady swallowed hard. "That has nothing to do with me."

"But it does. You borrowed the *Vampyre* from Pickering's library, aware the note was inside." She hadn't loaned the other books, probably because her suspicions had been confirmed. "You knew Lord Wrotham had hurt me and wanted to be sure. You know why, yet you let me live in fear. Don't expect sympathy when we've been hurt by the same man."

That's when recognition dawned.

When a terrible sense of foreboding churned in her stomach.

The dreadful certainty that something wicked had unfolded.

"What if Lord Wrotham hired men to hurt Miss Franklin?" A picture of the scene flashed into her mind. Now she thought of it, there was something organised about the chaos. "She was bludgeoned with a candlestick. If she doesn't recover, your fiancé as good as murdered her."

As if about to wretch, Lady Lucille slapped her hand to her mouth. "No. Anna does not deserve this. None of us do. She risked everything to tell me the truth."

"It's about time *you* told us the truth," Theo said, joining Eleanor. "This game has gone on for long enough."

It took Lady Lucille a moment to recognise Theo. "Game? Do you think I gain any pleasure from this? If the truth comes to light, I will be transported."

Eleanor gasped. "Transported? What have you done?"

The lady hung her head and cried. "I'm guilty of nothing but naivety. I'm like all the other foolish chits who believe titled men are moral."

Theo released a weary sigh. "Despite our differences, we're willing to help you."

She looked at him through teary eyes. "Unless you plan to kill Lord Wrotham, I see no other way you can help."

Kill Lord Wrotham?

Her situation must be dire.

"We'll not commit a crime." Eleanor glanced at Theo. She had everything to live for now. Every reason to believe they could be happy. "But Mr Chance and his brothers could use the information against Lord Wrotham. He does not need to know it came from you."

Theo cursed under his breath. "If I find out Wrotham hurt

Miss Darrow in her yard, he'll not walk without the aid of a stick."

The lady sniffed back more tears. "Why would you want to help me when I used you so cruelly? Wrotham hates you so much he relished stealing me away."

"We met twice," Theo said, his tone indifferent. "I had selfish reasons for wanting to court you, too." He reached for Eleanor's hand and clasped it tightly. "But I'm in love with Miss Darrow. Love has a way of softening one's heart."

Eleanor's heart swelled in her chest.

Theo wasn't ashamed to voice his feelings.

"Whatever you have done, my lady, it's helped us to realise what we mean to each other." She couldn't help but smile. "But we must put this dreadful business behind us. We have all made mistakes."

Lady Lucille looked at them with utter astonishment. "I encouraged Anna to steal your diary and the book hidden beneath your floorboards. She took the spare key from the drawer, had a copy made and entered the night you went to the Olympic. You have every reason to despise us both."

"I'm sure you were quite desperate at the time." Eleanor wanted to feel a burst of anger, a rage to make Lucifer quake, but she didn't. "Though I cannot understand why Anna would upend furniture and pull everything off the shelves."

"That wasn't Anna," the lady declared. "She swears the rooms were like that when she arrived."

"But I was away for two hours at most." She had gone straight to the Olympic and had arrived home to find the place in disarray. "Whoever it was must have been looking for my diary." Why hadn't Mr Franklin seen anything? He was forever watching the street. "Was it Anna who pushed me down the stairs?"

The lady frowned. "Why would Anna want to hurt you?"

Eleanor's head throbbed. But at least she knew who had been rooting under the floorboards. "The question we need to ask is, who hurt Anna? Mr Franklin is pedantic when it comes to protecting his property. He'll be annoyed he didn't confront the blackguards."

How had he not heard the intruders?

He watched the street with a hawk's intensity.

Surely Anna went in search of her brother before—

The blood in her veins froze.

Logic offered an alternative option. One that beggared belief. One her heart fought to reject but her mind could not.

"Why would Anna help you?" Eleanor said, wondering how they had formed a bond when they were nothing alike. "What is this truth she told you? Does it in any way relate to Mr Franklin? Might he have hurt Anna?"

Theo jerked his head. "Franklin? I've spent years studying gambling men. I know the truth when I see it. Franklin appeared distraught when speaking about his sister today."

Yes, his tears were genuine, his pain quite evident.

But Lady Lucille was quick to reveal the true nature of Mr Franklin's character. "Appearances can be deceptive. The man has ruined my life. He is cold and calculating and obsessed with ideas of grandeur."

Eleanor was taken aback. She knew the polite man who showed her every consideration, the hardworking man, the caring citizen.

"I thought Wrotham had ruined your life," Theo said, confused.

"They both have."

Theo could not keep his frustration at bay. "You're not making any sense. Stop being evasive. Tell us the truth, or we shall have no choice but to mention your involvement to the magistrate at Bow Street. I doubt your father would be pleased to know you aided a thief."

Knowing her back was to the wall, Lady Lucille gripped her pretty parasol and said, "Can I trust you? I have unwittingly committed a crime much worse than aiding a thief. Wrotham used me." Hatred dripped from those last three words. "He doesn't care if I hang."

"You have no choice but to trust us," Eleanor said, fearing Anna was at home with the person who'd hurt her. "Too many people know of your involvement. It's only a matter of time before Mr Franklin tries to silence you, too."

The lady contemplated her dilemma.

But realised she had no choice but to confess.

"It all began during one of my dress fittings. Bored, Wrotham visited the silversmith shop and somehow forged a bond with Mr Franklin." She angled her parasol, hiding from those out for an afternoon stroll. "Wrotham's father cut his allowance after a string of poor investments."

"How do you know this?" Theo said, sounding suspicious.

"Anna told me everything. She's been spying on her brother for the last six months. It's why I had my father insist on a long engagement. I wanted to be sure Wrotham's affairs were in order."

"I doubt Wrotham will ever get his affairs in order."

Theo was right. Based on his list of creditors, Lord Wrotham was a wastrel. Some members of the aristocracy saw it as their right to take what they wanted and never pay.

"He appealed to his father for funds, but the request was denied. I can only think that's what spurred him to lunacy. That, and the fact he believes he's above the law."

She had not told them anything useful or alluded to what criminal deed the men had committed. What would Lord Wrotham want with a silversmith? What crime carried a penalty of transportation?

Only one sprang to mind—forgery.

Eleanor stood for a moment, her mind working to fill in the missing details. Was Mr Franklin making worthless sovereigns? That would hardly generate the kind of money Lord Wrotham needed. Were they printing notes? If so, was Lady Lucille guilty of uttering?

"Then I assume he is working with Mr Franklin to replace his allowance." Eleanor could not believe they would be so stupid.

The guilty parties could receive the death penalty. The unwitting players could be transported for fourteen years.

Lady Lucille stepped closer, tears filling her eyes. "Miss Darrow, they are making plates to print notes and delivering them to a partner in Birmingham. Wrotham is responsible for delivery but uses others to carry out his criminal deeds." The lady clutched her chest. "I have made such a delivery on his behalf, on the way to visit my aunt in Chester. It's why I paid his bills. I'm terrified he'll use forged notes and I'll be implicated. I only know because Anna told me everything. "

And now Anna was injured and unconscious.

Had she confronted her brother?

"I knew nothing about their nefarious deeds." The lady gulped hard as tears slipped down her cheeks. "Like you, I am an innocent party."

"Like me?" Eleanor's heart pounded so wildly she thought she might swoon. "What has this to do with me?"

Panic flared in Theo's eyes. "You've got three seconds to explain how Miss Darrow is involved."

The answer came to Eleanor in a blinding light seconds before Lady Lucille said, "Mr Franklin didn't want Wrotham collecting the plates from the silversmith shop. Wrotham parks on Water Lane and collects them from Miss Darrow's coal shed."

Her vision blurred as the news hit like a hard blow.

She shuddered as if hearing the fiend's vile threats.

*If you tell anyone, you'll die.*

The villain's voice was coarse. It couldn't have been Lord Wrotham because he would struggle to disguise his eloquence. Her attacker was larger than the scrawny lord. Somehow, the devil had obtained a key because he had entered her bedchamber in the dead of night.

Eleanor froze in horror. Mr Franklin had attacked her in the yard. He'd put his grubby hands all over her body. He'd stood watching her at night.

"So, the notes in the book were a way of getting rid of Miss Darrow," Theo said, a stab of anger in his voice. "They sent her on a goose chase while using her premises to defraud the banks."

"Do you see why I was reluctant to tell you?" Fear tinged the lady's blue eyes. "Wrotham will deny everything and blame the Franklins. We're both friends with Anna. It will look like we conspired together."

"Trust me," Theo said, his expression as dark as the bowels of hell. "Wrotham will be dead before he can make any accusations. You need to visit the office of the Order in

Hart Street and have Lucius Daventry take your statement. He will assist us in bringing the real culprits to justice."

"Mr Daventry is a defender of the law," Eleanor added. "He will protect your identity. You have my word."

The lady's countenance brightened. "I shall go there directly." She paused. "There is something else."

"Yes?" Eleanor said.

"Wrotham is meeting Mr Franklin tonight. Since you've hired a man to guard your premises, they cannot leave the plates in your coal shed. They're making the exchange at midnight on the north side of Blackfriars Bridge. Anna read a note from Wrotham and sent word with a penny boy."

"Tonight?" There was a hint of excitement in Theo's voice. "Then there's no time to dally. It's imperative we catch them in the act."

A faint smile touched the lady's lips. "Do you really think we might bring an end to this nightmare, Mr Chance? I must admit, I had given up hope."

Theo gave a devilish grin. "Madam, nothing would give me greater pleasure than seeing my cousin rot in a dank cell. Daventry never fails. Come tomorrow, we will all be rid of Wrotham for good."

# Chapter Twenty

From Eleanor's dark bedchamber, Theo watched the silversmith shop through a gap in the curtains. Fog crept from the river like a silent thief, its ghostly tendrils curling around buildings and drifting through the streets.

"If Franklin doesn't leave soon, I'll lose sight of his premises."

While Daventry hid near Blackfriars Bridge with Aramis and Christian, Sigmund watched Wrotham's abode from an unmarked carriage.

Aaron moved closer to the window. "Perhaps I should wait outside on the street. Franklin doesn't know me, and I'm skilled at keeping to the shadows."

"We can't risk losing each other," Eleanor said.

"We'll stick to the plan unless the fog becomes so thick I cannot see." Upon sensing movement in the darkness, Theo narrowed his gaze. So far, he'd spotted nothing but drunkards and vagabonds. If only the gas lamp shone directly outside Franklin's door.

Aaron paced the floor. He was always calm under pressure, but the reason for his agitation became apparent. "I've waited a lifetime to punish the Earl of Berridge. That devil left four boys to sleep on the street. Nothing will please me more than seeing his son bound in chains."

Theo would count his blessings once Wrotham was stripped of his title and punished for forgery. He was wise enough to know the blame would probably rest at Franklin's door. Still, he hoped Wrotham would get his just deserts.

Eleanor had other concerns. "I pray Anna will make a full recovery. We should enter the house when Mr Franklin departs and ensure she is well."

"Half an hour won't matter," Aaron countered, his determination to hurt Berridge evident. "We must catch Wrotham in the act. If Franklin returns before making the exchange, it will ruin everything."

Theo had promised Eleanor they would rescue Anna Franklin, and he would not break his vow. "We'll have Gibbs bring Miss Franklin here. It will take two minutes to enter the shop and carry her to safety."

"I'd never live with myself if I left her," Eleanor said.

Aaron sighed. He was unused to negotiating with a woman. "Then you'd better pray Franklin doesn't return and catch you in the act."

Silent minutes passed before Theo spotted a figure in black emerging from the silversmith shop carrying a heavy valise. "Franklin is on the move. He's heading south towards the river."

"You're certain it's him?" Aaron said.

"As certain as I can be on a foggy night."

The tension in the air intensified.

"Let me knock on Mr Franklin's door," Eleanor

suggested. "If we're wrong and he's at home, I shall say I couldn't sleep because I was worried about Anna."

"Like hell you will." Just thinking about her alone in the house with Franklin brought bile to Theo's throat. "He'll think you have romantic intentions."

Aaron acted as peacekeeper. "As it's almost midnight, I suspect it is Franklin. Let's hope the Lord is on our side tonight."

Wearing dark outdoor apparel, and with Gibbs in tow, they crossed the street to the silversmith shop. The fog was thickening, falling over the street like a shroud. With the meeting place being close to the river, Daventry would struggle to spot the villains.

Eleanor knocked on the silversmith's door but received no reply. There wasn't a light in any window, though the curtains upstairs were drawn.

"Step aside." Aaron shooed them out of the way. "If we're wrong about Franklin, let him blame me for breaking into the premises." He didn't barge the door with his shoulder but removed a ring of metal implements from his pocket and fiddled with the mortice lock. "A crook named One-eyed Eric taught me this trick."

One click and Aaron opened the door.

Franklin had tidied the silver items from the floor and returned them to the cabinet. He'd even had the glass doors repaired. Had he staged the scene after losing his temper with his sister?

They found Miss Franklin asleep in bed, her head bandaged, her face deathly pale. Eleanor sat on the bed and checked Anna's pulse before exhaling with relief.

"She's alive, thank heavens."

"We must hurry," Aaron snapped. "Can you rouse her?"

Eleanor clasped Anna's hand and patted it gently. "Anna? Can you hear me? We're here to save you." When she received no response, she tapped the woman's face. "She's definitely breathing."

"We cannot wait." Aaron was at the door. "I'll head to the river and warn Daventry. It's imperative we find them with the plates in their possession."

Theo offered Eleanor a reassuring smile. "Another minute, then we must go. Try to rouse her again." He glanced at Aaron. "Go. We will meet you at the bridge."

Torn between leaving them and burying Wrotham, Aaron lingered in the doorway. He considered his dilemma before marching back to the bed.

Aaron pinched the end of Miss Franklin's nose and waited for her to breathe through her mouth. "Miss Franklin!" He shook her shoulders.

The poor woman's eyes shot open. She must have thought she'd died and gone to hell. "What? Help!" she cried weakly.

Aaron stepped back to let Eleanor speak. "Anna. It's me, Eleanor Darrow. We've come to help you. We were told you were hurt in a robbery at the shop. Is it true?"

Miss Franklin's eyes grew wide, then fearful. "Miss D-Darrow. You must leave before … before Geoffrey finds you here. He's in a t-terrible mood."

"We must go," Aaron barked. "Gibbs, carry Miss Franklin to safety. We'll discuss the whys and wherefores once we've found Franklin and Wrotham at the bridge." Aaron glared at Theo and jerked his head towards the door. "Need I remind you why we're here? Our pathetic cousin must suffer."

"W-wait," Miss Franklin whispered, her voice barely

audible due to her weakened state. "In the study … there are dyes and metal plates."

Theo instructed Gibbs to gather any evidence of forgery and then take Miss Franklin to Eleanor's shop. "Don't open the door until we return. Let's pray we're not too late."

"Wait," she said, gathering her strength. "Don't go to the bridge." She paused to catch her breath. "They're meeting at Mr Walker's apothecary. Geoffrey has a key."

Gibbs confirmed the possibility. "Walker is in Oxford visiting his supplier. He said he'll be away for two days."

They tried to remain calm while devising another plan.

"You can access Mr Walker's yard via William Street," Eleanor said, jumping to her feet. "It's why we saw Mr Franklin head south towards the river."

"Then there's no time to lose." Aaron instructed Gibbs to alert Daventry and then return to deal with matters at the silversmith's.

"How shall we proceed?" Eleanor asked as they hurried downstairs.

"We'll enter via the yard." Theo grabbed a silver candle-stick as they raced through the shop. He'd club Wrotham to prevent him from escaping.

Aaron cursed. "We need someone impartial to witness the exchange. We're biased. A magistrate might believe we invented the tale."

"Miss Franklin and Lucille Bowman will testify." Theo gripped Aaron's arm to calm his brother's temper. "Trust me. Fate is on our side."

From William Street, they ventured into the dim alley, and Eleanor directed them into Mr Walker's yard. The fog acted as a veil, and the array of wooden drying sheds gave them plenty of places to hide. The back door stood ominously open, and the sound of irate voices was carried on the cool night air.

"You're the one who dragged me into this mess," Franklin said with a sense of desperation. "Anna is far too inquisitive. I should have known she would discover the secret eventually."

"No one can prove a thing." Wrotham's voice dripped with arrogance. "My aunt is currently enjoying the hospitality of the Plume of Feathers in Edgware and will visit Birmingham tomorrow with our current consignment. The remaining plates will be dispatched next week, marking the end of our association."

His aunt?

Theo glanced at Aaron and grinned. Finding Mrs Dunwoody with forged plates would be the cherry on the cake.

Franklin breathed a long sigh. "What about Lady Lucille? Anna said she knows you're a crook."

"All peers are crooks." Wrotham's mocking laugh grated. "Don't worry about Lucille. The chit's father adores me. He wants his daughter to be the next Countess of Berridge. Lucille won't say a word. Besides, she delivered the plates and would be considered an accessory."

Theo felt a surge of unease.

Wrotham was right. Lady Lucille had no choice but to bow to his wishes if he escaped unpunished. Wrotham knew he could get away with murder.

"How do you know you can trust your aunt?" Franklin sounded anxious. Anxious and unpredictable. "How do I know I can trust either of you? We agreed I'd make one plate, but you blackmailed me to make more. When will it end?"

"Soon," Wrotham reassured him. "I need you to make another pouch of those pretty sovereigns, and we—"

"No! I've already risked my damn neck."

Aaron nudged Theo, his frustration palpable. "Where the hell is Daventry? We need him to catch Wrotham in the act."

Theo shrugged. "I'm sure he'll be here soon."

"Don't press me on the matter, Franklin." Wrotham was like a master puppeteer, using his status to pull the silversmith's strings. "No one can trace the plates back to us. I used an alias."

Delusions of grandeur had affected Wrotham's rationale.

Clearly, he had never encountered an inspector from the bank.

"If you're caught passing the coins, there'll be an investigation," Franklin countered. "And what about your valet? He only has to mention his connections in Birmingham and we're done for."

"Don't worry about my valet. He will be the victim of a terrible attack in the rookeries tomorrow night."

Wrotham was not a spineless fool after all.

Wickedness was in his blood.

But the privileged often lost sight of reality.

Franklin agreed. "Are you mad? What began as a small favour will see us both hanged." A pained howl escaped him. "I almost killed my sister in a fit of panic."

"They'll not hang a peer. It would cause civil unrest," Wrotham sneered. "Take control of the situation. Bribe your sister with jewels. Threaten to throw her out if she utters a word."

Franklin had heard enough. A thud and a clatter preceded him shouting, "Take the damn plates. I'm leaving. Don't contact me again."

"Have a care. You'll damage the goods."

"We can't let either of them leave," Aaron uttered. "Not until Daventry arrives. Where the hell is he?"

Theo's heart raced. If Wrotham left the premises, they would lose him in the fog. And it would help the prosecution if he was found taking the forged plates from the silversmith.

"I can stall them," Eleanor said *sotto voce*. "I can pretend I saw Mr Franklin and was worried about the apothecary."

Like the day Theo saw her lying at the bottom of the stairs, his blood ran cold. "I'll not send you into a viper pit."

"If we don't do something, our efforts will be in vain." She reached for his hand and clasped it tightly. "Mr Franklin attacked me. He entered my home and watched me sleep. I'll not rest if he escapes."

"Miss Darrow is right," Aaron uttered. "She can play the witless female and buy us time. Neither of them would be fool enough to hurt her."

Every fibre of his being fought against the suggestion. "I can't lose her."

"I shall take a weapon, say I suspected intruders. Trust me."

God, he wanted to believe she could succeed, but fear had him by the throat. "The minute they threaten you, I'll put them both on their arses. Play dumb. Don't mention the case."

Her chin trembled as she nodded. "I can do this."

He had never met a more courageous woman in his life.

The urge to declare his feelings overwhelmed him, but instead, it emerged as a demand. "You'll marry me when this is over."

A smile touched her lips. "That's hardly a proposal worthy of the King of Hearts."

"Desperate times call for desperate measures." She would get a proper proposal once they'd dealt with Wrotham.

"I suggest you hurry, Miss Darrow," Aaron whispered. "Before Franklin flees. We'll be right behind you."

Eleanor turned to Theo, grabbed his coat lapels and kissed him. "I love you."

"I love you."

He thrust the silver candlestick into her hand, but she refused it. "Franklin may recognise it and know I have been inside his premises. I shall survive on my wits."

And with that, she crossed the threshold.

"If anything happens to her, shoot me," Theo said.

Aaron gripped his shoulder. "Miss Darrow is a capable woman. I'm sure it's one of the many reasons you love her."

Miss Lovelace was a capable woman, too, but this was not the time to tease Aaron. Indeed, they crept into the house, keeping to the shadows.

"Mr Walker? Are you there?" Eleanor sounded like a concerned neighbour. "Do you know you left the back door open?" When no one answered, she shouted, "If you're one of those terrible men from the merchant ship, know I'm going to fetch a constable."

That got Franklin's attention.

From his hiding place in the storeroom, Theo heard the clip of footsteps before Franklin appeared in the doorway.

"Miss Darrow? Why are you not at home in bed?"

"Mr Franklin? Is that you? Oh, thank heavens. I thought you were one of those foul men from the merchant ships."

Wrotham was hiding in the shop, probably ducking behind the oak counter filled with dried herbs and pots of salve.

Franklin didn't move but continued blocking the doorway. "I thought I saw a thief entering Mr Walker's premises but was mistaken. I vowed to keep an eye on things while he's away in Oxford."

"That's extremely good of you, sir. How is Anna? I can spare time tomorrow if she would like company."

*Excellent! Keep him talking.*

"She woke for a little while and managed a few spoonfuls of vegetable broth. It's our grandmother's recipe and works wonders for an ailing constitution."

"You'll have to give me the recipe."

"I'm sure Anna will when she's recovered."

An awkward silence ensued.

Eleanor shifted her feet. "If all is well, I should return home."

Franklin gave an odd hum. "I would have expected to see Mr Gibbs. Does he know you've ventured out alone?"

Eleanor chuckled. "Oh, the poor man has barely slept these last few days. He had a second helping of stew and nodded off in the chair."

"And you did not think to wake him?" Suspicion coated Franklin's words. "I doubt he would approve of you sneaking about in the dark."

Theo feared she would stumble, but she spoke with confidence. "He'll be furious. I should return before he wakes. Don't mention my midnight adventure if you speak to him."

Unable to fight his attraction to her, Franklin stepped forward. "I'll escort you home. The fog has settled. There's no telling who's lurking about out there. This street isn't safe for a woman living alone."

The knots in Theo's stomach tightened. If Franklin laid a hand on her, he would gut him like a fish.

Franklin did lay a hand on her. More than one. He clasped Eleanor's upper arms and rubbed gently. Theo would have charged at the devil were it not for Aaron tugging his coat.

"I wouldn't want to see you get hurt, Eleanor." Despite the intimate use of her given name, the remark carried a veiled threat. Franklin must have sensed her fear. "You're afraid of me."

"Afraid? No, I'm not," she said in a playful tone.

"You flinched when I touched you."

"Because you're not usually so familiar."

"You're lying. You looked over my shoulder as if you'd seen someone inside the shop. How long were you lingering outside?"

Wrotham didn't give her time to answer. He suspected she had come to spy and called to Franklin. "Bring her here. Don't let her feminine wiles sway you. We cannot afford a mistake."

Franklin froze and muttered, "I've hurt one woman. I'll not hurt another." He bowed his head. "Run, Eleanor. Go, before it's too late." When Eleanor failed to move, Franklin said, "I am escorting Miss Darrow home. We will continue this conversation when I return."

Wrotham appeared in the darkness, a few feet behind Franklin. "If you leave, I'll expect your full co-operation. You'll fulfil one more order." A mocking chuckle escaped him. "Women are your weakness, not mine."

Wrotham sounded like a seasoned criminal, not a dandy whose valet dressed him each morning. Unlike London's most dangerous rogues, his lackey wasn't afraid of him. They had reached a stalemate.

Theo's heart pounded in his chest.

One snap decision, and Franklin could break Eleanor's neck. Indeed, he stared at her as if in a trance, unsure what to do.

"You'll dangle from the scaffold if you fail to deal with her," Wrotham's bitter voice echoed from the darkness. "End it now. I'll take care of things. I shall be the one to tell my cousin his betrothed has met her maker."

Eleanor gasped when Franklin firmed his grip. He snarled at her like a blood-thirsty beast, anger bloating his cheeks. "You should have stayed at home, Miss Darrow."

Unable to wait or risk losing her, Theo stepped out from behind the tall cupboard and met Franklin's gaze. "Release her," he muttered.

Recognition dawned in Franklin's eyes, but he did not raise his hands and surrender. "I'll not let that bastard escape unpunished." Fury built inside him, his shoulders rising, his chest expanding. A growl escaped him as he turned on his heel and charged at Wrotham.

Chaos erupted.

Daventry burst in through the front door.

Theo raced to Eleanor and pulled her into his arms.

Aaron charged to Daventry's side while Franklin punched Wrotham to the floor and smacked his head repeatedly on the wooden boards.

Another fight ensued when Aaron dragged Franklin away. One punch from Aaron's fist left the silversmith unconscious.

For lengthy seconds, no one moved, only breathed.

"Cole, fetch a doctor for Lord Wrotham," Daventry said

to his agent. "Hurry. And fetch Harper from *The Morning Post*. He lives at 7 Fleet Street, a minute's walk from here. I'll not have Wrotham worm his way out of this."

"I'll fetch Harper," Aramis said.

While Theo consoled Eleanor, Aaron checked Wrotham's pulse. Blood circled his head in a crimson halo. His lip was cut, his eye bruised.

"Make sure Harper knows he happened to be walking by." Daventry crouched, opened the leather valise and examined the metal plates. "There are five here, all for different banks. One for the Bristol Bank, another for Attwood and Spooner."

"How much did you hear?" Theo asked.

"Enough to make a statement saying Wrotham was blackmailing the silversmith to commit bank fraud. Franklin will hang, of course. He was hardly an innocent party."

"Mr Franklin hurt his sister," Eleanor said, wrapping her arms around Theo's waist. "I believe he hit her with a blunt object. She will need a doctor, too. I doubt her brother sent for one."

When the doctor arrived, Daventry's agent went to find a constable and summon the Home Secretary. The journalist from *The Morning Post* arrived, half-dressed and breathless. He looked over the scene, spoke to Daventry and left.

It was six in the morning when they left the premises. Franklin was arrested, and his sister taken to the infirmary. Wrotham was stretchered to the doctor's home, though it was doubtful he would make a recovery. They'd all given their statements and were warned by the Home Secretary to keep this sorry business to themselves.

Theo faced Eleanor, draping his coat around her shoulders. "If you've no objection, I shall remain here with you."

He stroked her cheek, marvelling at the softness of her skin. "I suspect we'll both sleep past noon."

He could spend his life with her in bed.

She fell into his arms and rested her head against his chest. "I don't care what happens as long as I'm with you."

They stood on the pavement, holding each other, waiting for Daventry to confirm they were free to leave. Once they'd rested, he would remind her of his desire to marry.

Daventry came to speak to them. "We're heading to the Plume of Feathers in Edgware." He gestured to Theo's brothers, who were gathered on the pavement, deep in conversation. "I assured the Home Secretary we would take Mrs Dunwoody into custody before she reaches Birmingham with the fraudulent plates. Your brothers are keen to join me."

Theo straightened, the fire of vengeance burning in his veins. "After all the despicable things that woman said, I'll relish seeing her squirm." He turned to Eleanor and lowered his voice. "Will you come, too?"

She looked at his brothers before cupping his cheek. "I'll wait for you here. I think it's something you need to do as a family."

"You're part of that family now."

She swallowed hard, evidently moved by his statement. "Something you need to do as brothers. As you had the locks changed, I presume you have a key to the shop."

He nodded. "Get some rest. I'll return shortly."

Theo escorted her into the house, kissing her tenderly before joining his brothers in the carriage. They followed Daventry to Edgware, stopping at the inn for a description of the matron's coach before parking a mile from the Feathers and lying in wait.

"Daventry doubts Wrotham will survive his head injury," Aramis said. "That means our dear brother Aaron is heir to an earldom."

Christian laughed. "The news is bound to put Berridge in the grave. Aaron could be the earl before All Saints' Day."

"I will never be the Earl of Berridge," Aaron said firmly. "Our father traded his familial rights for money to pay his debts."

"The King might see it differently," Theo said, though a gaming hell owner was hardly considered good stock.

"Even if the King had a momentary lapse in judgement, I'll never relinquish my right to own Fortune's Den. I'll never place my faith in the aristocracy again."

There was no time to press Aaron on the matter.

Daventry's coachman blocked the road with his carriage, forcing the approaching vehicle to stop. Theo looked out of the window and saw Mrs Dunwoody gawping back.

Satisfaction slithered through him.

They alighted and stood on the side of the road while Daventry approached her carriage and yanked the door open.

"What's the meaning of this?" Mrs Dunwoody complained with the usual sharp sting in her voice. She stabbed her finger at them. "I should have known that rabble would take to highway robbery."

"And yet your nephew has been arrested for fraud," Theo called, making no mention of Wrotham's injuries. "Don't look so surprised, madam. You're to join him in Newgate."

The matron used her haughty manner as a crutch. "Is that the best you can do, boy? Threaten an ageing woman with vicious lies?" She glared at Daventry. "Close the door, sir, and move your vehicle. I don't know who you are or why you're stooping to their level, but I suggest you find better friends."

Daventry produced the magistrate's writ. "I have a warrant to search you, this vehicle and any luggage you carry. I'm acting on behalf of the Home Secretary, investigating a case of fraud."

Mrs Dunwoody paled but found the strength to argue. "A warrant? Do you know who I am, sir? I'm not some bawd making a living from ill-gotten gains. I don't know what those ingrates are paying you, but you'll rue the day you crossed me." The woman tried to close the carriage door. "Drive on, Wilson."

Daventry looked at the coachman. "Move this vehicle and you'll join her in a cell. You'll remove all luggage and place it on the ground, or I'll arrest you for aiding a felon."

While Mrs Dunwoody sat in the carriage, pretending her world wasn't crumbling around her, Wilson followed orders. He placed the valise, small portmanteau and vanity case before Daventry.

"That's all, sir."

"Open them."

"Mrs Dunwoody has the keys, sir." Wilson bent his head. "I ain't worked for her that long. I've a family to feed. I can't afford to be caught up in nasty business."

"Then prove your innocence and tell me everything you know. I'm looking for any heavy metal items she might have stowed away."

"I saw her shoving something in the cupboard under the seat."

Daventry slapped the fellow on the back. "Thank you, Wilson." He opened the carriage door and beckoned Mrs Dunwoody out. "I'll not ask twice, madam."

"If you want me out, you'll have to drag me out." Mrs Dunwoody crossed her arms as if it made her impenetrable.

Aaron groaned. "Allow me to speed up the process." He strode to the carriage and addressed the matron. "You think I'm a beast and a barbarian. You don't know how right you are." He hauled the lady out of the carriage and flung her over his broad shoulder. "Search the vehicle, Daventry, before I deposit Mrs Dunwoody in a hedge."

"Argh!" Mrs Dunwoody kicked and screamed and thumped Aaron's back. "Put me down, you dunderhead."

Daventry rummaged in the cupboard, removing a valise. When he threw it to the ground, it landed with a thud and the metal plates fell out. "Well, are they not unusual items to take on a road trip?"

Aaron lowered the matron to the ground so she could answer for her crimes. The glint of satisfaction in his eyes was undeniable.

"What? I've never seen those before."

"Are you planning to produce forged notes, madam?"

"Don't be ridiculous. They don't belong to me. They must belong to Wilson." She pointed a shaky finger at the coachman. "Look at him. Does he not look like a shifty fellow?"

Aaron folded his arms across his chest. "Wrotham confessed. He said you were involved in transporting the goods. I hope you like long journeys and hot weather, madam, and aren't afraid of venomous snakes."

Mrs Dunwoody did not hit Aaron with a cutting remark. She did not raise her hem and make a run for it.

She cried, "Snakes!"

Then fainted.

# Chapter Twenty-One

*Burial Ground, Shoemakers Row*
*Three days later*

Eleanor stood at her mother's graveside, staring at the small headstone and reading the simple epitaph. It said nothing about the complex nature of the woman who'd left her child and sought a new life. It gave no context. Was Ivy troubled or selfish? Was her heart made of glass or stone?

Despite Eleanor's thoughts, the atmosphere was not sombre but peaceful. The sun's rays broke through the trees, the early autumn leaves a painter's palette of oranges and golds. A gentle wind caressed her face, like a purifying breath from the heavens.

Life was good.

She was happy.

The past belonged in this place of quiet reflection. A place where one could close the wrought-iron gate and leave the bad memories behind.

The pad of footsteps on the narrow path signalled Emily's arrival. Eleanor did not turn around but waited for her sister to join her. If she looked at Emily, her resolve might crumble.

"Coming here doesn't help ease the grief," Emily said, gazing upon the moss-covered stone. She crouched and placed a posy of dried wildflowers on the grave. "There must be questions you want to ask. Things you want to know."

"Can one ever truly understand a person's motives?"

People told stories from their own perspective. They were flawed, altered to cast the teller in a good light. Eleanor doubted her father would admit to being cold and unloving or that his presence cast a morbid shadow over the house. With his proud bearing, he'd have claimed to be a man of principles who always did his best.

"Mother loved you," Emily said.

Eleanor felt an odd flutter of hope in her chest but knew to ignore it. "Love is conveyed in actions, not words."

Love was a fresh flower in the vase by her bed. It was a soft kiss on the forehead as she drifted to sleep. It was a sprint across town on a cold rainy night, so they might share the same bed.

"It's why I know this is the last time we will ever speak," she said, her heart breaking because she had witnessed how deeply Theo loved his siblings and had longed to feel the same about Emily. "You hurt me. You destroyed any trust I had."

Emily gripped Eleanor's arm, forcing her to turn from the grave. "You know I had no choice but to do Uncle Jack's bidding. He's a monster."

"Is he a monster or a drunken fool who doesn't care how you make money?" Jack Rogers was the obvious scapegoat.

"I took an inventory of my stock. Shall I list the missing items? The stolen yards of ribbon? The gloves and stockings you've pilfered since you began working for me?"

She had been too trusting.

A fool to think she and Emily were anything alike.

"You think I stole those things?" Emily released Eleanor like she had the plague. "Yes, I took the silk, but only because Jack made me."

Eleanor sighed. "I met your Aunt Daisy at St Clement's. She said you have our mother's wild streak. That you believe you're owed something in life but refuse to work. That's why Uncle Jack threatened to throw you out."

Emily jerked. "And you believe that evil hag? You believe a stranger over your own flesh and blood?"

"You trashed the shop as an excuse to steal more stock. You came back to see what else you could steal, but we surprised you. You pushed me down the stairs, Emily. Anna said you told her about my fall, though I had not told a soul."

Emily hadn't mentioned their mother out of concern for Eleanor. She had not wanted to ruin her little enterprise by receiving a negative reaction.

Knowing she was cornered, Emily used tears to incite pity. "It's all right for you," she sobbed, though her cheeks remained dry. "You've had a comfortable life. Your father left you money to rent the shop and buy stock. What about me? My father left me beholden to my uncle."

Why was that? Eleanor wondered.

Perhaps Emily was too much like their mother. Indeed, Eleanor was grateful her father had invented a fictitious role model.

"You're not my responsibility," Eleanor said.

Emily sniffed back absent tears. "But we're kin."

She thought of how much Theo loved his sister Delphine, yet they shared no blood ties. Blood ties were a crutch selfish siblings used to assert their will.

"We're different people. I would have worked hard to forge a bond, not deliberately set out to hurt you. What if I'd died from my injuries? Would you have wept or been the first to hire a solicitor to claim the contents of my shop?"

"I know it looks bad, but I can change."

"I would have to see proof before I could ever trust you again." Eleanor took one last look at her mother's grave. Daisy had confirmed Eleanor's unfortunate ancestry. "You're lucky I've not given your name to the officers at Bow Street. I suggest you find work. Strive to do better and pray for forgiveness. Goodbye, Emily."

With a heavy heart, Eleanor left her sister and navigated the path back to Shoemakers Row. Thoughts of Theo slipped into her mind, reviving her broken spirit. She was counting the hours until she saw him again, until passion over-whelmed them and they lost themselves in each other's bodies.

When she arrived at her shop, she was greeted by the alluring smell of Theo's cologne, and noticed her sewing box on the counter next to a fresh plum tart.

"Theo!"

Her heart fluttered, the urge to kiss him, to touch him, drumming a potent beat in her blood. They'd agreed to dine together tonight, but she'd returned home yesterday to find him naked in her bed.

She searched every room, sad he wasn't there.

Surely he'd bought the tart because plums were an aphrodisiac.

The urge to cut a slice proved tempting. That's when she saw the note.

*Something to devour later.*

Why had he moved her sewing box? At one time, she'd considered hurling it into the fire. Yet the box had united them, and had swiftly become her most cherished possession.

She lifted the lid but found the box empty.

Perhaps he'd left her a secret note.

A quick fiddle with wooden appliqués and the drawer popped open.

There were two notes hidden inside. One that sent her temperature soaring because he said not to worry about plates and cutlery. He would eat his pie off her belly. One inviting her to join him at the Olympic tonight in the family box. She was to come in the same pink gown she'd worn the night he'd kissed her.

How odd. The Olympic was closed on a Monday.

A smile touched her lips. What was he up to?

She knew one thing for certain.

Whatever he had planned would exceed her expectations.

*The Olympic Theatre*
*Wych Street, Drury Lane*

Theo had sent Godby to collect Eleanor from the modiste shop and to give her a note. Mr Sawston, the manager, was waiting to greet her at the theatre door. Then he'd agreed to leave them alone and spend the next two hours supping ale at the White Hart tavern.

All was quiet. There wasn't another soul in the building. The gaslights were lit but dimmed. Supper awaited them on a table in the box. He knew Eleanor disliked champagne so had taken a bottle of Aaron's best claret and poured it into a crystal decanter. More importantly, the ring he'd purchased from Woodcroft jewellers was tucked safely in his coat pocket.

His heart thundered in his chest when he heard footsteps in the corridor. Would she play her part as requested? Could she remember all the things she had said to him that night?

He took his seat and waited for her to enter.

"Good evening, Mr Chance." Her voice held the soft, teasing quality of a woman eager to make love. "You're a hard man to find."

He glanced at her while struggling to contain a surge of emotion. Swathed in a pink satin cloak, she looked confident and beautiful even though she'd had a difficult day.

"Missing me already, Miss Darrow?" He'd not stopped thinking about her since he'd left her bed this morning. "I should think you've seen enough of me to last a lifetime."

"Not nearly enough. I'm sure you know why I'm here."

He stood. The need to touch her had him veering off script. Closing the gap between them, he lowered the hood of her cloak to reveal her lustrous red hair. "You held me spellbound that night. You've held me spellbound every night since. I can barely catch my breath now."

"I thought you despised me."

He captured a curl and let it slip through his fingers. "I was hard for you then. I'm hard for you now. I've always wanted you, Eleanor."

She stepped closer, brazenly cupping his cock in his trousers. "Is this not where you claim I'm infatuated and desperate for your attention?"

He inhaled sharply as her palm slid over his erection. "Aren't you?"

"Undoubtedly. You're like a drug."

She released him and pushed him into a velvet seat. He'd hoped to surprise her tonight, yet she was always one step ahead.

"I don't recall asking you to sit," he said, watching her hike up her satin skirts and straddle him. He gripped her thighs, drawing her over the solid bulge in his trousers.

"As you said, I am suffering from an addiction I cannot control." Her voice dropped to a sensual whisper. "I mean to hound you night and day until you give me what I want. And I'm not talking about the sewing box."

"I know what you want," he uttered, reaching between them to unfasten his trousers. "But I'll make a trade."

"A trade?" Having undone the button, her cloak slipped off her shoulders, revealing the gown that showed her figure to perfection.

"I see you've come armed to the teeth tonight," he said, admiring the rapid rise and fall of her breasts. "Did you hope your pretty countenance would leave me defenceless?"

"By whatever means, you're at my mercy." She moistened her lips. "You'll give me one thing I crave—your love." When his hands settled on her bare buttocks, she said, "I want it now, Theo."

He entered her, their moans echoing through the auditorium.

"You were made for me, love, but I hadn't planned on reaching this part so soon." His heartbeat thumped in his throat as she took him slow and deep. "Wait!" He'd hoped to propose before sating their desires. "I need to say something." All the things he'd omitted to say that night.

"Say what?" Her lips parted as she sat on his lap, taking him to the hilt. "Is something wrong?"

Everything was perfect.

"No. There's nothing wrong." He gazed into her eyes, eyes as striking as the emeralds in the ring he'd bought her. "I never told you how incredible you were the night you charged into this box. As incredible as you are now."

She blinked because she struggled with compliments. "I so desperately wanted to hate you, but then you kissed me and sent my world spinning."

He cupped her nape and brushed his lips over hers, recalling the instant spark that had rocked his world, too. "Something magical happens when our mouths meet."

"Something magical happens when you enter the room. I cannot explain it, but every cell in my body thrums with excitement."

He studied her, drinking in the gorgeous sight. "Marry me. Let me take care of you. Let me love you for all eternity."

Tears filled her eyes. "I belong to you, Theo. I felt it the first time you accompanied Delphine to her fitting. I called her back a week early, hoping to see you again."

"Aramis offered to escort her, but I paid to take his place."

Her eyes brightened. "You did?"

"I might have made my intentions clear, but Delphine spoke of your blossoming friendship, and I couldn't take that away from her."

"Your love for your sister only enhanced your appeal." To show how attracted she was to him, she came up on her knees and sank slowly back down. "I love you. I feel like I've always loved you."

He reached into his pocket and gave her the velvet ring box. "I hope you like it. It should fit. I measured your finger with string while you were sleeping."

She chuckled. "What else do you do while I'm sleeping?"

"Watch you." And count himself amongst the luckiest of men.

She opened the box, joy evident in her eyes. "Theo, it's beautiful. It's exactly what I would have picked for myself."

"You're beautiful." He drew the ring from the box and placed it on her finger. "You're the love of my life, Eleanor."

She examined the ring before pouring everything of herself into a kiss that curled his toes and had his cock swelling inside her.

As always, their passion overwhelmed them, and they took their lovemaking to the floor.

"We'll revisit this position later, when we're less encumbered." He held her hands above her head, interlacing their fingers, and drove deep. "Though you're wearing my ring, you've still not said you'll marry me."

A mix of a giggle and a pleasurable moan escaped her. "I love you. Of course I'll marry you. How can I not? You've aroused me to the point of madness, and there's not a plum pie in sight."

*Fortune's Den*
*Aldgate Street*
*Four weeks later*

"Did I not say you'd be married by the autumn?" Aramis grinned and thrust his outstretched hand at Theo. "You owe me a hundred pounds, but consider it a wedding gift." He glanced at Eleanor, busy talking to Delphine and Miss Lovelace in the drawing room—when she wasn't looking Theo's way. "Your bride looks at you like you're a hog on a roasting spit, and she's waiting to devour you whole."

Theo laughed. He couldn't stop staring at her, either.

The last month had been glorious. They'd been married for two hours, yet it was the happiest two hours of his life. As they'd not spent a night apart since his proposal at the theatre, he would lay odds Eleanor was already with child.

Delphine noticed them looking and joined them. "Remind me not to leave town for the next three months. I believe my husband placed a bet on Aaron being married before Twelfth Night."

Aaron had retired to his study to talk privately with Lucius Daventry and so they did not need to speak in whispers.

"I fear your husband must put his hand in his pocket," Christian said. "We all knew of Theo's attraction to Eleanor. With Aaron, it's much more complicated."

"I'm not so sure." Delphine checked over her shoulder,

then stepped closer. "Miss Lovelace called him a prized ape last week and could have sworn she saw him smile. Have you ever known Aaron smile at a woman?"

"I've never known him smile at anyone," Theo said.

Aramis offered another snippet of gossip. "Sigmund said Aaron has been training in the basement every night for the last month. There's to be a fight soon. Brutes coming from as far afield as Manchester."

"He's hoping they'll thrash Miss Lovelace from his mind." Theo feared his brother was on a downward spiral. His fists had got them out of a predicament when they were children. Perhaps Aaron prayed the same would be true now.

"He's doing it to make her hate him," Delphine offered. "Wait until he hears of her new plan." She paused for dramatic effect. "Miss Lovelace is to open the club to gentlemen every Thursday. He'll be furious."

Theo was glad he would miss the family meeting tomorrow. "She'll never manage a club full of men. Not on her own."

Delphine raised her hands, signalling the next words to leave her mouth would be shocking. "She's opening the club to men and women and has planned a host of themed evenings."

"The lady is courting trouble," Aramis said. "She'll attract nothing but scoundrels out to rid her wallflowers of more than their pin money."

"I believe that's the plan. She's keen to play matchmaker."

"Good grief. Has she lost her mind?" Christian countered.

"Has who lost their mind?" Aaron said, joining them. The man moved with a panther's silent grace.

"Eleanor," Theo was quick to say. He'd explain all to his wife later. "She was considering hiring Anna Franklin when she settles into new premises." It was not a lie.

Not wanting to work in New Bridge Street, she had given notice. The upstairs apartments were too small for a married couple, and so Theo had purchased a house on The Strand.

"Personally, I wouldn't trust a woman who had stolen from me," Aaron said. "But Eleanor's heart is as huge as yours. I suspect she'll give Miss Franklin an opportunity to prove her worth."

"Without Miss Franklin, we wouldn't have known about Wrotham's treachery," Theo reminded him.

"Wrotham is dead," Aaron blurted. "He succumbed to his injuries last night. They'll not transport Franklin for forgery but hang him for murder."

They all fell silent. While they lived to punish their estranged family, they were not heartless men. Mrs Dunwoody had received the lesser sentence of seven years transportation and loss of her assets.

"Forgive me," Aaron said, his gaze sliding to Eleanor and Miss Lovelace. "It's your wedding day. It's a time to celebrate the future, not dwell on the past."

"Good." Aramis gripped Aaron's shoulder. "You may as well know, Naomi is with child. You'll be an uncle in the spring."

The muscle in Aaron's cheek twitched. "Someone fetch me a brandy? On second thoughts, bring the decanter."

Everyone laughed but Aaron.

Keen to join the revelry, Eleanor approached with Miss Lovelace. "What's so amusing?"

Theo reached for her hand. "We were discussing how quickly our family has grown." He turned to Miss Lovelace, who was dressed in a fetching turquoise ensemble. "Do you think you'll ever marry?"

"Me?" The lady pressed her hand to her chest and chuckled. The girlish laugh sparked a light in Aaron's dark eyes. "Heavens no. I have enough to deal with managing the club."

Aaron couldn't wait to offer his opinion. "If you married well, your husband would provide for you."

"You mean if I marry for money."

"What other reason is there?"

The lady scanned Aaron's broad shoulders and impeccable attire. "I wouldn't expect you to understand. I wouldn't settle for anything less than a man who'd wait hours in the rain just to spend a minute in my company."

Aaron snorted. "I doubt such a man exists."

Theo begged to differ but remained silent.

"Which is why I'm happy to remain a spinster."

"I thought you were a wallflower."

Miss Lovelace shrugged. "Some women are hard to define."

The air thrummed with palpable tension. Aaron would probably beat his sparring partner to a pulp tonight.

Theo caught Eleanor's covert jerk of the head, meaning she wanted to speak to him alone upstairs.

He cleared his throat. "Would you excuse us for a moment?" He turned to the alluring lady who he prayed had the means to overthrow his brother. "Did you know Aaron has an interest in medieval history?" He wanted her to know his brother had brains and brawn.

"Early, High or Late Middle Ages?" Miss Lovelace asked as Theo took Eleanor's hand and made a quick retreat.

They raced upstairs, keen to spend a private moment together.

"I'm glad we're staying in a suite at Mivart's Hotel tonight," he said, cupping her cheeks and kissing her wildly. "Aaron will be like a bear with a thorn in his paw once he learns of Miss Lovelace's plans."

"Theo, we must help them." Eleanor was so excited she could barely stand still, and it had nothing to do with his fervent kisses. "Miss Lovelace admitted she likes riling his temper, and you know what that means."

"What does it mean?"

"That she wants his attention." Eleanor hugged herself and laughed. "If she didn't care, she would ignore him. She would refuse his assistance, refuse to enter this house."

No man wanted to dash his bride's hopes on their wedding day, but they'd vowed to be honest. "Aaron will do everything in his power to push her away. She's not strong enough to withstand his harsh temperament."

He could not imagine Aaron holding a woman tenderly, kissing her, and making love to her like she was life's most precious gift. All was lost. Unless Daventry had something special in his box of tricks.

"Never underestimate a woman on a mission," his wife reminded him. "Admit I caught you off guard when I stormed into your theatre box."

He smiled at the cherished memory. "You knocked me sideways. Kissing you was a means of bolstering my defences, though it left me wanting. I left the theatre deter-mined to have you."

She straightened and braced her hands on her hips. "You sound rather sure of yourself. Perhaps my desire came from desperation."

He laughed, capturing her chin. "I'm the King of Hearts. No other man could make you ache like I do. No other man knows the secret door to your heart. I'm a scoundrel who's in love with one woman. A scoundrel who'll love you until your dying day."

She smiled as she kissed him, giving everything of herself. "You're my kind of scoundrel." She ran her hands over his chest. "What say we leave our guests waiting and put those questionable morals to the test?"

I hope you enjoyed reading *My Kind of Scoundrel*

Is Miss Lovelace courting trouble by welcoming men into her club? Will the ghosts of the past haunt Aaron now he's living alone at Fortune's Den?
Find out in …

*The Last Chance*
*Rogues of Fortune's Den - Book 5*

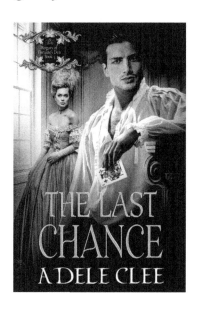

Printed in Great Britain
by Amazon